Writers and Their Mothers

Dale Salwak
Editor

Writers and Their Mothers

palgrave
macmillan

Editor
Dale Salwak
Glendora, USA

ISBN 978-3-319-68347-8   ISBN 978-3-319-68348-5   (eBook)
https://doi.org/10.1007/978-3-319-68348-5

Library of Congress Control Number: 2017961850

Cover illustration by Jenny Vong

Printed on acid-free paper

This Palgrave Macmillan imprint is published by Springer Nature
The registered company is Springer International Publishing AG
The registered company address is: Gewerbestrasse 11, 6330 Cham, Switzerland

For our mothers

Preface

The idea for this collection goes back to 2013, when I was reading Alexander McCall Smith's *What W. H. Auden Can Do for You* and came upon the following words: "There may be no book on the mothers of poets, or artists in general, but it might one day be written and would be, I think, an enlightening read."

This book considers some of the provocative questions he suggested: personal and anecdotal, philosophical and practical. What were the early maternal influences on an artist and how were they manifested in the work? Was there truth in Georges Simenon's claim that novelists were united in their hatred of their mothers? Or of Gore Vidal's assertion, "Hatred of one parent or the other can make an Ivan the Terrible or a Hemingway; the protective love, however, of two devoted parents can absolutely destroy an artist"? What were, in Carl Sandburg's words, the "silent working" of their inner lives as children become writers? What happened to writers who were wounded by their mothers? What were the links between childhood joy and sorrow and the growth of individual genius?

I invited twenty-two prominent novelists, poets, and literary critics from both sides of the Atlantic to write a new chapter about the profound and frequently perplexing bond between writer and mother (and in one instance, stepmother). I cast my net wide, providing the focus and theme, making suggestions for possible approaches, but ultimately leaving it to each contributor to decide on their own methods. Thus prompted, the contributors bring to life in compelling detail the thoughts, work, loves, friendships, passions and, above all, the influence of mothers upon their literary offspring from Shakespeare to the present. Part I is biographical; Part II is autobiographical. All but two of the essays were produced expressly for this volume.

Many of the contributors evoke the ideal with fond and loving memories: understanding, selfless, spiritual, tender, protective, reassuring and self-assured mothers who created environments favorable to the development of their children's gifts. At the opposite end of the parenting spectrum, however, we also see tortured mothers who ignored, interfered with, smothered or abandoned their children. Their early years were times of traumatic loss, unhappily dominated by death and human frailty.

An edited volume is only as good as its contributors. I had a splendid field to choose from and am profoundly grateful to all of them. Some forged on through the demands of other deadlines, illness (their own or a loved one's) or in one instance the inexpressible sadness of losing a daughter. The late Kenneth Silverman, whom I have known as a very good friend and highly respected scholar for more than thirty years, produced his essay on Walt Whitman, his final piece of writing, while undergoing treatment for lung cancer. My own mother, now ninety-six and still living in her home, read with immense and varied pleasure each of these essays as they arrived. Their truthfulness and sensitivity moved her deeply, sometimes to tears.

Finally, I would like to express my great debt to Ben Doyle, commissioning editor at Palgrave Macmillan, whose many conversations with me shaped the project; to Camille Davies, also at Palgrave Macmillan, for guiding me through the thicket of permissions, contracts, and myriad other details that an editor inevitably encounters; to Jeffrey Meyers, who suggested a structure for the book and, along with Rachel Hadas and Edwin A. Dawes (Chairman of the Philip Larkin Society), generously helped me to acquire some of the contributors; and to Ann Thwaite, who assisted at an early stage with the title as well as the focus of the project.

Glendora, USA   Dale Salwak

Acknowledgements

Grateful acknowledgement is made to the following for permission to reprint unpublished and previously published materials:

Extracts from William Golding's unpublished manuscripts and journals. Copyright © 2017 William Golding Limited. All rights reserved. Quotation from *The Double Tongue* by William Golding (London: Faber and Faber, London, 2013; first published 1995).

Extracts from Philip Larkin's unpublished letters. Copyright © 2016 The Estate of Philip Larkin. Reproduced by permission of The Society of Authors as the Literary Representative of the Estate of Philip Larkin.

"Mother Tongue: A Memoir" from *On Modern British Fiction* by Ian McEwan (London: Oxford University Press, Oxford, 1990). Copyright © Ian McEwan. Reproduced by permission of the author c/o Rogers Coleridge & White Ltd., 20 Powis Mews, London W11 1JN.

"My Mother Enters the Work Force" from *On the Bus with Rosa Parks* by Rita Dove (New York: W. W. Norton & Company, 1999). Copyright © Rita Dove. Reprinted by permission of the author.

"My Wicked Stepmother" by Martin Amis. Published by the (London) *Daily Mail*, 4 January 2014. Copyright © by Martin Amis. Reprinted by permission of the author c/o The Andrew Wylie Agency, 17 Bedford Square, London WC1B 3JA.

"A Crack of Air," "The Cry," "The Message," "Throes," "Watching," "Worst Words" from *Collected Poems* by Anthony Thwaite (London: Enitharmon Press, 2007). Reprinted by permission of the author and the publishers.

Every effort has been made to trace all copyright-holders, but if any have been inadvertently overlooked the publishers will be pleased to make the necessary arrangements at the first opportunity.

Contents

Notes on Contributors

Catherine Aird is the author of more than twenty detective novels and short story collections, most of which feature Detective Inspector C.D. Sloan. She holds an Honorary M.A. from the University of Kent at Canterbury and was awarded an M.B.E. Apart from writing the successful Chronicles of Calleshire, she has written and edited a series of local histories and has been active in village life. She lives in East Kent.

Martin Amis is the author of ten novels, the memoir *Experience*, two collections of stories, and six collections of non-fiction. He lives in New York.

Judy Carver is the younger child of William Golding and his wife Ann. Born in 1945, she was educated at Godolphin School, Salisbury, the University of Sussex, and St Anne's College, Oxford, where she did research into an eighteenth-century anthology of poetry. She married in 1971, and worked in publishing for several years until she had children. In 2011, the year of her father's centenary, Faber and Faber published her memoir, *The Children of Lovers*, which described life growing up in a household dominated by her father's extraordinary talent and her parents' intense, creative marriage. Further details: www.william-golding.co.uk

Anthony Daniels, born in 1949, is a retired psychiatrist who worked for many years in an inner-city hospital and prison. He is the author of many books, including *Romancing Opiates*, in which he traced the origins of modern attitudes to addiction to De Quincey and Coleridge. He has written literary essays and book reviews for many publications, including the *TLS*, the *Sunday Telegraph*, the *National Review*, the *Spectator*, *The* (London) *Times* and the *New Criterion*. His memoirs of his life in prison (as a doctor) were published in June, 2017, under the title *The Knife Went In*.

Rita Dove, recipient of the 1987 Pulitzer Prize in poetry, served as U.S. Poet Laureate from 1993 to 1995. The author of numerous poetry books, most recently *Sonata Mulattica* (2009) and *Collected Poems 1974–2004* (2016), she has also published short stories, a novel, a play and, as editor, *The Penguin Anthology of Twentieth-Century American Poetry*. Among her many recognitions are the 2011 National Medal of Arts from President Obama and the 1996 National Humanities Medal from President Clinton. Rita Dove is Commonwealth Professor of English at the University of Virginia.

Margaret Drabble, DBE is a novelist and critic, born in Sheffield in 1939. After a brief and inglorious career as an actress with the Royal Shakespeare Company she became a full-time writer, and has published nineteen novels, most recently *The Dark Flood Rises* (2016). Her work has been translated into many languages. She has also published various works of non-fiction, including biographies of Arnold Bennett and Angus Wilson, and edited the Fifth and Sixth editions of the *Oxford Companion to English Literature* (1985, 2000.) She is married to the biographer Michael Holroyd, and has three children from her first marriage to the actor Clive Swift.

Lyndall Gordon is the author of seven biographies, including *Lives Like Loaded Guns: Emily Dickinson and Her Family's Feuds*, *The Imperfect Life of T. S. Eliot* and most recently *Outsiders: Five Women Writers Who Changed the World*. Amongst her awards are The British Academy's Rose Mary Crawshay Prize and the Cheltenham Prise for Literature. She has also written two memoirs, *Shared Lives* and *Divided Lives: Dreams of a Mother and Daughter*. She is a Fellow of the Royal Society of Literature and lives in Oxford, where she is a Fellow of St Hilda's College.

Rachel Hadas is the author of more books of poetry and essays than she can quite count. Her most recent poetry collection is *Questions in the Vestibule* (2016, Northwestern University Press); her verse translations of Euripides' two Iphigenia plays will be published by Northwestern in 2018. The recipient of honors including a Guggenheim Fellowship, an American Academy of Arts and Sciences Award in Literature, and the O.B. Hardison Poetry Prize from the Folger Shakespeare Library, Rachel Hadas is Board of Governors Professor of English at Rutgers University–Newark.

Adrianne Kalfopoulou has had work published on Sylvia Plath in *Women's Studies, an Interdisciplinary Journal*, and *Plath Profiles*. She is the author of two poetry collections, and a book of essays, *Ruin, Essays in Exilic Living*. A third poetry collection, *A History of Too Much*, will be published in 2018. She is a poetry and non-fiction mentor for the Mile-High MFA program at Regis University, and heads the English Program at Deree College in Athens, Greece. Some of her work is available at: www.adriannekalfopoulou.com

Reeve Lindbergh, a daughter of aviator-author Anne Morrow Lindbergh, was born in 1945 and grew up in Connecticut. She graduated from Radcliffe College in 1968 and moved to Vermont, where she lives near St. Johnsbury with her husband, writer Nat Tripp. Her work has appeared in a number of magazines and periodicals including the *New York Times Book Review*, *The New Yorker* and *The Washington Post*. She is also the author of two dozen books for children and adults. Her next book, *Two Lives*, about her family past and rural present, will be published by Brigantine Media in 2018.

Ian McEwan has written two collections of stories, *First Love, Last Rites*, and *In Between the Sheets*, and fifteen novels, *The Cement Garden*, *The Comfort of Strangers*, *The Child in Time*, *The Innocent*, *Black Dogs*, *The Daydreamer*, *Enduring Love*, *Amsterdam*, *Atonement*, *Saturday Solar*, *On Chesil Beach*, *Sweet Tooth*, *The Children Act* and *Nutshell*. He has also written several film scripts, including *The Imitation Game*, *The Ploughman's Lunch*, *Sour Sweet*, *The Good Son*, *The Innocent*, *On Chesil Beach* and *The Children Act*. He won the Booker Prize for *Amsterdam* in 1998.

Gardner McFall is the author of *The Pilot's Daughter and Russian Tortoise* (poems), an opera libretto entitled *Amelia* (commissioned by Seattle Opera), and two children's books. She edited *Made with Words*, a prose miscellany by May Swenson, and wrote the Introduction for the Barnes & Noble Classics edition of Kenneth Grahame's *The Wind in the Willows*. For over a decade she taught Children's Literature at Hunter College/CUNY, and lives and works in New York City.

Jeffrey Meyers has written fifty-four books, thirty-one of which have been translated into fourteen languages and seven alphabets, and published on six continents. In 2012 he gave the Seymour lectures on biography at the National Libraries of Australia. He has recently published *Remembering Iris Murdoch* in 2013, *Thomas Mann's Artist-Heroes* in 2014, *Robert Lowell in Love* and *The Mystery of the Real: Correspondence with Alex Colville* in 2016.

Andrew Motion was the UK Poet Laureate from 1999 to 2009. He is the co-founder of the Poetry Archive, and now teaches at Johns Hopkins University; he lives in Baltimore. His book-length elegy for his parents, *Essex Clay*, is published in the Spring of 2018.

Martha Oliver-Smith was born in Rhode Island into a family of writers, scholars and artists. She earned an MA in literature from the University of Nevada at Reno and an MFA in writing from the Vermont College of Fine Arts. She taught high school English and college writing courses for 36 years before retiring to write the biographical memoir *Martha's Mandala* (2015), based on her grandmother's life as an artist who struggled with mental illness. She lives with her husband in Vermont where she is working on a second memoir about her mother, the author Martha Bacon.

Tim Parks is a novelist, essayist, travel writer and translator based in Italy. Author of fifteen novels, including the Booker short-listed *Europa*, he has translated works by Moravia, Calvino, Calasso, Machiavelli and Leopardi. While running a postgraduate degree course in translation in Milan, he writes regularly for the *London Review of Books* and the *New York Review of Books*. His many non-fiction works include the bestselling *Italian Neighbours* and *Teach Us to Sit Still*, a memoir on chronic pain and meditation. His critical work includes the essay collection *Where I'm Reading From*, and most recently, *The Novel, A Survival Skill*, a reflection on the relationship between novelists, their writing and their readers. His most recent novel is *In Extremis*.

Philip Pullen was born and brought up in Coventry and is familiar with most of the haunts of the young Philip Larkin. He studied at University College, Swansea and the University of Leicester and holds a PhD in the sociology of education. He spent most of his working life teaching in further and higher education and also served for 10 years as one of Her Majesty's Inspectors (HMI). He is a committee member of the Philip Larkin Society and is currently working on a biographical study of Eva Larkin, making use of the extensive Larkin Archive located in the History Centre, Hull.

Hugh Macrae Richmond has degrees from Oxford and Cambridge, and is Professor Emeritus of English at the University of California, Berkeley, where he heads the Shakespeare Program devoted to "Shakespeare in Performance" and staging some forty plays, with five video documentaries in national distribution: *Shakespeare and the Globe, Shakespeare's Globe Theatre Restored*, and *Shakespeare and the Spanish Connection* as well as *Milton By Himself*. He has published *Shakespeare's Sexual Comedy, Shakespeare's Political Plays, Shakespeare's Tragedies*

Reviewed, Shakespeare's Theatre, as well as *Renaissance Landscapes, Puritans and Libertines*, and *The School of Love*. The Program's two websites are Shakespeare's Staging and Milton Revealed.

Dale Salwak is professor of English literature at Southern California's Citrus College. His publications include *Living with a Writer* (Palgrave, 2004), *Teaching Life: Letters from a Life in Literature* (2008) and studies of Kingsley Amis, John Braine, A.J. Cronin, Philip Larkin, Barbara Pym, Carl Sandburg, Anne Tyler and John Wain. He is a recipient of Purdue University's Distinguished Alumni Award as well as a research grant from the National Endowment for the Humanities. He is also a frequent contributor to the (London) *Times Higher Education* magazine and the *Times Educational Supplement*.

Kenneth Silverman (1936–2017), a native of Manhattan, was Professor Emeritus of English at New York University. His books include *A Cultural History of the American Revolution*; *The Life and Times of Cotton Mather*; *Edgar A. Poe: Mournful and Never-ending Remembrance*; *HOUDINI!!!*; *Lightning Man: The Accursed Life of Samuel F. B. Morse*; and *Begin Again: A Biography of John Cage*. A fellow of the American Academy of Arts and Sciences, he has received the Bancroft Prize in American History, the Pulitzer Prize for Biography, the Edgar Award of the Mystery Writers of America, and the Christopher Literary Award of the Society of American Magicians. He has loved the poetry of Walt Whitman since, at sixteen, he heard his English teacher read aloud, "Give me the splendid silent sun."

Ann Thwaite has spent her life as a writer, with two spells of teaching in Japan. She wrote and reviewed children's books for many years. She and her husband Anthony have lived in Tokyo, Richmond-upon-Thames, Benghazi and Nashville, Tennessee, but have been settled in Norfolk in East Anglia for the last forty-five years. Her five biographies, of Frances Hodgson Burnett, A.A. Milne (Whitbread Biography of the Year 1990), Emily Tennyson, the poet's wife, and the father and son P.H. and Edmund Gosse (Duff Cooper Prize, 1985) have all been highly praised. *Goodbye Christopher Robin* (from her Milne life) is now a major motion picture and mass market paperback.

Anthony Thwaite had early success as a poet, publishing widely while he was still at Oxford. His *Collected Poems* was published in 2007 and his most recent book, *Going Out*, when he was eighty-four. He was a BBC radio producer, literary editor of the *Listener*, the *New Statesman* and *Encounter*, and has lectured and taught in many countries. He was awarded an OBE for services to poetry, and both he and Ann are Fellows of the Royal Society of Literature and have honorary degrees from the University of East Anglia. Hull University awarded him an honorary doctorate for his work on Philip Larkin, whose poems and letters he has edited.

David Updike is Professor of English at Roxbury Community College, Boston. He is the author of two collections of short stories, *Out of the Marsh* and *Old Girlfriends*. His stories and essays have been published in *The New Yorker*, *The New York Times Magazine*, *Newsweek*, and *The John Updike*. He has written six children's books and a young adult novel, *Ivy's Turn*. He lives in Cambridge, Massachusetts, with his wife Wambui, and is the father of one son, Wesley.

Part I

Biographical

1

Shakespeare's Mother(s)

Hugh Macrae Richmond

Within great achievements we can often detect the contributions of talented women. Pierre Curie was even outdistanced by his wife Marie. Eleanor Roosevelt now earns her own recognition alongside her husband's. Rosalind Franklin's photographs provided data for the Nobel Prizes of the "discoverers" of DNA. We still talk of the Countess of Pembroke's *Arcadia*. But no one has ever talked of Mary Arden's contribution to the plays of her son William Shakespeare. Yet, despite the popular view that we know very little about Shakespeare, there is something relevant known about his antecedents. His grandfather, Richard Shakespeare, was a tenant farmer of a branch of the prominent Warwickshire Arden family. His son John was more ambitious, moving to Stratford to develop his skills as a craftsman and entrepreneur, with sufficient talent, sociability, and ambition to work his way up the municipal hierarchy to become its head, aided on the way by marriage into the genteel family who were his father's landlords. Their upper-class connections would inspire his own ultimate success in sharing their gentility through the award of a heraldic crest. His son William carried that social climbing to the ultimate pinnacle of official appointment to the royal court of King James I.

© The Author(s) 2018
D. Salwak (ed.), *Writers and Their Mothers*,
https://doi.org/10.1007/978-3-319-68348-5_1

His mother Mary Arden's resilient character suggests what she could contribute to the potential for William's meteoric career. Her father was prosperous, and though she was his eighth child it was she that he designated as his executor and a principal heir. The view that she and her husband were illiterates conflicts with their numerous legal and administrative responsibilities. Another shared trait of the married couple was inheritance of rooted Catholic family traditions, for which the Ardens even suffered executions. This ominous maternal context invites the careful elusiveness of William's communication of any personal political and theological views.

Socially Mary Arden was well above her husband in social rank, and she was certainly temperamentally and physically resilient. She lived about seventy years, outliving her husband after bearing eight children, a likely model for feminine dynamism, reflected in her son's registration of his high expectations of women in both his life and art. The fact that he married a woman eight years his elder suggests acceptance of female superiority in sexual relationships, a ratio also present in the pattern of the adulterous romance with the Dark Lady outlined in the *Sonnets*, in which the Lady seems to have held the initiative to a disconcerting degree.

However, it has often been assumed by critics that an author's life and professional aims have little to do with the nature and status of his writings. Feminists have also urged us to admit the irreducible patriarchy of Elizabethan life and letters, supposedly reflected in Shakespeare's plays. As for mothers in the scripts, the very title of my colleague Janet Adelman's influential study, *Suffocating Mothers: Fantasies of Maternal Origins in Shakespeare's Plays*, suggests the negative readings they may receive. The blurb summarizes that book thus: "In her original and highly charged account, Adelman traces the genesis of Shakespearean tragedy and romance to a psychologized version of the Fall, in which original sin is literally the sin of origin, inherited from the maternal body that brings death into the world." In Adelman's account, Shakespeare's confrontation with maternal power has devastating consequences both for masculine selfhood and for the female characters in whom that power is invested: the suffocating mothers who must themselves be suffocated. Ironically, the seeming corroboration of such a sinister status lies in Puritan tirades such as John Knox's hysterical rodomontade against *The Monstrous Regimen of Women*—in which, paradoxically, he is denouncing the dominance (regimen) of many great Renaissance monarchies by women rulers, from the time when Marguerite de Navarre headed France during her brother Francis I's imprisonment by the Emperor Charles V. That successful regency (ended by her securing of her brother's release) provided a precedent for the far longer Regency of France by Francis's daughter-in-law Catherine de Medici—at the same time as England was ruled by Mary I, and later when Elizabeth I also ruled in England, while threatened by Mary, Queen of Scots from her northern kingdom. So that domestically and politically it could be said that William Shakespeare experienced something approximating to matriarchy at all levels of society.

Looking at Shakespeare's scripts we find his experience of womanhood in general, and mothers in particular to be a central feature, unlike their minimal roles in the work of his nearest contemporaries in talent and achievement: in their best-known plays neither Christopher Marlowe nor Ben Jonson reflect deep concern with women's family status as mothers. By contrast the numerous examples of mothers in Shakespeare's plots invites creation of a whole range of subcategories of distinctive family structures in which mothers are decisive—present, or even when absent. For some mothers are literally too powerfully present, others disastrously absent; some prove evil, while several prove essential to the happy resolution of story lines, while victims like Juliet, Ophelia and Cordelia notably lack supportive mothers.

The easiest mothers to dispose of are the disastrous ones, since they do not reflect any great insights into maternal misconduct born of first-hand experience: they are mere caricatures manipulated to suit plot designs, not felt knowledge of feminine wickedness. I have in mind Tamora, the ruthless Queen of the Goths in *Titus Andronicus*, or the wicked queen who, in the interest of her daughter, tries to kill the more attractive Marina in *Pericles*; and her analogue, Imogen's enemy in *Cymbeline*. There is little to be learned from these stereotypes. A little more interesting are failed mothers, such as Lady Capulet, who deserts her daughter Juliet at a time of crisis, to support her husband's fixation on Juliet's forced marriage—with almost no index of motivation. It is very revealing that the most interesting group of questionable mothers in Shakespeare is defined by their over-concern with family well-being, and particularly with that of their sons: Constance relentlessly presses the claim to the English throne of her son Arthur in *King John*, to poor effect; Gertrude's over-emotional fixation on Hamlet complicates his concerns with her behavior, and it undercuts his capacity to act rationally, as when he kills Polonius in her bedroom. Volumnia's obsession with the guiding of the military reputation of her son Coriolanus verges on coercion, and it leads audiences to a misreading of the hero's autonomy in his actual consistently positive actions.

Paradoxically it is just this near morbid interference with male autonomy that marks out the next, more positive maternal category in Shakespeare: the successful manipulators, who resolve the calculated tangles which beset their male dependents. I have in mind the Countess in *All's Well* who contrives the overcoming of her son Bertram's resistance to her ward Helena's love for him. Even more impressive is the triad of afflicted mothers who confront Richard III, and whose chorus of curses heralds his defeat at Bosworth. Less obvious is Queen Isabel who proposes her intervention in the Anglo-French treaty which ends the war in *Henry V* by the marriage of her daughter, a similar role to that of the Abbess whose intervention ends *The Comedy of Errors*, and to Thaisa's, who achieves a similar resolution in *Pericles*—all three being women endowed with matriarchal status and social power.

One of the great paradoxes of mothers' roles in Shakespeare is that some of the most significant are the ones that are not there. Their absence creates a deep distortion of each of the play worlds involved: *The Taming of the Shrew, The Two Gentlemen of Verona, Love's Labor's Lost, The Merchant of Venice, Much Ado, As You Like It, Twelfth Night, Henry IV, Othello, King Lear*. In the comedies the young women lack maternal advice in the face of male volatility, in dealing with which their seemingly widowed fathers are of little assistance—only the mental agility of the heroines can save them and their obtuse lovers from such disasters as those which befall the naiver Juliet, Ophelia and Desdemona. Some fathers even constitute a threat to their daughters, from excessive interest in their marital options, as seen in the ridiculous will of Portia's father; or the racism of Brabantio in repudiating Desdemona's marriage to the Moor, Othello; or Lear's frustrated over-reaction to Cordelia's inept emotional obtuseness at his abdication, on the occasion of her carefully planned marriage. Of course the most extreme example of disastrous unconfined paternal interest is the incestuous relationship in the opening scenes of *Pericles*, whose discovery almost precipitates the hero's murder. For Shakespeare, a competent mother's absence from the scene constitutes the risk of impending social ruin, as a result of paternal volatility or incompetence.

So how does Shakespeare express his sense of effective maternal interventions? With sons there is usually an uneasy sense of intense monitoring of the kind seen in Gertrude and Volumnia. With daughters the mothers are far more poised and effective, as we see with the Countess of Auvergne, who unfailingly supports Helena in the face of her son Bertram's outrageous conduct, which is frustrated by help from another mother, Diana, who saves her daughter from Bertram's predations by bonding with the Countess and Helena. A similar matriarchal dominance appears in *The Merry Wives of Windsor*—though Ann Page escapes it to marry the suitor of her own choice, while the other males are totally outmaneuvered by the Wives. In *All Is True*, a similar matriarchal authority marks the Catholic Queen Katherine of Aragon, who successfully protects her daughter Mary from Henry VIII's erratic behavior, and consistently displays superior insight and wisdom to her male persecutors, before the heavenly derived masque that provides a mystical celebration of her virtue.

There remains one erratic mother in the canon, Lady Macbeth. Shakespeare accurately indicates that she is a mother, despite questioning by such scholars as L. C. Knights in his notorious essay "How Many Children Has Lady Macbeth?" In trying to mock A. C. Bradley's literalism about the reality of Shakespeare's characters, Knight neglects the fact that, historically, Macbeth's wife did have a son by a previous marriage, Lulach, who inherited Macbeth's throne by his mother's provenance. The play's text reflects this strikingly in her notorious lines of reproach to Macbeth's cowardice in refusing to assassinate King Duncan:

> What beast was't, then,
> That made you break this enterprise to me?
> When you durst do it, then you were a man;
> And, to be more than what you were, you would

Be so much more the man. Nor time nor place
Did then adhere, and yet you would make both:
They have made themselves, and that their fitness now
Does unmake you. I have given suck, and know
How tender 'tis to love the babe that milks me:
I would, while it was smiling in my face,
Have pluck'd my nipple from his boneless gums,
And dash'd the brains out, had I so sworn as you
Have done to this.

[I.vii.47–60]

We must be shocked by this subversive asseration, but it reflects the same determination to ensure a virile outcome at any price which we see in Joan of Arc in *Henry VI Part 1*; and in Queen Margaret of Anjou throughout *Henry VI*, in advocacy of her son and husband; and above all in Volumnia's cult of her son Coriolanus's heroism.

Shakespeare has no doubt that women are as capable as politicians as on the battlefield itself, a view initiated in his longest female role and one of his earliest, Queen Margaret, who figures prominently in all four plays of his first English tetralogy—the three parts of *Henry VI* plus *Richard III*—in which she appears successively as romantic heroine, wife, political Machiavel, mother, and prophetess. This type of multiple characterization of a uniquely talented historical woman climaxed in Shakespeare's deployments of Cleopatra. The latter may be Shakespeare's supreme celebration of female dominance, and it is notable that at the height of her power in the play Cleopatra chooses to incarnate herself as the goddess Isis, publicly presiding over her family. Isis is seen as the ideal mother and wife, and patroness of nature and magic. Isis is identified as the mother of the falcon-headed Horus, symbol of kingship. Isis is also known as protector of the dead and goddess of children. Her name Isis means "throne" as seen in her head-dress, which is a throne. Personifying the throne, she also represented a pharaoh's power: he was depicted as her child, sitting on the throne she provided.

In this iconic kind of role we encounter other authoritative mothers in Shakespeare's last plays, ones probably written near or after his mother's death in 1608: *Pericles* and *The Winter's Tale*. In the first we see the supposedly dead Thaisa, buried at sea by her husband Pericles, restored to life and enshrined as a priestess by her rescuers, only to be restored to her mourning husband at the end of the play. This resurrection recurs even more memorably when Hermione returns from the death that even the audience had been deceived into believing has occurred in the first act. In *Shakespeare, Catholicism and Romance*, Velma Bourgeois Richmond points out that Hermione first reappears as a seeming statue in a chapel, echoing the concealed icons of the Virgin Mary banished by the Reformers, and her resurrection suggests the transcendence of mortality by that figure. This transcendence is the key to the much-favored artistic theme of the assumption of the Virgin, favored by such painters as Titian and Rubens. However, the motif is even more literally echoed in the deathbed masque honoring Queen Catherine of Aragon, near the end (IV.ii) of what was probably Shakespeare's last play, *All Is True*—now usually known as *King Henry VIII*. There the complex stage directions require the Queen's coronation by "six persons in white robes" who are "inviting her to a banquet" and "promising eternal happiness." The recurrence of this pattern of maternal resurrection, in the years following the death of Mary Arden Shakespeare, suggests the playwright's thoughts about such an option for mothers like his own, to become revered figures comparable to his stage characters. At least the awareness of the possibility of the transcendence of mortality perceived by most commentators in his last plays is most vividly incarnated in their maternal figures. Throughout his career Shakespeare treats the role of mothers with the most profound attention, surely embodied from his own experience of a resilient mother.

2

John Ruskin and Margaret

Anthony Daniels

John Ruskin's life was both triumphant and tragic. He was one of the most prolific authors of any age, whose books were recognised from the first as being of singular importance; he was a gifted draughtsman, Slade professor at Oxford, by far the greatest art critic of his time, a sage whose social thought influenced Tolstoy and Gandhi, a popular lecturer, a man who from early adulthood was known to be distinguished and remarkable. And yet one would not have wanted to *be* Ruskin, for he was a tormented soul, experienced several periods of madness and the public humiliation of having his marriage annulled for non-consummation.

It is doubtful whether the multi-volume products of his phenomenal industriousness are now much read either for pleasure or illumination, at least outside academic circles, although at least some of them have never gone out of print since his death in 1900. His prose style, ornate, often self-consciously eloquent and discursive, is not such as to appeal to an age of sound bites and tweets, in which even a single page of print may seem to many to be of Himalayan proportions; he places too great a demand on our time to remain part of our mental furniture, since no settled doctrine is to be found in the millions of words he published. His particular

© The Author(s) 2018
D. Salwak (ed.), *Writers and Their Mothers*,
https://doi.org/10.1007/978-3-319-68348-5_2

kind of evangelical earnestness also seems to us strained, exaggerated or even ridiculous. He is, in short, very dated.

It is difficult to place Ruskin on the ideological spectrum, perhaps because that spectrum is (to change the metaphor) a Procrustean bed into which every thinker must be squeezed. In the very first sentence of his autobiography, *Praeterita*, he describes himself as a Tory of the old school, but he was the inspiration of Christian socialists and of Ruskin College, Oxford, which is devoted to providing higher educational opportunities for those too poor to have received a proper or intensive education in their childhoods. His radical criticisms of modernity and of the commercial and industrial society around him from the standpoint of an idealised, or at least a superior, past, are such that they could please both a conservative right and a radical left. The following, for example, from Tim Hilton's *John Ruskin: The Early Years*, could be endorsed enthusiastically by either:

> Though we have abolished slavery, we literally bargained daily for the lives of our fellowmen … evils, arising partly from pressure of population, but more from the carelessness in masters and consumers, from desire of cheapness, or blind faith in commercial necessities …

Ruskin's thought was Protean rather than systematic; the term *Ruskinian* has connotations without very clear denotations. There is something in his writing for every ideological taste.

There is no doubt that Ruskin was in many respects a peculiar man (assuming there to be a standard of normality from which he deviated). The sources of a man's character are always a matter of speculation in which plausibility counts for more than strict scientific reliability or proof. In the face of the irreducible individuality of man no individual's conduct will ever be entirely and indubitably explicable.

It is tempting to blame Ruskin's odd, intense and durable relationship with both his parents for such characteristics as his sexual impotence and what his biographer, Tim Hilton, calls his paedophilia, which was really his eroticised feelings for young girls rather than any actual sexual practice. And it is likewise plausible to attribute Ruskin's astonishing literary and other industriousness to his sexual failure or frustration.[1] His inclination throughout his life was to distract himself from unhappiness by incessant hard work: so that we might say that, by a chain of causation, we owe at least a large part of his *œuvre* to his relationship with his mother.

That relationship was exceptionally close, but in a strange way, for it was also distant. He lived with his mother most of his life, until her death aged ninety in 1871. On the evidence of his autobiography, *Praeterita*, his feelings towards her were ambivalent, to say the least, as perhaps is only to be expected of someone whose mother was so powerful and so controlling of him as a child. When Ruskin was lodged as a student in Christ Church, Oxford, in 1837, his mother, Margaret, took lodgings herself in the High Street, to which her son repaired each evening, until he left the university. He was the only student of whom this was true, and is one of the very few students (if any other) of whom it has *ever* been true. Even if he experienced no mockery from his fellow-students because of this arrangement, which strikes me as unlikely, Ruskin must have been to some degree humiliated by it.

Much in *Praeterita*,[2] written in his later sixties, may not be literally true: for example, he says that as a young child he had few or no toys, but this claim is not borne out by collateral evidence. Nevertheless, what he says on the subject of toys is revealing, at least as to his state of feelings:

> No toys of any kind were at first allowed … On one of my birthdays, [my aunt] bought the most radiant Punch and Judy she could find … I must have been greatly impressed. My mother was obliged to accept them; but afterwards quietly told me it was not right I should have them; and I never saw them again.

The fact that he remembered, or thought he remembered, having no toys, and then having a gorgeous Punch and Judy removed from him on the very sour grounds that he should not have them, could surely only have caused him rage towards his mother. Whatever the real cause of this rage, even supposing his memory to have been mistaken in detail or even in outline, it must have existed.

His first mention of his mother in *Praeterita* is one that hardly reflects tender feelings: 'My mother, being a girl of great power, with not a little pride, grew more and more exemplary in her entirely conscientious career

…'. Even taken at its most literal best, suggesting a woman of iron probity, this is hardly an affectionate description, and she does not sound like someone fun to be with, let alone to be with all one's life.

By our standards, at any rate, his upbringing was harsh, though Ruskin says that it had its benefits:

> I had a bunch of keys to play with …; as I grew older, I had a cart and a ball; and when I was five or six years old, two boxes of well-cut wooden bricks. With these modest, but I still think, entirely sufficient possessions, and being summarily whipped if I cried, did not do as I was bid, or tumbled on the stairs, I soon attained serene and secure methods of life and notions …

This sounds like serenity through fear; and, as Dickens remarks, nothing is awoken so early in a child as a sense of injustice, and it is surely unjust to punish a small child—with whipping!—for tumbling on the stairs. No doubt parents were harder on their children then than now, but as described, the normal protective reflexes of a mother seem to be singularly lacking.

Margaret Ruskin was by far Ruskin's most important teacher when he was a child. His description of his mother's regime puts one in mind of John Stuart Mill's *Autobiography*, published a decade and a half before Ruskin's. Mill, of course, was taught by his father rather than by his mother, who is but a ghost in Mill's book; but in her own way she was just as unbending, though she was pious where Mill's father was strictly rationalist.

She was a nonconformist Protestant, that is to say a Protestant who did not subscribe to the doctrines, or assent to the privileges of, the Church of England. Her belief was literalist and her early indoctrination of her son may go to explain some of the deep *angst* that Ruskin felt later in his life when he wrestled with the nature and content of his religious belief, or whether he had any religious belief at all. It is a common experience that early religious indoctrination by parents causes those who later question the beliefs with which they have been indoctrinated great anxiety and feelings of guilt, even if they come to the conclusion that the indoctrinated beliefs are without foundation or even absurd. If James Mill's militant rationalism can be regarded as a religion, then his famous son, John Stuart Mill, underwent a religious crisis in his early adulthood in the course of which he came to the conclusion that his father's whole philosophy and outlook on life was insufficient and omitted important dimensions of human life. Intellectual rejection, however, is not the same as emotional liberation, and Mill, like Ruskin, retained the scars and open wounds of his early training for the rest of his life. This must have been a common enough experience in an era in which the strenuous indoctrination of children must have seemed almost a parental duty.

Ruskin described his Bible training under the direction of his mother in *Praeterita*, and it is not one which many people would wish to have undergone. He says that she had 'solemnly dedicated me to God' before he was born (he was, significantly, an only child, on whom all his parents' concern and ambition was fixed in a form undiluted by concern for other children). Ruskin writes of this 'dedication' (whose precise meaning he is at a loss to understand) that 'Very good women are remarkably apt to make away with their children in this manner.' Again, these are hardly words of approbation, let alone affection; they imply that Ruskin thought his mother had done something that she was not entitled to do and which he experienced as an injustice, a feeling that had evidently rankled with him until late in his life.

The making away with him included having decided his career for him from the very first. Again, this could hardly have been an experience unique to Ruskin: even today, parents often push their children in the direction of one career or another and appear vicariously to live their ambitions through them. In Ruskin's case, it was the Church of England that his mother destined him for, a choice that must have seemed almost hypocritical to him, in so far as it was motivated by a desire for social advancement rather than by an adherence to theological truth.

In his mother's desire that he should enter the church, Ruskin saw the domestic weakness of his father, often absent on his business as an importer and salesman of sherry, in which he made a considerable fortune:

[My mother] would try to send me to college, and make a clergyman of me … My father, who had the exceedingly bad habit of yielding to my mother in large things and taking his own way in little ones, allowed me, without saying a word, to be allowed to be thus withdrawn from the sherry trade as an unclean thing …

Of course, Ruskin would not have been suited to the business of buying or selling sherry, nor would his father, a man who much regretted his own lack of formal education and strove successfully for the rest of his life to make up for it, ever have wanted him to pursue it. Ruskin's irony here is directed at his mother, not at his father.

Of the Bible training proper, Ruskin writes:

I have next with deeper gratitude to chronicle what I owe to my mother for the resolutely consistent lesson which so exercised me in the scriptures as to make every word of them familiar to my ear in habitual music—yet in that familiarity, as transcending all thought, and ordering all conduct.

This is a clear recognition that the influence of an early and thorough indoctrination extends far beyond the conscious acceptance or rejection by ratiocination of whatever doctrine is indoctrinated: that it has a durable influence that lies deeply and perhaps ineradicably inscribed in the character.

Margaret Ruskin had a method of indoctrination:

This she effected not by her own superior or personal authority, but simply by compelling me to read the book thoroughly for myself. As soon as I was able to read with fluency she began a course of Bible work with me, which never ceased till I went to Oxford. She read alternate verses with me watching, at first, every intonation of my voice, and correcting false ones till she made me understand the verse, if within my reach, rightly and energetical … In this way she began with the first verse of Genesis, and went straight through to the last verse of the Apocalypse.

There is an odd contradiction in this passage: the assertion that his mother did not teach by her own superior or personal authority is obviously false; no child as young as was Ruskin would have submitted of his own will, without the exertion of parental authority, to a 'course of Bible work' such as this: a course that lasted until the age of eighteen. Moreover,

Ruskin later says that if he had failed to grasp the meaning of any Bible text, on his mother's own interpretation of it, she would have continued to teach him it until the day she died.

This intensive daily instruction in the Bible, lasting for his entire childhood and well into his adolescence, not surprisingly left a mark on Ruskin's personality and style as a writer. As Mill wrote clear, straightforward, muscular expository prose, Ruskin wrote in the prose of an Old Testament prophet, calling down his anathemata on the evils of the modern world, and even, at the end of his long life, turning himself physically into such a prophet. He wrote prose like no one else's, which marked him off from every other writer, and for this he had truly to thank his mother.

The deficiencies of the upbringing he received at the hands of both his parents were clear to him. Having first enumerated its advantages (his parents lived in perfect harmony with one another, and he never heard a cross word between them, giving him a strong sense of security), he enumerated the disadvantages: First, he wrote, I had nothing to love.

This sentence stands by itself in *Praeterita*, bald and naked so to speak. It has a tremendous charge in its unequivocal simplicity and finality, and one can almost feel the intense emotion off bitterness and regret that Ruskin must have felt in writing it. Freud, in one of his more illuminating statements, said that a son who has once experienced his mother's love feels forever like a conquering hero; with the likely corollary that one who has not done so can never quite have confidence in the reality or desert of his own success ever afterwards.

Ruskin continues: 'My parents were visible powers of nature to me, no more loved than the sun and the moon: only I should have been annoyed and puzzled if either of them had gone out.' This had lasting consequences for his emotional life: 'I grew up selfish or unaffectionate, but that, when affection did come, it came with violence, utterly rampant and unmanageable, at least by me, who "never before had anything to manage".'

This would be bad enough if Ruskin had managed early to separate himself from his parents; but far from this, he lived so inseparably from them that it seemed to his wife, Effie Gray, that they were far more important to him than she, another reason why she chose to leave him, by no means an easy decision to take in Victorian England. Ruskin spent much of his life living with people who were no more to him than visible powers of nature, without malign intent, perhaps, but inescapable. He describes how he was not allowed to pick the fruit in the garden at Herne Hill until his mother had declared it ripe for picking; and he could not choose a peach for himself. No doubt there might have been a good reason for not allowing a small boy to eat unripe fruit, but the prohibition lasted beyond a normal age for it, and permanently protecting a child from the consequences of his acts is hardly a way of encouraging independence.

Having written nothing that could be interpreted as affectionate towards his mother, and having described her as a woman that surely nobody would want for his own mother, Ruskin rather curiously goes on to say: 'The reader has, I hope, gathered that in all I have hitherto said, emphasis has been laid only on the favourable conditions which surrounded the child whose history I am writing, and on the docile and impressionable quietness of its temper.' This is surely a remarkable thing to say of a childhood in which there was 'nothing to love' (it is notable that he here uses the word *nothing* rather than *nobody*, as if inanimate objects rather than people were the proper locus of his affections, a peculiarity that might explain his early sensitivity to and obsession with art). The reader will almost certainly have gathered the precise opposite of that which Ruskin hoped he had gathered, for if what he had described was 'only the favourable conditions' that formed his docile nature of his temper, one may surmise what the unfavourable ones were: His impressionable quietness of temper (though he was certainly capable later of expressing his rage against his father when, completely dependent financially on him until he died when Ruskin was forty-five years old, his father did not accede to his requests for money, thus combining dependence and entitlement, not a combination to result in a happy frame of mind).

Of course, it is possible that Ruskin's memory was not accurate, or that he was deliberately misleading himself or the public; modern scholarship had found that *Praeterita* does indeed contain many inaccuracies. But it does not follow that all in it is false, especially in essence; and you do not have to be a full Freudian to believe that an inaccurate memory may have a significance of its own. The fact that Ruskin chose to reveal his mother's control over the fruit in the garden half a century later suggests that Ruskin at least *felt* that his mother had been too domineering. And since it is unlikely that he was entirely mistaken in his description of his mother's insistence on biblical study, and since it is undoubtedly true that she followed him to Oxford, Ruskin's feeling was not without reason.

Although it seems highly reasonable to ascribe Ruskin's inability to form a satisfactory adult relationship with a woman to the close and intense but cold relationship with his mother, other explanations are possible: for example, that he was homosexual, either acknowledged or unacknowledged to himself, which accounts for his horror on seeing his wife's body, and that this homosexuality had nothing whatever to do with his relationship with his mother. His later bouts of madness were almost certainly unconnected with that relationship, and the pattern suggests that he was manic-depressive (his paternal grandfather, John Thomas Ruskin, had committed suicide in a state of intense depression). Possessed and capable of social charm, but incapable of close relationships except in fantasy or by correspondence, and which have a marked infantile quality, Ruskin was happiest when alone. It is difficult to resist the conclusion that his ferocious industry, in which he tackled so many things from drainage to J. M. W. Turner's immense bequest to the British nation to geological science, as well as being the author of one of the largest corpuses of published writing ever accomplished, was an attempt to keep an underlying unhappiness at bay, and that the source of at least some of this unhappiness is to be found in his early experiences of and with his mother.

Notes

1. It is notable that his two most famous followers, Tolstoy and Gandhi, also had some peculiarities with regard to sex.
2. All quotations from *Praeterita* are from the 1907 edition, ed. George Allen.

3

Ambitious Daughter: Louisa May Alcott and Her Mother

Gardner McFall

When Louisa May Alcott and her younger sister May sailed to Europe in April 1870 in the glow of *Little Women*'s great success, she referred to them in her journal as "two ambitious daughters." May was off to become a painter and Louisa, at the age of thirty-seven, had achieved her girlhood dream of becoming a recognized author, able to bring financial security to the Alcott family with Parts 1 and 2 of *Little Women* appearing in 1868 and 1869, respectively. How Louisa managed this in the nineteenth century, when women could not attend college or vote, when married women could not legally own property or inherit money, and social conditioning aimed to reduce them to sweet, silent, models of self-sacrifice feels like nothing short of a miracle. As Meg bemoans women's state in *Little Women*: "men have to work, and women to marry for money. It's a dreadfully unjust world." Yet Louisa May Alcott had a not-so-secret (at least, not to her) champion in her corner: her mother, Abigail May Alcott, known as "Abby" or "Abba" to her husband and brother and "Marmee" to her four daughters; she enabled Louisa not only to break through gender barriers of the day, but pursue her ambition of becoming a writer and produce the first classic girls' book, based on her own "simple and

© The Author(s) 2018
D. Salwak (ed.), *Writers and Their Mothers*,
https://doi.org/10.1007/978-3-319-68348-5_3

true" experience (as she referred to it), with Marmee heroically at its center. In doing so, whatever critics may feel about the book, Louisa May Alcott secured a place in the canon of children's literature.

Every daughter intimately knows the abiding power of her mother. She thrives on her praise, and can wither under her censoring eye. Nancy Friday has written in *My Mother/Myself: The Daughter's Search for Identity*: "My mother ... was my first and most lasting model ... whatever else happens to us in relationships to father, peers, teachers—the tie to the mother is the one constant, a kind of lens through which all that follows is seen." Born to Dorothy Sewell May and Colonel Joseph May, Abba grew up in a liberal, aristocratic Boston family that valued moral virtue and education. According to Sanford Salyer's early biography of Abigail May Alcott (*Marmee: The Mother of Little Women*), her own mother was "a power behind the scenes, a gentle, pervading influence. She knew how to get inside the minds of her children, studied their failings and possibilities, and guided them with a calm wisdom." Two of Abba's favorite maxims were: "Love your duty and you will be happy" and "Hope, and Keep busy," an instruction she tucked in Louisa's journal in 1845 and which the March sisters adopt as their motto in a moment of family crisis in *Little Women*.

Duty, industry, and generosity bordering on self-denial, were three gender-specific virtues Abba learned in her own home and later communicated to her daughters. Compared to her older, beloved sister, Louisa May Greele, for whom Louisa May Alcott was named, Abba was in Salyer's words "strong, forceful, moody and impulsive." Louisa inherited her mother's character traits as well as her dark eyes and hair; according to Eve LaPlante in *Marmee & Louisa: The Untold Story of Louisa May Alcott*, she had a childhood memory of being told she was "the spirit and image of her mother." Her father Bronson noted that "the elements of their beings are similar; the will is the predominating power." Quick tempered, they both struggled to control their anger, a bond they shared; Marmee counsels Jo about this in *Little Women*: "I am angry nearly every day of my life, Jo; but I have learned not to show it; and I still hope to learn not to feel it, though it may take me another forty years to do so." In giving Marmee these words, Alcott expressed not just the condition of women then but what it continues to be in modern times as articulated by Friday: "We bear a burden of anger all our lives … society would rather we always wore a pretty face, women have been trained to cut off anger."

Although Abba was unable to attend Harvard like her brother Samuel Joseph, she borrowed his books and absorbed the ideas he brought home. Like him, she grew to be a women's rights activist and abolitionist, who, with her husband Bronson, sheltered runaway slaves. She was a woman ahead of her time. Headstrong and intelligent, a natural storyteller, she once had aspirations of becoming a writer and certainly continued writing poems as an adult. Louisa recorded in her journal on Christmas 1843 "the piece of poetry which Mother wrote for me." Abba defied her father's wish that she marry a cousin, preferring to wait and marry, if ever, for love, and spent her twenties exploring her place in the world, not tied to a wife's domestic duties. Her ambitions prompted her in 1819 to tell her parents, "I am not willing to be found incapable of anything." She said, quotes LaPlante, that "No woman's intelligence should be trammeled and attenuated by custom as her body is by fashion."

Abba's will and fervor regarding women's worth and independence informed her ability over many years to shoulder the family's financial burdens. The man she married, Bronson Alcott, a friend of Emerson and Thoreau, implemented his progressive views of education at Boston's Temple School, which Louisa attended from ages three to seven, until the school closed, but he was incapable of providing for his family as men were expected to at that time. Insolvency and transience marked Louisa's childhood. While Bronson fostered an intellectual atmosphere at home when he was there, and apparently was a brilliant conversationalist abroad, he held conventional views of how girls should behave, and criticized Louisa for being undisciplined and willful. He much preferred Louisa's older sister Anna who was blonde, sweet-tempered, and docile, who wrote about others in her journal, not herself. Leaving home at key junctures in Louisa's life, to travel to England for a year and a half when she was eight and nine, or just take a room apart from the family in order to read and think, which he did for eighteen months during her infancy, it fell to Abba to shoulder the duties of parenting and bread-winning alone.

Over the years, even Anna and Louisa worked to support the family, taking in sewing and teaching to supplement Abba's income, derived at various times from boarders in her home, social work, and requests to her brother for money. In her mother, Louisa saw a powerful figure, capable of acting independently of a man, indeed standing in a man's position by way of supporting the household, and, at critical points when Louisa's voice might have been silenced by cultural mores and values, in the ways Carol Gilligan (*In a Different Voice*) and Mary Pipher (*Reviving Ophelia*) have cogently examined concerning girls' development today, Abba gave Louisa the unwavering encouragement to follow her inclinations and talent.

Friday quotes child psychiatrist Dr. Sirgay Sanger: "There's a crucial growth period from five to ten ... when little girls' passivity and underachievement is too often accepted as normal." The ages five to ten were central to Louisa's development. In "Recollections of My Childhood," where she refers to herself as a tomboy, she credits her mother with giving her a sense of freedom, by allowing her to run freely outside and "learning of Nature what no books can teach ... I remember running over the hills just at dawn one summer morning, and pausing to rest in the silent woods, saw through an arch of trees, the sun rise over river, hill, and wide green meadows as I never saw it before." Madeleine B. Stern reveals that when she was eight, Louisa wrote a two-stanza, rhyming poem, entitled "To the First Robin", to which her mother reportedly responded: "You will grow up a Shakespeare!" She preserved the poem and urged Louisa to keep writing.

Although all the members of the Alcott family had journals, Abba especially encouraged Louisa to write about her life there; she often left notes in Louisa's journal for her to read, telling her in one to "make observations about our conversations and your own thoughts. It helps you to express them." In her book *The Alcotts: Biography of a Family*, Madelon Bedell notes that Abba wrote her brother: "I encourage her writing. It is a safety valve to her smothered sorrow which might otherwise consume her young and tender heart." Bedell suggests that Abba may have been speaking from her own smothered sorrows. In any event, she understood that Louisa channeled her emotions into her writing, and that she was happy when immersed in imaginative work.

Nothing is so valuable to a child trying to understand her place in the world as having her mother's attention and praise. This matters to children of both sexes, of course, but it is especially true for girls, who, by virtue of being female, understand themselves in relation to the world through her. The mother serves as a model to imitate or reject; she demonstrates what's possible or what to avoid. Evidently, Abba's favorable response to her poem motivated Louisa to continue writing; when she was ten, she records in her journal giving her mother "a moss cross and piece of poetry" for her birthday. Urging Louisa on, Abba presented Louisa with a pencil case in 1842 on her tenth birthday, with a note quoted by LaPlante: "Dear Daughter ... I give you the pencil-case I promised, for I have observed that you are fond of writing, and wish to encourage the habit."

Such acceptance from her mother combined with permission to pursue her talent informed Louisa's early sense of herself as well as her ambition, which was large; an 1843 journal entry indicates that she wished to be as famous as Jenny Lind. Of course, in time, she became more famous. Abba's views must have counter balanced the social tutelage she was receiving from her father and his friend, the English transcendentalist Charles Lane, who convinced Bronson that he should move his family to a commune they named Fruitlands during the family's unhappy years 1843–1845. In a January 1845 journal entry (Louisa was twelve), she recorded some of her "lessons." Among the virtues she was striving for, according to her list, were the stereotypically female virtues of "silence" and "self-denial"; the vices she wished to surmount included "activity" and "willfulness," clearly traits considered undesirable in a girl. In her book *In a Different Voice: Psychological Theory and Women's Development*, Carol Gilligan says: "The notion that virtue for women lies in self-sacrifice has complicated the course of women's development by pitting the moral issue of goodness against the adult questions of responsibility and choice." In *Reviving Ophelia: Saving the Lives of Adolescent Girls*, Mary Pipher writes:

> Girls have long been trained to be feminine at considerable cost to their humanity. They have long been evaluated on the basis of appearance and caught in myriad double binds: achieve, but not too much; be polite, but be yourself; be feminine and adult; be aware of our cultural heritage, but don't comment on the sexism. Another way to describe this feminine training is to call it false self-training. Girls are trained to be less than who they really are. They are trained to be what the culture wants of its young women, not what they themselves want to become.

If this restricting socialization is true today, Louisa's triumph over the more rigid rules governing girls in the nineteenth century is all the more remarkable. She managed to yoke female sacrifice or duty to her goal of becoming a writer. If she could earn money from her writing to take care of her family, she could fulfill her duty as a daughter and her wish for her independent, adult self simultaneously. These twin impulses were arguably fueled in part by well-channeled anger. Aware of her family's relentless poverty, she wrote in "Recollections of My Childhood" that as a girl she'd shaken her fist "at fate embodied in a crow cawing dismally on the fence nearby—'I will do something by-and-by. Don't care what, teach, sew, act, write, anything to help the family; and I'll be rich and famous and happy before I die'."

Louisa knew whom she could count on, writing in her journal at thirteen: "People think I'm wild and queer; but Mother 'understands and helps me," and at seventeen: "I can't talk to anyone but Mother about my troubles." Discovering an encouraging note from Abba in her journal, she also wrote: "I wish some one would write as helpfully to her, for she needs cheering up with all the care she has. I often think what a hard life she has had since she married—so full of wandering and all sorts of worry … I think she is a very brave, good woman; and my dream is to have a lovely, quiet home for her, with no debts or troubles to burden her."

Abba continued giving Louisa talismanic gifts. She assured Louisa had her own room in March 1846 when the family occupied their Concord house known as Hillside; Louisa was thirteen when she wrote in her journal: "I have at last got the little room I have wanted so long, and am very happy about it. It does me good to be alone, and Mother has made it very pretty and neat for me. My work-basket and desk are by the window, and my closet is full of dried herbs that smell very nice. The door that opens into the garden will be very pretty in summer, and I can run off to the woods when I like." LaPlante reveals that Abba saved money to give Louisa a fountain pen that year on her fourteenth birthday, with a card reading: "Dearest, accept from your Mother this pen and for her sake as well as your own use it freely and worthily." As quoted by Bedell, she also wrote to her on this occasion: "believe me you are capable of ranking among the best."

In the fall of 1851, at eighteen, Louisa published a poem entitled "Sunlight" in *Peterson's Magazine* under the pseudonym "Flora Fairfield"; it was her first paid publication. She also sold her first short story "The

Rival Painters", which was published under her initials the following year, an accomplishment ascribed to Jo in *Little Women*: "how proud Mrs. March was when she knew it." In real life as well as in the fiction, Marmee was indeed proud of her daughter's first literary success. For Christmas 1852, she bought Louisa a new desk, the culmination in a long series of presents and commendations, expressing her confidence in Louisa and support of her work. She believed, quotes LaPlante, that Louisa was "a fine, bright girl [who] only needs encouragement to be a brave woman."

Over-determined to say the least, Louisa survived adolescence intact with a writer's profession in view and gratitude to her mother who understood and had empowered her. She was twenty-two when her first book, *Flower Fables*, was published in December 1854, earning her thirty dollars; she gave the volume to her mother with a letter on Christmas day:

> Into your Christmas stocking I have put my "first-born," knowing that you will accept it with all its faults (for grandmothers are always kind), and look upon it merely as an earnest of what I may yet do ... Whatever beauty or poetry is to be found in my little book is owing to your interest in and encouragement of all my efforts from the first to the last; and if ever I can do anything to be proud of, my greatest happiness will be that I can thank you for that ... and I shall be content to write if it gives you pleasure.

A decade later, at Christmas, Louisa presented her mother with her first novel, *Moods*, which she dedicated to her, inscribing the copy on Abba's sixty-fourth birthday: "To Mother, my earliest patron, kindest critic, dearest reader I gratefully & affectionately inscribe my first romance." In a Christmas letter to her that same year, she continued: "Now if it [*Moods*] makes a little money and opens the way for more, I shall be satisfied, and you in some measure repaid for all the sympathy help and love that have done so much for me in these hard years. I hope Success will sweeten me and make me what I long to become more than a great writer—a good daughter."

By now Louisa had been published in the *Atlantic Monthly*, an accomplishment of which she was justly proud; *Hospital Sketches* (based on her experience as a Civil War nurse in Washington, DC) had been serialized in the *Boston Commonwealth* and would soon be published in book form. Only two years before, she'd told her father (and she reiterates the story in her 1888 "Recollections of My Childhood"): "I think I shall come out right, and prove though an *Alcott*, I *can* support myself. I like the independent feeling; and though not an easy life, it is a free one, and I enjoy it."

Louisa's repayment to her mother had begun in earnest. In January 1864, she'd recorded in her journal that she'd earned "by my writing alone nearly six hundred dollars since last January." For her, there was no looking or turning back as duty to be a good daughter merged with authorship and virtue with ambition. She would not follow the conventional path for girls of the day toward marriage and motherhood. She balked at marrying Jo off to Laurie in *Little Women*, writing in her journal in November 1868: "Girls write to ask who the little women marry, as if that were the only end and aim of a woman's life." While Louisa had numerous flirtations with different suitors and at least one marriage proposal about which she sought her mother's advice and on determining she did not truly love the gentleman declined, Louisa's "children" would be her books and, as Susan Cheever has written in *Louisa May Alcott*, she would be "married to her family and their needs." She had seen firsthand in her parents' relationship how difficult and stifling marriage could be. Not even seeing her sister Anna happily married to John Pratt would change her view: she famously wrote in her journal in 1860: "Very sweet and pretty, but I'd rather be a free spinster and paddle my own canoe."

Abba aided Louisa in her writing by being a first reader and a sometime narrative conspirator (Louisa used material from her mother's life and journals in her fiction). She cheered her on, and took care of her when she fell into a frenzied trance of composition, making her clothes and bringing her cups of tea. Not that Abba lived through Louisa; she had three other daughters to guide, though Lizzie, her third daughter died in 1858. She was always very dedicated to her women's rights work. Yet Abba certainly felt maternal gratification and pride in Louisa's accomplishments; she probably saw in her what she might have become if her own circumstances had been different.

Louisa repaid her mother not only with her books and inscriptions, but undiluted devotion and love. In the published Journals and Letters, there's not a negative word about Abba, while what Madeleine B. Stern calls in her introduction to Alcott's *Journals* her "love-hate" relationship with her father is tempered by reduced expectations for him and acceptance of his being a "philosopher in a money-loving world." Numerous times, she records the pleasure of providing her mother with material comforts, with "keeping the hounds of care and debt from worrying her."

As Abba aged and fell ill, Louisa took care of her, putting aside her writing as necessary. When she returned from her 1870 trip to Europe with May, she found her mother "feeble and much aged", writing in her journal, "I shall never go far away from her again." In 1873, she found that "Marmee [was] never to be our brave, energetic leader any more." She died on November 25, 1877 after falling "quietly asleep" in Louisa's arms; after her death, Louisa wrote: "My duty is done, and now I shall be glad to follow her." Louisa, Abba's good, ambitious daughter had fulfilled her early wish to make her mother burden-free; yet somehow knowledge of that completed mission did not fully comfort Louisa. A month later, she wrote: "a great warmth seems gone out of life, and there is no motive to go on now."

Louisa May Alcott lived a little more than a decade after her mother died, and, though she published books and continued to care for her family, the great love of her life was gone. This mother-daughter relationship, what LaPlante calls "perhaps the most famous mother-daughter pair in American literary history," stands like a balanced scale of gifts given and gifts repaid, freely. Pipher writes about negotiating the dangerous terrain of adolescence and moving into adulthood: "Growth requires courage and hard work on the part of the individual and it requires the protection and nurturing of the environment. Some girls develop under the most adverse conditions, but the most interesting question to me is, Under what conditions do most girls develop to their fullest?" For Louisa May Alcott, whose adverse conditions were poverty, awareness of her parents' unhappy marriage, and the strictures of the nineteenth century itself, Abba was her protector and nurturer; she mediated the environment in which the budding author evolved and ultimately thrived. Fortunately, Abba lived to see her daughter's huge, unprecedented success, what, according to Cheever, Louisa's publisher of *Little Women*, Thomas Niles, called "a triumph of the century." By the end of December

1869, LaPlante tells us, *Little Women* had sold 36,000 copies and Louisa was the most popular author in America.

If developing to one's fullest means achieving a youthful dream, Louisa did so. If it came at a cost (for some critics that cost would be marriage and biological motherhood) that is often how big dreams are achieved. Louisa chose to take care of her family and repay her mother for the greatest gift a mother can give her daughter: permission to hold on to her true voice (not the voice culture imposes), and protection while she becomes herself.

4

Walt Whitman and His Mother

Kenneth Silverman

Often people would say—men, women, children, would say—'You are a Whitman: I know you.' When I asked how they knew they would up with a finger at me: 'By your features, your gait, your voice: they are your mother's.' I think all that was, is, true: I could see it in myself.

Walt Whitman's comment illustrates the opening of "Song of Myself": "every atom belonging to me as good belongs to you." It pleased Whitman to think that people noticed his strong resemblance to Louisa Van Velsor, his mother. Her marriage to a carpenter produced nine children. When twenty-four years old she gave birth to her second child, Walter. What survives of their relationship is a correspondence of about three hundred letters between mother and son, one hundred seventy of them from her to him.

Mother and son not only looked alike, but were emotionally very close. He addressed his letters to "Dearest Mother" and might close a letter with "Love to you, dearest mother." Louisa had a sense of humor and a sense of irony. She satisfied his view of her as a "cheerful woman," playfully closing her letters as "your dear mother," "good bie Louisa Whitman," "your mother L Whi," or simply "LW."

© The Author(s) 2018
D. Salwak (ed.), *Writers and Their Mothers*,
https://doi.org/10.1007/978-3-319-68348-5_4

Walt idolized his mother. As he speaks of himself in "Starting from Paumanok," he had been "rais'd by a perfect mother." But his intense love for Louisa existed apart from his poetry. She was not a literary person. His letters to her were often prosaic, style-less: "I felt quite disagreeable yesterday," he wrote, "but went to bed early, & had a good sleep—to-day, Tuesday, I have felt all right." His great closeness to his mother deeply influenced his poetry without taking it in. He once said that "Leaves of Grass is the flower of her temperament active in me." But there was more to be said: "Who could ever consider Leaves of Grass a wonderful thing: who? She would shake her head. God bless her! She never did," he wrote; "She stood before Leaves of Grass mystified, defeated." Louisa inspired something she could not appreciate.

Whitman wrote nothing to his mother about the ongoing printing and publication of his works, information he did give to others. He did however mention or send her reviews of his works that appeared in newspapers and magazines: "Mother, I send you the part of the N.Y. Times. containing a good long piece about me." And he did occasionally tell Louisa about his poetry, presumably one time in 1868 when overseeing a revised edition of *Leaves of Grass*, containing "Drum-Taps": "so your writin again leaves of grass,'" she commented, "well if it dont hurt you i am glad." Even if not tuned into his poetic work, she had great faith in him, he believed, and felt that he would accomplish wonderful things.

In their correspondence, Walt and Louisa often expressed concern about each other's health. He told her when feeling ill with a sore throat or faintness: "walt if you are sick or any thing the matter i hope you will let me know immedtely." Louisa was proud of her ability to write letters: "i fell quite smart considering i have to work so hard." And when writing to Walt she often mentioned her lameness and dizziness, both when suffering them and being relieved. As she put it: "i have been troubled with the dissiness in my head but to day i feel intirely free." She had spells of rheumatism as well that disabled a hand and arm. She relieved the spell by taking "sulphur vapor" treatments. "I feel very anxious about you," Walt wrote to her, "I am afraid you are more unwell than you say—I think about it night & day." In writing to others too, he often mentioned his mother's physical health and state of mind, always wanting her to be active and cheerful. Louisa had been making do on an uncertain income for forty years, while rearing eight children. Walt often sent money to her—two dollars, five, ten.

Part of Louisa and Walt's love for each other was their mutual love of the large Whitman family—her seven other sons and daughters/his seven brothers and sisters. He wished letters from her to concern them: "I want to hear family affairs before any thing else," he told her, "write all about things home." Whitman also wrote to Louisa through other family members, asking them to show her the letters he had written to them: "i don't know what i would doo if i dident get any letters," Louisa said. She once noted that letters to her from other family members had fallen off: "but the good old standby if he should fail me i should have nothing to look for but i gess there is no danger is there walter dear as long as you have your old mamma."

"I wrote my mother voluminously from the war," Walt recorded, "my dear, dear mother. She in Brooklyn, alone—I wrote every day or so." He had much to report. Late in 1862, he began ten years of government employment in Washington. He worked as a clerk in the Interior Department's Bureau of Indian Affairs, then as a copyist of official documents in the Attorney General's office. Becoming transformed into an important city, wartime Washington was then a huge hospital, nurturing thousands of injured soldiers. Walt reported to Louisa back home in Brooklyn what he saw many times, "awful loads & trains & boat loads of poor bloody & pale & wounded young men."

The schedules of Walt's clerkships gave him time to help treat the injured troops, as he began doing in January 1863. He told Louisa that he generally went to the hospitals from 10 to 4 and again from 6 to 9, some days not going to both or even skipping a day when he felt "somewhat opprest." He visited the wounded troops, both Union and Confederate, not only in the hospitals but also in the camps. He reported to Louisa the illness and butchery he witnessed and cared for: a "heap of feet, arms, legs, &c. under a tree," jaundice, pus, gangrene, tetanus, scurvy, consumption, putrefied wounds, delirium—one soldier believing "there was a great cat gnawing at his arm, & eating it." Walt himself served at amputations, changed dressings, watched troops dying of pneumonia. "Poor souls," Louisa replied, "i think much about them and always glad to hear you speak of them."

When going among the wounded, Walt brought with him a haversack with food, preserves, crackers, berries, oysters, note-paper, small sums of money, and other treats to distribute: "I have given the men pipes & tobacco, (I am the only one that gives them tobacco)—O how much good it does some of them—the chaplains & most of them are down upon it—but I give them & let them smoke ..."

It particularly pleased Walt to enter the wards finely cleansed and clothed, to give the wounded men an impression of refreshed manly health, encouraging them to survive and return healthy to their prewar selves. "Mother, I have real pride in telling you that I have the consciousness of saving quite a little number of lives by saving them from giving up & being a good deal with them—the men say it is so, & the doctors say it is so ... I know you will like to hear it, mother, so I tell you." He believed, he said, that "no men ever loved each other as I & some of these poor wounded, sick & dying men love each other."

Louisa was deeply concerned about the ongoing war. She told her son that almost every night before going to bed she browsed in his "Drum-Taps" (whose war poems happen to contain the line "My sacred one, my mother"). It seemed to Walt that his mother never tired of hearing about the soldiers. "I sometimes think she is the greatest patriot I have ever met, one of the old stock—I believe she would cheerfully give her life for the Union, if it would avail anything." She missed him and often urged him to visit her and stay a while: "dont you think you can come Walt i doo so wish you can."

His letters to her involved mention of serious wounds and illness. "I know you like to hear about the poor young men, after I have once begun to mention them," he told her. His mother responded to his depictions of the wounded: "O the poor soldiers i doo so hope that poor fellow will live it is so sad to suffer so much." Walt especially wanted Louisa to know what he felt when treating the troops. When present at sickening wounds, operations, and deaths he kept "singularly cool," he said. But hours afterward, when recalling the events at home or out walking alone, "I feel sick & actually tremble."

However much involved in war work, Walt remained concerned about the health of "My sacred one, my mother." For her part, Louisa wanted and needed her son's love, and his presence: "don't you think you can come Walt i doo so wish you can i know you will if you can get away." Occasionally Walt was able to take breaks from his work in Washington to stay with Louisa in Brooklyn and later in Camden, New Jersey. "The great recompense of my journey here is to see my mother so well, & so bravely sailing on amid many troubles & discouragements like a noble old ship." When finding her less than healthy, he could even look after her himself. "Mother has been quite sick, & I have been sort of nurse ... she is much better this morning under my doctoring."

At home, Walt and Louisa always breakfasted together, "& it is first rate," he wrote: "I think my mammy makes the best coffee in the world, & buckwheats ditto." One morning, apparently around breakfast time, mother and son learned of the assassination of Lincoln. Walt had seen Lincoln often, had what he called a "good view" of the president in Washington, and once stood close to him. He and his mother shared their horror: "not a mouthful was eaten all day by either of us," Walt wrote. "We each drank half cup of coffee, that was all. Little was said. We got every newspaper morning and evening, and the frequent extras of that period, and pass'd them silently to each other."

Louisa tried to follow national political developments: "once in a while I see the tribune. i like so to read the speakery in the house." Thus she followed the trial of President Andrew Johnson, not only in itself but also because it could affect Walt's job:

> "i suppose there will be stiring times to Washington," she wrote to her son: "well Walt we have lived to see something that never was i suppose known before in America the impeachment ! i think it rather sad but notwithstanding exactly as it should be."

However absorbed in his literary career and clerical work, Walt kept track of Louisa's advancing age: "dear old Mother, as she gets older & older, I think about her every day & night":

> ... my dear mother is very well indeed for her age, which is 67—she is cheerful & hearty, & still does all her light housework & cooking.

... Mother's age I think begins to just show—in a few weeks, she will commence her 70th year—still she does most of her light housework.

... Mother is quite well for an old woman of 74.

... hearty dinner with my mammy (who has this month entered on her 76th year, but to my eyes looks young & handsome yet).

... Mother is towards eighty ... now shows the infirmities of age (indeed rapidly advancing) but looks finely, & is cheerful hearted.

At his Washington desk in January 1873, Walt suffered a stroke that left him dizzy, nauseated, and partly paralyzed. "Mother you must not feel uneasy," he wrote to Louisa, "though I know you will." On the wall at the foot of his bed he tacked up a picture of her. Receiving electric shock treatment on his left leg and thigh he could begin sitting up, taking medicines. Suffering in body and spirit, feeling feeble, he nevertheless wrote to her about his progress every few days: she "mopes and worries a good deal about me." By late March he was able to spend a little time at the office.

Just as Walt began to feel almost exuberant about his chances for recovery, his mother began to fail. He hastened to Camden a few days before her death on May 23, four months after his stroke: "I was just able to get from Washington to her dying bed, & sit there." After her burial he returned to Washington for a few weeks but felt so depressed and restless that he obtained a two-month leave of absence and fled back to Camden. There he lived in his "inexpressibly beloved" mother's rooms, frequently sitting in her old armchair.

For Walt, now fifty-four years old, Louisa's death was a profound loss. "Every day every night comes the thought of my mother." It left him feeling emptied. After two weeks in her room, he felt that "the blank in life & heart left by the death of my mother is what will never to me be filled." In July the death remained vivid in his mind: "time does not lift the cloud from me at all." Though he gained physical strength in August, his feelings kept hurting: "mother's death—I cannot be reconciled to that yet—it is the great cloud of my life—nothing that ever happened before has had such an effect on me."

Walt felt no better at the beginning of the new year: "Every day & every night comes the thought of my mother ... that thought remains to temper the rest of my life." In May, a year after Louisa's death, the grief remained, "a sorrow from which I have never entirely recovered, & likely never shall—she was an unusually cheerful woman."

Walt Whitman had lost something more than a mother, a friendly double of himself: "my darling dear mother: she and I—oh! we have been great chums: always next to each other: always."

5

The Maternal Embrace: Samuel Beckett and His Mother May

Margaret Drabble

'*I am what her savage loving has made me*'

Beckett's relationship with his mother, as with his Mother Country, was close and combative. May was a formidable woman, and however far he travelled, he never escaped her. The shadow of her presence looms in many of his deeply if obscurely autobiographical plays, poems and novels, and he discusses his difficulties with her in letters to his closest friends. When he was twenty-seven, at the beginning of his professional writing life, he committed himself to intensive psychoanalysis in London (paid for by her) in an effort to come to terms with their embattled relationship, which was making him physically ill. But he remained inextricably involved with her, responded to her demands over the years (despite the advice of his analyst), and he attended her in her last illness in the Merrion Nursing Home by the Grand Canal in Dublin, though he had long been resident abroad. He sat (as he recalled in *Krapp's Last Tape*) on a bench by the weir, gazing at her bedroom window, 'in the biting wind, wishing she were gone … the blind went

© The Author(s) 2018
D. Salwak (ed.), *Writers and Their Mothers*,
https://doi.org/10.1007/978-3-319-68348-5_5

down, one of those dirty brown roller affairs, throwing a ball for a little white dog, as chance would have it. I happened to look up and there it was. All over and done with at last.'

She died on 25 August 1950, having survived her husband Bill by sixteen years, and after suffering for some time from Parkinson's disease, an illness which has been seen to affect and inform the complex psychology and choreography of ageing in several of her son's plays.

I first became interested in May Beckett when reading James Knowlson's fine biography of Beckett, *Damned to Fame* (1996), from which she emerges as a strong-willed, somewhat dour, volatile and dominating figure, with a conventional and rigid respect for religion and propriety, but a far from conventional temperament. She was a large-featured, stoutly dressed and upholstered woman who liked gardening and dogs and donkeys and wore large hats adorned with flowers and birds. She produced a wayward, brilliant, rebellious yet eternally mother-entangled son, and much of his work springs from their conflicts, which were at times dramatic: there were scenes of plate-throwing at the Beckett home, and on one occasion, with some drink taken, he concluded their quarrel by throwing a pudding 'into the veronica hedge near the kitchen door.' The dynamics of this intense mother-son relationship, as described by Knowlson (and, as I later discovered, by Beckett's earlier biographer, Deirdre Bair) were intriguing, and I decided to explore them. I used to find Beckett's work challenging and compelling as well as painful and at times incomprehensibly repellent and nihilistic, yet here, in his mother's life and her power over him, seemed a clue to its darkness, and a way into the strange landscape of his mind.

Maria Jones Roe, usually known as May, was born on 11 March 1871, the daughter of a wealthy miller and exporter of grain. She trained as a nurse after the failure of her father's business, and was employed at the Adelaide Hospital in Dublin, where she met William Frank Beckett (Bill) whom she married in 1901: she was tending him when he was admitted for what seems to have been a depressive episode. Her personality thereafter had some of the dictatorial traits of an old-style hospital matron, and she was to rule the Beckett household of Cooldrinagh, in Foxrock, a leafy suburb of Dublin, with histrionic authority. She quarrelled noisily with her servants as well as with her son and was described by those who knew her as 'ill-tempered' and 'tricky'.

Her family was fiercely Protestant: the Becketts were also Protestant, and their considerable wealth came from the building trade, property dealing and quantity surveying. Bill's depression, said to have been caused by his family's refusal to accept his intention of marrying a young Catholic woman with whom he was in love, appears to have been uncharacteristic: he was much less devout than May, and became known around Dublin as a club-bable man and an outdoor man, who enjoyed golf, swimming and walking. He did not accompany her on her regular visits to Tullow Parish Church.

Cooldrinagh, the house where Samuel was to be born, was built for May and Bill in 1903: it was grand and spacious, a comfortable Edwardian family home 'in Tudor style' with bow windows, mahogany panelling, a verbena-covered porch, a gravelled driveway, a croquet lawn and a planta-tion of larches. Its name means 'back of the blackthorn hedge', and was taken from the name of May's father's mill at Leixlip. Its features appear again and again in Beckett's prose. The larches in particular obsessed him, and a larch tree appears ominously in *Molloy* as the site of the grave of the foul-smelling 'uniformly yellow' dead dog that the mother-figure in the novel buries there: Molloy, witness to the interment but not, as he insists, gravedigger, comments that 'It was a larch. It is the only tree I can iden-tify with any certainty. Funny she should have chosen, to bury her dog beneath, the only tree I can identify with certainty. The sea-green needles are like silk and speckled ... '

The house is still there, though deliberately obscured from view by high hedges and fencing. The neighbourhood prided itself on its gentility, and still does: as I and my friend and guide Niall MacMonagle peered through the cracks in the fence and tried in vain to attract the attention of the man who was mowing the lawn, a passer-by stopped to chat to us and told us that the Becketts were still well remembered, and that Foxrock has always declined to have a public house or a betting shop. This is a little odd, as Foxrock is also the home of the famous Leopardstown Racecourse, which features prominently in Irish fiction and is the back-drop of Beckett's 1956 radio play, *All That Fall*. But so it is. When Niall and I were investigating the house and visiting the church, in 2016, Cooldrinagh was on the market, described as 'a wonderful example of the Arts and Crafts style ... steeped in history', in a sales catalogue that also emphasised its privacy. The asking price was 35,000,000 euros.

Frank Edward Beckett was born promptly in July 1902, and was by all accounts a healthy, happy little boy. Samuel, born in the new family home at Cooldrinagh, followed on 13 April 1906: he was a more delicate and often sickly child, requiring much attention. The house certainly had the possibilities of enabling the kind of happy childhood that Samuel at times insisted he had enjoyed: lawns, shrubberies, outhouses, dogs, a donkey and donkey cart, chickens, trees to climb, wigwams, hiding places. The boys were left in charge of a Catholic nanny, Bridget Bray from the County of Meath, known as Bibby, who told them scary stories and played wild games with them, while May led a ladylike existence of tea parties (with wafer-thin bread and butter) and gardening and dog shows and walking her Pomerians. (Pomerians are a feature in Beckett's work.) One of Sam's odder and most provocative amusements, as he relates in *Company*, consisted of hurling himself from the top of a sixty-foot high fir tree, trusting the 'great boughs' to break his fall. His mother unsurprisingly was not at all pleased by this activity, and told him he was a very naughty boy.

The artist Beatrice Elvery, in her memoir *Today We Will Only Gossip* (1964, published under her married name, Beatrice Glenavy), gives us a pleasant and normative glimpse of May: her mother Mary Theresa Elvery was a great friend of May, who lived less than a mile away, and they would visit one another frequently, 'May flying on her bicycle with some new cutting or plant for my mother's garden'. Beatrice's sister Dorothy, an amateur painter, is responsible for an extraordinary early photograph of little Sam, aged four, kneeling outdoors in the porch of Cooldrinagh in a nightshirt on a pillow at May's feet as if in prayer: she was planning a painting to be called 'Bedtime', the set topic for a competition for the Taylor Art Scholarship, and she asked May to pose with Sam for an image from which she could work. Sam recalls this scene in *How It Is*: the verbena, the red tiles of the veranda, the hum of insects, and his mother's huge hatted head towering over him, her eyes burning with 'severe love'.

This episode reveals that May had friends with artistic interests, and was not innately hostile to the arts. The neighbourhood, although genteel, was not Philistine. (This was, and is, Ireland: the tone of much of Edwardian stockbroker suburban life in England would have been very different.) Sam's father's sister, his much loved Aunt Cissie Beckett Sinclair, was very musical, a talented pianist who loved to sing: she was also a gifted artist, and trained with the Elvery sisters at the Dublin Metropolitan School of Art. So May might well have been proud to discover in due course that her son was deeply interested in literature, and that he intended to be a writer.

Will and May were committed to providing an orthodox education for their sons: they first attended the 'Misses Elsners' Academy', a kindergarten run by two German sisters, and at the age of nine Sam left for a school in Dublin called Earlsfort House, where he was happy, admired the teachers, and excelled at games (tennis and croquet) and English composition. He then moved on at the age of thirteen as a boarder to the distinguished Portora Royal School at Eniskillen, in Fermanagh, which had a long tradition of educating the sons of prosperous Protestant families. He did well there too, both in sports and studies (developing a great love of cricket). In October 1923, aged seventeen, he entered Trinity College Dublin (predominantly Protestant) to study English, French and Italian, moving on after graduating with distinction to teach briefly in Belfast, then to Paris, where he became a lecteur d'anglais at the École Normale Supérieure, a position of prestige.

All seemed to be going according to plan, and Sam seemed set for a successful career as a scholar and academic. We do not know if May suffered from what we now call the empty-nest syndrome, or whether she was content with her Foxrock life of visits and church activities and gardening. Later evidence suggests that she would not have been happy for him to have settled permanently in Paris (and not at all pleased to learn that he had become friendly there with the notorious Irish exile James Joyce, who was already influencing Beckett's prose, behaviour and aspirations). She wanted him nearer home, back in Ireland, where she could have some control over him. And he came back in 1930, to a post as a lecturer to Trinity College.

He returned from Paris looking skinny and in his own word 'scrofulous', and was welcomed home by his parents, who fussed over him and tried to fatten him up. He moved as soon as he could from Cooldrinagh to rooms at Trinity, where he was able to lead a freer and more Bohemian life. But he returned to Foxrock in the summer to recover from a bout of pleurisy, and while he was there May happened upon some of his writing that he had left lying about, was (predictably) disgusted by it, and kicked him out of the house. It is not known which of his works-in-progress she came upon, but there are many possibilities of obscenity and blasphemy that would have caused extreme offence. In fact, there was hardly anything he wrote that she might have found acceptable. Did he leave it, whatever it was, lying around on purpose? Maybe his analyst was to ask him this question. The quarrel seems to have lasted for months, and he appears to have been as much upset by it as she was.

He was not happy teaching at Trinity, although he had good friends around him. He was not happy in Ireland. He knew he needed to get away.

He decided with much agonising to ditch his career at Trinity, and resigned formally (by telegram) in January 1932, after heading off for Germany. Several years of often lonely wandering on the continent and in England followed, during which he worked on his fiction and on translations, made efforts to publish, made contacts in the literary world and intensified his friendship with Joyce and (unhappily) with Joyce's daughter Lucia. Back in Foxrock, May waited. After his sickly reappearance in 1930, maybe she suspected that ill health and poverty would bring him back. And eventually he gave in. After miserable months in London, he wrote to his parents asking for his airfare home, and 'crawled home' with his tale between his legs (interview with Lawrence Harvey, March 1962). He tried to readjust to Cooldrinagh, playing the piano, sawing logs, and taking long walks with his father, which he always enjoyed, while he continued to work at his creative writing. But he was ill at ease in the Dublin he had tried to desert, and physically unwell. He was admitted to the Merrion Nursing Home in December 1932 for an operation on a cyst on his neck, and on a hammer toe. His parents and brother, laden with books, visited him regularly. He was slow to recover and the operation on his neck did not heal well. May fussed over him and worried about him, with some reason. In May 1933 the cyst was lanced again, and May and Bill devoted themselves to trying to nurse him back to health, but he was frustrated and angry and started to drink more heavily. (This was the period during which he threw the pudding into the veronica hedge.) Both Bill and May were anxious for their son to take a 'proper job', for he was financially completely dependent on them, and on loans from Frank. (Sam's relationship with Frank bears some resemblance to James Joyce's with his brother Stanislaus: both writers were greatly in debt to their hard-working, more prosaic brothers.)

Beckett might have regained his health, and he might have come to consider more seriously one of the academic posts which had been dangled before him, but in June 1933, catastrophically, Bill suffered two massive heart attacks, and died. This was a disaster for both sons and mother. The obedient Frank, who had at one time tried to escape, was trapped forever in the family firm, and May went into deep and ostentatious mourning, which, much as he had loved his father, got on Sam's nerves and drove him to distraction. He protested against 'the vile worms of melancholy observance' (letter to Tom MacGreevy, July 1933) and his health now got worse and worse, his supposed convalescence deteriorating into night sweats and panic attacks, insomnia and urinary problems. A doctor friend, Geoffrey Thompson, advised him to seek psychoanalysis, then illegal in Ireland, and somehow he persuaded his mother (on whom he was now financially dependent) to allow him to move to London and to sign on with Dr Wilfred Ruprecht Bion (1897–1979), practising at the Tavistock Clinic, and then at the beginning of what was to be a highly distinguished career. He started on 27 January 1934, and nearly two years of treatment followed, which seems to have focused largely on his relationship with May, who had both cosseted and constricted him all his life. Bion and Beckett were intellectually compatible, and got on well socially as well as in their analytic relationship. The London years were often painfully lonely for Beckett, but they were also productive.

He was also beginning to make progress as a writer. From May's point of view, it was unfortunate that the very titles of his first two published works were so unlikely to be well received in Foxrock. This was not yet the successful author-son of whom she could be proud. His poem "Whoroscope," written and published in Paris in 1930, was ripely blasphemous and obscene, and his volume of stories, *More Pricks than Kicks*, published by Chatto and Windus in 1934, was not the kind of volume to display prominently on the library shelves at Cooldrinagh. It even upset his liberal-minded and artistic Aunt Cissie, although she eventually came round to it. But the battle for recognition and acceptance from May continued.

However, in the summer of 1935, a most extraordinary interlude in their relationship occurred. Sam, still based in London, invited his mother to accompany him on a three-week holiday in England, an episode the strangeness of which has in my view not been sufficiently registered. It is true that she paid for everything, but he seems to have gone along with the plan willingly enough. He hired a car, prone though he was to motoring and cycling misadventures, and drove her to various cathedral cities (including St Albans, Canterbury, Winchester, Bath and Wells, an itinerary which involved covering many hundreds of miles) and on to the West Country, spending several days in West Somerset and North Devon. This is a long time to spend alone with a difficult widowed mother, and one doubts if Bion would have recommended it. But Beckett was enthusiastic about their sight-seeing, and seems to have been able to enjoy himself. These travels strike me all the more forcefully because I know this part of the West Country very well, and am writing these words at Porlock Weir, overlooking the Bristol Channel, and a few minutes' walk from the Anchor Hotel where the Becketts must have stayed. I know what he called 'the demented gradients' of Porlock Hill all too well, and am surprised (as was he) that his hired car survived them. In Lynmouth, a few miles west of Porlock, they stayed in the Glen Lyn hotel, and followed in the footsteps of Shelley, Wordsworth and Coleridge. Sam was able to escape by going for a swim. Maybe May risked what we now call the Granny Walk along the beautiful Valley of the Rocks, with its wild goats and strange rock formations, and he felt obliged to introduce her to the Doone Valley, named for the fictitious heroine Lorna Doone. It is my view, naturally, that the great beauty and many literary associations of the landscape wrought on both their souls, to such a degree that they were even able to discuss his analysis peacefully over dinner at the hotel.

He described this holiday in a letter to one of his closest friends, Tom MacGreevy, later a director of the National Gallery of Ireland, and the recipient of many of Beckett's confidences. This letter tells us that they had originally intended to spend a night in Minehead, a seaside resort a few miles east of Porlock Weir, but 'one look' at it was 'enough'. This was (and remains) a characteristically superior view of Minehead, a pleasant but modest lower middle-class resort, with many 'dreary semi-detached gabled houses' (N. Pevsner, 'The Buildings of England', 1958). I like it very much and have spent many happy hours there, but it is not surprising that the Becketts moved on to the wilder and more romantic Porlock Weir, above which Coleridge wrote 'Kubla Khan'.

Beckett returned to London refreshed, having visited Lichfield by himself after leaving May with family (including a 'loathed cousin') at Newark, and with a new Lichfield-inspired idea in his head: he thought he might write a play about the melancholic and troubled Samuel Johnson, famous son of Lichfield. But instead he immersed himself in the creation of what was to be his first major novel, *Murphy*, set in London, and much of it closely based on his exhausting solitary tramps around the capital and his hours of study in its libraries. He worked and walked obsessively in what he described as a 'boiling over', while continuing to correspond regularly with May. But at the end of the year, in December 1935, he found himself back at Cooldrinagh, ostensibly for his annual Christmas visit, at the end of his analysis, and he stayed there in a truce that lasted for some months. He was suffering from pleurisy, and May was delighted to devote herself once more to nursing him. They rubbed along together as best they could. She kept him, in his view, short of money, and urged him to seek what she reasonably called 'gainful employment'. One can see her point of view. He had excellent academic qualifications, and had carelessly thrown away his appointment at Trinity College. But he thought the world owed him a living. He seemed to expect to live off her forever, drinking with his friends in town or hiding in his study writing books she would never want to be seen reading.

Luckily for both of them, some ill-judged and doomed sexual attachments convinced him that he had to get away from Dublin again, and in September 1936 he set off for Germany after what Knowlson described as 'a tense, though fond farewell to his mother on the front porch of Cooldrinagh'. She was glad that he was getting away from the two unsuitable young women with whom he had been involved, but she had little faith in his future. He could now expect a small annuity from his father's estate, but it would not be enough to support him. She cannot yet have had any intimation that he would become self-sufficient, successful, and world famous.

With Sam away on the continent, May reorganised her life. She sold Cooldrinagh, and moved into a nearby bungalow, New Place, in the same refined neighbourhood of Foxrock, taking with her some of the domestic staff, including the gardener, Christy. Her contacts with Sam over the next few years were overshadowed by the threat of war and her own deteriorating health. Sam came back to Ireland reluctantly, and his return visits were marked by several disastrous episodes—a libel action against his uncle Harry Sinclair, a serious car collision, bouts of heavy drinking, and the traumatic death of a Kerry Blue terrier bitch, Wolf, of which both mother and son were very fond. She had it put down and buried it while he was out of the house, which made him 'very upset'. (Deirdre Bair suggests that this was done out of malice and a desire to cause pain and regain control, as he had to nurse her through two days of prostrated grief, but her motives were probably more mixed.) Tensions ran very high whenever they were together, as Sam struggled against her persistent claims on him. He resolved to move permanently to Paris, but even after he had settled there the tug-of-war and flux of their relationship continued: a characteristically melodramatic episode occurred in January 1938 when Beckett was randomly stabbed in Paris in the street by a pimp, and ended up in hospital. His mother, his brother Frank and Frank's newly wedded wife at once flew over to be with him, and Sam was touched by May's concern. 'I felt great gusts of affection and esteem and compassion for her when she was over … what a relationship!' For a few days she had him where she needed him to be: dependent, grateful, in need of her care.

But the balance was beginning to shift, as his reputation grew and he became more confident of his literary power, and as she began to age and weaken. On his infrequent but regular visits to New Place he noted her increasing frailty: she had Parkinson's, was stooped and shaking, could hardly write, and was depressed and lonely. Letters to friends describe her as 'shaky' and 'poorly'; her eyes were 'heart-rending - the eyes of an issueless childhood, the eyes of old age' (letter to Georges Duthuit, 2 August 1948). He accompanied her to Tullow church when he was in Foxrock and took charge of her medication, seeking advice from doctor friends, and acquiring Swiss drugs for her condition. They were nearing the end game. He tried to get her to come on a visit to France, but it couldn't be managed. Years later he was to write to a newly bereaved relative (Peggy Beckett) that May was 'seventeen years in black and sorrow hardly daring to smile … her religion didn't seem to help her at all' (22 April 1971).

It was a long, slow decline, and the end came, as we have seen, in the summer of 1950. She had a fall and broke her leg, but it was not the fall that killed her: it was, as he recorded, 'Parkinsonian encephalitis'. She had also been in great mental distress. He was there for her last days, but, inevitably, he was relieved when she died and it was all over at last. He had longed for it all to be over at last.

And yet he was what she had made him. She had forged his genius by her power and her relentless claims upon him. Memories of her are threaded through his prose and poetry, and she was a constant creative presence, as well as a destructive one. The liberating vision that Krapp receives on the pier at Dun Laoghaire was in fact experienced, he claimed, in May's house in Foxrock, probably in the summer of 1945. That was where he started to write *Molloy*. She was a part of him, for better and for worse. His anguished compassion for the old, the frail, the grief-stricken, the despairing was rooted in her. She rocked it into him from the cradle.

In a late, short play, *Footfalls*, written many years after her death, he evokes a mother-daughter relationship, in which he gives the speaker the name May, transposed at one point to Amy. It is a tale of unutterable sadness: May is neither bitter nor grotesque, like the mothers in *Molloy* and *End Game*, but infinitely sad. She walks and walks, barefoot on the floorboards, and grieves and paces, and paces and grieves. Some commentaries have connected this play with Jung (Beckett went with Bion to hear Jung speak in London during his analysis) and the famous Jungian case of the girl who was never fully born. But I connect it with May Beckett, haunting Cooldrinagh, haunting New Place, haunting her son. The play was first performed in 1976, with Beckett's favourite actress, Billie Whitelaw, as May, and the stage directions describe her 'dishevelled grey hair, worn grey wrap hiding feet, trailing'. It is a play of ageing and endless psychotic repetition. 'Slip out at nightfall and into the little church by the north door, always locked at that hour, and walk, up and down, up and down.' May was frozen by 'some shudder of the mind', and Beckett's pity for her, as for all suffering things, is immeasurable. He took up the theme again, a few years later, in *Rockaby* (1981), where an old woman (again Billie Whitelaw) with unkempt grey hair rocks herself monotonously as she delivers a monologue with the refrain 'time she stopped'. And stop at last she did, as the blind came down. But she never left him.

6

William Golding's Mother

Judy Carver

A small girl runs along the clifftop. She is about seven, and in one hand she carries a covered enamel pitcher. It is full of cream from the farm. She and the rest of the family will have it with late summer blackberries. The day is bright though breezy—this is, after all, the north coast of Cornwall.

But the ground is not as gentle as it looks. A tussock of grass trips her, throws her to the ground, and spills the cream. It spreads in the dirt, useless.

My grandmother Mildred told me this story often, perhaps forgetting I had heard it before, but I think more likely re-living it herself. Strangely,

---

My thanks are due to Professor John Carey, Alison Golding, the late Theo Golding, the late Eileen Hogben, and Elizabeth Hogben. Much of this account depends on my memory. I've done my best to be truthful. I have also drawn on many unpublished pieces of writing by my father. In particular, I have used and quoted from a manuscript by him which he calls 'Men Women & Now'. It was probably written in 1966 but just possibly the previous year. The description of my grandfather Alec surrounded by a crowd of children is actually taken from my father's novel *Free Fall*, first published in 1959, a few months after my grandfather's death. The character of the teacher Nick Shales, described here, was acknowledged by my father as a portrait of Alec, and is completely recognisable to his family. There is also an untitled account by him, written sometime around the spring of 1969, which I have called 'It was 1940', since this is how it begins. I have also quoted from my father's immense journal which started in autumn 1971 and continued up to the night before his death in June 1993. This is indicated in the text.

© The Author(s) 2018
D. Salwak (ed.), *Writers and Their Mothers*,
https://doi.org/10.1007/978-3-319-68348-5_6

she would smile as she did so. Her childhood was very vivid to her even in old age (she was seventy-four when I was born). Cornwall and its countryside, its coast, and its legends were a large part of her life, especially her imaginative life. During the half-century of her marriage in landlocked, chilly Marlborough, she had the local Newquay paper sent up to her every week. The papers arrived rolled into cylinders, wrapped in brown paper, and she would open them eagerly. She told many Cornish stories, but these were generally too full of the supernatural to get past my parents' anxious censorship. One ghost story has survived; my father turned it into French as a piece of homework for a class he and my mother took. It is neatly marked up by the young woman who taught them in Truro in the 1980s, but it has my father's sparseness and his taste for the one vital detail—perhaps this was also Grandma's style. They were quite right not to let her tell it to me—I find it profoundly disturbing even now, in my seventies. Like the spilt cream story, it causes you pain. Grandma's stories were not for the faint-hearted.

Grandma lived a third of her life during the reign of Queen Victoria. Her parents, Thomas and Mary Elizabeth Curnoe (*née* Husband), married in February 1869. February is not the most obvious choice for a wedding, but their first child, a boy called John, was born four days after the wedding. Grandma was born in November 1870, when the little boy would have been nearly twenty-two months. He had died eight weeks earlier, of scarlatina.

My grandmother's birth certificate does not give her a name, and I suppose one should hesitate to interpret that fact. Eventually she became Mildred Mary Agatha, and the photos we have of her as a child make much of her. She is nicely dressed, in the pleated, swagged and cluttered costumes of the period, and—possibly for photographic reasons—she looks very straight and unflinching at the camera. And we know from her own account that she ran happily around the countryside near Newquay. She still hankered after the windswept cliff tops as an old woman; this suggests her childhood did contain happiness. There may not have been many toys—she was shyly appreciative of the dolls' house my grandfather made me, and no dolls of her own survived. Perhaps they were handed on to her sister. However, there were definitely books; once at Marlborough I was reading *Little Women*, and she said to me, 'Of course, I always liked Jo best.'

Poor Grandma—I looked up at her wrinkled face and hid my incredulity that someone so ancient had actually read Louisa May Alcott as a child. I hope she didn't understand. And I am so pleased she liked Jo best. Did she see herself as Jo? My father's imagined portrait of her as a young woman (long before he knew her) is reminiscent: "She was a gaunt, leggy, humourous [sic] girl, I fancy, dark-haired and striking but not pretty."

We do have a photograph, a family group in which she is about twenty-five or six, and I can see the humorous quality—she looks quite satirical. Perhaps the photographer has made some comment about her. And she does look tall compared with the others, though in fact like all our family she was rather short. She stands at the back, and her face is kind rather than pretty. It may be my imagination, but I think she already looks somewhat defeated, as if she would not struggle to be at the front.

As a child and young woman, she had piano lessons; she played all her life. I remember her playing the *Moonlight Sonata*. She and my grandfather, Alec Golding, played duets before they were married. He was a very reasonable violinist; and from somewhere in that strange Newquay home she produced a violin—a good one—and gave it him. What schooling she had was local. Until she met my grandfather, the furthest she had been from Newquay was Modbury in Devon, to visit her aunt.

Grandma was born in the village of Crantock, across the river Gannel from Newquay, in the Old Albion pub where her grandmother was licensee. My father did not know until after her death that she was born in a pub. She and my grandfather were teetotal, and anyway the raffishness of the idea would not have pleased either of them. My father comments admiringly, 'She carried that secret to the grave, with all the hardness and more success than Lady Dedlock.'

The 1870s were a bad time in Cornwall. Cornish tin and copper could not compete with the cheaper discoveries in South America. Harsh as a miner's occupation was, the lack of it was terrible for many Cornish families. Some moved to other mining areas in Britain: Wales, Lancashire, Yorkshire. A friend of mine from Burnley, Lancashire, is surnamed Trevithick, an utterly Cornish name; her family, she said, had walked the hundreds of miles from Cornwall. No sooner had the mining collapsed than the fishing industry began a long decline as well. The shoals of herring, whose sudden appearances had been so intermittent that they were heralded by a special watchman called the huer, first diminished and then quietly failed to turn up. My grandmother's father was a mining engineer, and soon after her birth in 1870 he took long, unpredictable trips to mines in distant parts of the world—to the western United States, Ballarat in Australia, and maybe South America. Family legend says it was a good thing he went—he and his wife quarrelled so violently that one of them might have murdered the other.

I assume they had married because of the imminent birth of their first child. It's hard to think of any other reason for the closeness of the two events. No doubt there had been pressure from her parents. My father believed that his ancestors, particularly the female ones, were tenacious defenders of the fragile respectability of their families, struggling against the chaos that would overwhelm them if they let things slip.

So, by the time the little boy died, my great-grandmother was irrevocably tethered to her husband by yet another child—a child she may have resented. This is a grim beginning for Grandma's childhood, with the death of her little brother, her parents' volatile emotions, the decline of mining and fishing, and Thomas Curnoe's unpredictability, let alone his failure to provide for the family. To support their grass-widowed daughter, her parents William and Mary Husband purchased a boarding house in Newquay—a tall, gaunt house on Mount Wise, a long, narrow road up above the town and harbour, with sea views. They had caught the tide of the next big thing in Newquay—tourists. The railway was already there, originally designed for mining and fishing. Newquay, with its glorious beaches and picturesque, somewhat disused harbour was a good holiday destination. A small building boom began.

The house was named Karenza, the Cornish word for charity or love—I hope it's too cynical to see this as a family joke. Here the Curnoe females, hard at work running Karenza, endured the sporadic reappearances of the nominal head of household, the intermittent arrival of comparative wealth, and no doubt the swift decline afterwards to genteel poverty. My great-grandfather Thomas Curnoe is said to have declared, 'Tes come in minin' and tes goin' in minin'.' I can hear those words in the voice of my grandmother, my father and my aunt. It was a good story, which does not mean it was untrue.

We still have some of Thomas Curnoe's gold, a few bits, some turned into jewellery. The gold was real, though not plentiful, and so was its disappearance. He made several unsuccessful investments in Cornish tin and lost almost everything more than once, despite its being a very bad bet. I wonder if the succession of losses was partly designed to give him permission to go on his travels again. There are documents making him a citizen of the State of Nevada—my father fantasised about an alternative family, a group of little Curnoes and a bigamous wife, but there is no evidence for this. Meanwhile the house was carefully protected, passing from the Husbands to their daughter, and to her alone.

Grandma's mother had a reputation as a fierce woman, often full of anger—though my father remembers her buying him another cinema ticket when he, as a small boy, had gone to the local cinema in Newquay and had naturally lost the first one. Revealingly, he seems to have felt that such kindness was uncharacteristic. The idea of her quarrelling with her husband to the point of violence was something he accepted as plausible. He also remembers a terrible scene at Karenza when Grandma was giving him a bath. He was aged about two, and he recalls that the bathroom was 'one of Karenza's glories'. Grandma had allowed him to play— to slide down the long slope at one end of the bath, landing in a swoosh and a great soapy wave at the other end. My great-grandmother burst in, 'uttering bloody knives', he says. Grandma sank under the attack to a diminished and frightened figure, cowed by her own mother's rage. She was described to me by her niece as a frightened woman, frightened of her mother.

My grandmother did eventually have three more siblings: two brothers Tom and Will, and a much younger and very beloved sister Mary Victoria Estie, always called by the last of these names. But the little boy who died in October 1870 seems to have preoccupied her. Many decades later, a married woman of thirty-five, she was pleased that her own first child, Jose, was born in 1906 on the anniversary of her brother's death.

To my father, Estie was the family beauty. She had, he said, two handfuls of beauty, and one of them was the handful my grandmother should have had. For him, and for our family, the beauty of a woman was a huge thing—and its absence a potent source of pain. My grandmother's lack of it was for my father the tragedy of her life, and a source of that deep disappointment he saw in her. I don't know whether this is true. Maybe she didn't mind. She and the beautiful Estie were said to be particularly fond of each other. But then emotions in a family are rarely simple. My father may also have remade her in terms of his own preoccupations (which were often of pain and humiliation). Beauty in particular meant a lot to him, and he was very proud of my mother's wonderful looks. He was, after all, a novelist and had thirty-three years after his mother's death in which to reimagine her—to shape her according to his priorities.

Was Grandma's marriage an escape? She met my grandfather when he got a teaching job in Newquay and was booked into Karenza as a paying guest. This was in 1900. Their marriage took place in January 1906, and my father puzzles about the delay—he and my mother got married in 1939 five months after they met. Was Grandma doubtful about her prospective husband? Was she weighing up an escape from Karenza, and the life of the put-upon daughter, versus marriage to someone she was probably not in love with? It's not an unusual—or unliterary—choice. Besides, she was thirty-five to Alec's twenty-nine, and my father reported that she felt she was past it. But I don't know whether this comes from anything other than his novelist's imagination. Maybe they were, as my grandfather Alec says in his diary, patiently waiting till he got a good enough job.

They married in Truro Cathedral and the photographs of the occasion make everyone, except the luscious Estie, look defensive and slightly startled. Grandma is in a splendid white dress, Alec uncomfortably defiant in a suit. On the marriage certificate Grandma slices five years off her age.

At her marriage, Grandma moved from Newquay, a place defined in so many ways by the sea, to Marlborough in Wiltshire, 'about as far from the sea', says my father, 'as you can get in England' (about 60 miles). It is a small market-town, now pretty and picturesque, but then rather dusty and neglected. It had been a staging-post on the Great West Road, and coaches had come through the town on the journey between London and Bath. Passengers had patronised its many inns. Willoughby, the dangerously attractive anti-hero in Jane Austen's *Sense and Sensibility*, stops there for a pint of porter on his frantic journey from London to Somerset. But these days had long gone. Nevertheless, Marlborough in 1906 had two railway stations, a royal forest dating back to Norman times, and a boys' public school (that is to say, fee-paying and only for the very prosperous). My father felt Marlborough 'sloped up' towards this institution. My grandfather was a teacher at the other school, the grammar school, and the ruthlessly measured distinction between the two coloured my father's entire life. This is no exaggeration, and I am sure I owe my own expensive education to it. If class weren't so serious a matter in England, it might be thought of as the national hobby. British people, at least in the twentieth century, and possibly still, were born and bred experts in its gradations and boundaries. My grandmother was no exception. To her pitch-perfect awareness of class, she added an intense curiosity about people. In 'Men Women & Now' my father writes:

I remember her standing by the dining room window, looking through the muslin curtain at the passersby, but standing well back in case she should be detected ... Sometimes if the specimen or the victim, whatever it was, was far enough off, she would lift the corner curtain for a clearer look ... It was a direct curiosity about individuals, went on sometimes for hours, and in the days when she was spry, became almost a dance.

Meanwhile, my father would be doing something abstract—standing by the fire and contemplating a galaxy, perhaps; and receiving her ejaculated remarks with a nod, or yes or no; until my mother would exclaim with vigorous impatience—'Alec! You're not listening!'—as indeed he was not, contemplating radioactivity, or the instruments of the orchestra.

Eventually my grandmother enlisted an ally in these arts.

> I remember once, returning on leave [from the navy during World War II]. My mother was looking out of the window, 'gunning' as we called it, while Ann [his wife] was sitting by her and sewing. They talked of the passersby and Ann helped my mother's inspired deductions with her wider social knowledge. So my mother took off.
>
> 'That must be the Parkinson boy. He's back from Egypt then. He'll be sneaking down to see the Willis girl while he can, because his mother's still in hospital –'
>
> I remember how wide my eyes and mouth fell open with astonishment at this accurate assessment made from behind muslin, so that Ann, who is post-suffragette[,] laughed till she pricked herself.

He saw this whole process as mysterious but emphatically feminine—he refers to it as 'witchcraft'. He was admiring, though undoubtedly suspicious, of women's capacities, and I saw this many times. In the days when British telephones gave a small but audible click before they rang, my mother and I were both able to hear it while my father, a bit deaf (something he inherited from his mother), could not. In the brief gap between the click and the ring, my mother and I would each stretch out an arm towards the phone, which would then, obediently it seemed to my father, burst into life. Witchcraft, he would mutter again, and I don't think he was joking. Similarly, for him, and probably for his father and brother, too, much of my grandmother's knowledge of other people's lives appeared out of nowhere, as if in defiance of the laws of physics.

Perhaps because women's capacities were always opaque to him, he could be sentimental about them—even, oddly, about motherhood. It was very important for him to see the whole process as deeply instinctive. When my first child was about two, back in the 1970s, I worried about taking my son in a car without a baby seat—this was before it became mandatory. I was doubtful about my capacity to hold on to my small son, if there were an accident. My father replied, 'You wouldn't be able to let go.'

Luckily, this was never tested. He idealised motherhood, and this prevented him from seeing many of its frustrations and difficulties, even in the case of his own wife. In particular, he refused, almost to the end of his life, to accept that the relationship between my mother and her two children was not perfect—when is it ever? This is all the more puzzling, since his attitude to his own mother seems to have been ambivalent, at least until late middle age. He once told me (admittedly he was slightly drunk at the time) that he never had a mother—'You're my mother,' he added. I certainly didn't feel like it.

He wrote much about his early childhood, and one of the most astonishing things in these writings, at least to me, is that my bearded, bluff, broad-shouldered father wanted as a child to be a girl. He thought of girls as superior beings, gorgeous, knowledgeable and skilful. He was thrilled to wear a tortoiseshell slide in his hair. He wished to be of the same stuff as them, soft, beautiful, neat … Later, he simply adored them. Aged about seven, he fell terribly in love with a little dark-haired Belgian girl, a refugee in World War I. She vanished suddenly from his life, and he suspected his parents had ensured that the tentative friendship should end. He remembered the little Belgian girl painfully for the remaining seventy years and more of his life.

The old house in Marlborough, where he grew up, was dominated in the most gentle way by my grandfather, with his rationalist, atheist (or at least agnostic) beliefs. My father and my uncle Jose, both much bigger than Alec and his wife, and both very athletic, were pupils at his school, and frequently taught by him. He was a popular, engaging teacher, and my father describes him as surrounded by crowds of children who were 'questioning, watching, or just illogically and irrationally wanting to be near'. Alec was small, not handsome and not striking. But he was in some way charismatic. People wanted to be near him.

Back at home as well, this meant that the two sons belonged far more to their father's world than their mother's. This is not to say that it was an unimaginative world. My grandfather had a superb capacity not only for imagining things such as gravity, the solar system, or the laws of thermodynamics, but also for passing them on, for dramatizing them. The state-funded school, under-resourced as you might expect, naturally lacked science equipment, so my grandfather mimed many experiments to his fascinated pupils. My father, in his seventies, could still vividly evoke them and describe them in detail. And Alec, like his wife, was a good story-teller. But the world he described, unlike hers, was calm and rational, predictable, and obedient to the laws of nature. For a while my father stuck with it.

This state of affairs lasted throughout his boyhood, and for part of his time at Brasenose College, Oxford. He admits in his journal that he studied science at university to please his father, gradually coming to the realisation that he could not bear it. The cost of his attempt to stay with science was great. He was in any case unhappy at Oxford, but the grimness of his studies there exacerbated this. Eventually, he had what he described to me as a breakdown. The college suggested he make himself scarce for the summer term of his second year. During the vacation, he had a showdown with his parents. He wished to study English.

My kind and generous grandparents agreed that he should do this. They also agreed that he should have an extra year, since he was effectively starting his bachelor's degree again. However, he completed the three-year course in two years, and was given a 'good' second class degree.

So my father abandoned the world of scientific enquiry and allied himself to one of his great loves ever since childhood—the use of words. It had been too hard following the way of his father—he needed to allow some other influences to be felt. I think he needed to pay more attention, and possibly respect, to my grandmother.

Grandma often demonstrated a clear belief that the world was not rational, not benevolent, not reliable. She shouted at me in real terror when I started to open an umbrella indoors, bringing as she thought terrible bad luck on us all. She had a whole list of the small inadvertencies (putting a shoe on a table, for example; standing a loaf on its end) which would result in the sinking of a ship. Her stories left you with emotions and perhaps a question; they did not provide you with certainty about the physical world—in fact, they did the opposite. I suspect for my father she brought with her, up from Cornwall, the sense of the nearness of death and the real possibility that the dead might decide to visit you.

If you look through the history of any family, the deaths are likely to strike you with what appears excessive frequency. But it does seem to me that my grandmother grew up surrounded by the awareness of death, as well as a sense of the effect bereavement had on people.

The beautiful Estie married, and went to live in Newport, Monmouthshire, where her husband Edgar Haydn Davies was a marine engineer. Then, alas, she died, relatively young, in her early forties, of pernicious anaemia, now treatable but then fatal. Two years later her husband also died, and a few years after that her first child, a son, died too. Eileen, the surviving child, was adopted aged thirteen by my grandparents and came to live in Marlborough. Particularly for my grandmother she was a very welcome addition. My grandmother, by then almost sixty, talked to Eileen as she did to no one else, and much of my adult knowledge of Grandma comes from these conversations. It must have been an interesting sight for the family. Eileen looked so like her mother that she was on one occasion—back in Newquay—mistaken for Estie's ghost.

The simple presence in the house of another woman made a great difference. My father describes the situation before this by saying, 'We were cruel to her, I think, building by instinct a male world to which she conformed.' With Eileen, my grandmother could build a different one, and a very strong relationship developed. Eileen was the one who nursed her in her last years, and Eileen was the one to whom she said her last words.

By the time Eileen moved to Marlborough, my father was at Oxford. His ideas about women in adolescence were more than normally hesitant, ill-informed and even contradictory. He laments the fact that he did not grow up with a sister—that he could not envisage how women were made, what their bodies were like under their clothes. This ignorance led him to horrified speculations about the processes of birth and of defecation. There was no way for him to pacify his curiosity with information—biology at school stopped well before human procreation. It may be that this aided his rejection of his mother's ideas, though it must be said that he completely agreed with her about the terrors of the dark. However, in rejecting most of his mother's world, he mixed that rejection as an adolescent with something like contempt. This, of course, is not unusual. Even in later life he would revisit this stance. In February 1977, aged sixty-five, he had a nightmare about Egyptian mummies, recorded in his journal. In the nightmare he figures as childlike at least, if not a child. He sets down his belief that the nightmare was retribution, justly inflicted.

> During the evening I had spoken disrespectfully of my mother to the others, saying that—after Ann had said I looked like her—she had not my feminine sort of face.

Given the family preoccupation with beauty, this was cruel as well as disrespectful.

Once at home I was reading Austen's *Northanger Abbey*, laughing over the appalling John Thorpe, the callow, graceless brother of the heroine's best friend. My father said,

'Have you got to young Thorpe and the hat?'

He took it from me, flicked back the pages and read aloud.

'"Ah, mother! how do you do?' said he, giving her a hearty shake of the hand: 'where did you get that quiz of a hat, it makes you look like an old witch?'"

And then he added: 'Ghastly. Ghastly but exact. To my shame, of course.'

Grandma herself could be sharp and very direct, suddenly emerging from her remote world to pronounce acerbically or even harshly. She could also be violently angry, like her mother, at least according to my father's account. She once threw a pot of boiling tea at him when he was a boy. Luckily it missed. On another occasion, she threw a pair of trousers at him, presumably forgetting that one pocket contained a knife. Once, at night, when he was small, and in bed in an adjacent room, he begged and begged for a light. Eventually, exasperated, she flung into his darkened room a candlestick, a candle and a packet of matches.

Her intuitive knowledge of people could sometimes make her cruel, particularly if that awareness bore some relation to her own daydreams. When my father was about to go up to Oxford, and was silently envisaging the distinguished and liberated time he was going to have, he describes how 'she crashed straight into the daydream as if she had a kind of stethoscope to my head'.

'Don't think you're going up there, swaying about!' she declared.

These occasional bursts seem to have been the exception. She helped and protected him at university when he had got into debt and what he describes as 'real, bad trouble'. He specifically says she was loyal. On one occasion in his childhood, she persuaded Alec that they should intervene when he was in trouble at school. 'After all', she said, 'it's his world.' My father adds: 'It was simple and accurate and one of the times I have found my situation understood wholly. It defined to me all the sorrow and desperation that I could not define for myself.'

In return, he seems to have understood her in a particularly personal sense. He recognised their common nature. He says: 'She was, as I am, a fantasist, a person whose tumultuous life, torrid, complex, is lit behind the smooth skin of a brow.'

He watched her move about the house, abstracted, happily absorbed, communicating, he thought, to others, to those he believed she valued more than her real family. Her daydreams, he thought, were social, 'hobnobbing' with the great. And some of the disappointment he attributed to her might have been her frustration at the gap between her brilliant imaginings and the mundane streets of Marlborough. Indeed my father reports that his parents in later life grew isolated; they retreated, he said, 'into their poor fortress'. He also said that his mother was 'defeated'.

She was pleased by my success, and took vicarious satisfaction in it. My books and fame were a kind of door into the wide world—that door that she must have looked at so often, pushed at occasionally, and known would never open for her.

I believe he came finally to accept her uncanny awareness of people. But it was difficult, nevertheless, for him to come to terms with the power she had had in his life, a power I suspect he had tried for many years to deny. As a child, he had a recurrent nightmare, one he gives to the anti-hero in his novel *Pincher Martin*.

The dream concerned the cellars under my father's house at 29 the Green Marlborough … The nightmare was this. I would be down there in the dark. I would be small, the cellar vast and dark. An old woman, hideous, a crone, would be advancing on me. I would be turning in terror to run away towards the stairs that led up to the living quarters of the house. I suppose the time always to have been night. As I turn away I find my legs, my whole movements slowed into that peculiar dream rhythm like wading through treacle or trying to run underwater. She, the crone, of course, can advance as fast as she likes. Then, I suppose, I wake up. That was the recurrent nightmare, it's [sic] tone, terror. I don't think I ever had the dream as an adult, and I was fifty before I read in Jung a possible explanation of the dream itself.

I don't know whether it's necessary to look at Jungian psychology to understand what was going on. Maybe the old crone is the Terrible Mother, maybe she is his feared and fearsome grandmother, she of the bloody knives. Or maybe the dream, perhaps like a piece of music, is simply itself and does not have a separate meaning. But I do not mean to be cheaply dismissive of Jungian ideas. My father owed them a great deal. During a very distressing period of his life, characterised by inability to write, by abuse of alcohol and fairly constant despair, he found help and comfort through reading Jung's works. As a result, he started a dream diary, and this dream diary contains much that is revealing about his mother, especially early on. It eventually turned into a more quotidian work, but the early stages of it undoubtedly helped him recover and—crucially to him—start writing again.

One of the first works he produced after this dark time clearly shows him remembering his mother with more appreciation, with subtlety and especially self-reproach. He openly acknowledged (to John Carey, his biographer) that Mr Prettyman and Miss Granham in his 'Sea Trilogy' (which began with the publication in 1980 of *Rites of Passage*) were portraits of his parents. Miss Granham (the name comes from a hill just outside Marlborough) is initially viewed by the narrator as someone he can patronise; gradually, throughout the three novels, he comes to realise her superiority to himself, and eventually, through the tossing of the ship, and his attempt to steady her, he finds to his astonishment that she has a womanly form.

In 'Men Women & Now', an unpublished work written in or around 1966, there is a remembrance of his mother in old age. At the time he wrote it, she had been dead a mere six years.

When she was very old, moving towards a second childhood and dying slowly, she spoke to me in a way she had never spoken before. "I've been a bad mother to you, Bill" she said, in her worn voice. I knew, or guessed what she meant, and tried to deny her knowledge, shouting raucously against the barrier of her deafness. She was thinking, I believe, of her remoteness, her physical remoteness. She felt she had given me as a child, too little cuddling, too much bottle via Lily [his nurse], too little bosom and rest. It may be so. I think it was so, though I denied it to her, as if I had anything to put against her intense perception of people! A woman of nearly ninety, and a man of nearly fifty, poking back all those years, to the smells, the milk and the nappies! So I denied my knowledge, and she knew I denied it, knew it accurately. I tried to shout more, but already she had gone back inside, back to that secret life which was her true being; and now drifting away on the tide, hobnobbing with whatever it was.

My father's last novel, *The Double Tongue*, was left in draft at his death and published posthumously. It is the only one of his works with a female narrator. She is a plain child, rather neglected by her stern parents. It takes an outsider to give her an escape route from her family. Once free of them, she reveals her remarkable talent: she has an uncanny understanding of people, together with the capacity to prophesy. She becomes the priestess of Apollo at his shrine of Delphi and settles there during a very long life, witness to the fading of classical Greece and its glories, and the inexorable rise of the upstart Rome.

Near the end of her life, the priestess decides to investigate the god's mystery. She makes the descent to the sacred cleft in the rock:

When the winter came … when, I say, that deadly wind blew down and sifted the unmelting snow along the cobbled street, I returned to the oracle, as was my right, and opened one leaf of the door. I passed … down the steps past the niches, round the tripod and stood before the curtains. The key with the double labrys was hanging round my neck. I pulled the drawstrings slowly and the curtains slid back. There was a double door behind them. I stood before it for a long time but the only thought that came to me was that whatever happened it did not matter much. So I put the silver labrys into the silver lock and turned the key. The doors were easy enough to open. There was the solid, impenetrable rock of the mountain behind them.

Are we back in the cellar? If so, the old crone has disappeared; in her absence, the astute but retiring prophetess calmly explores the mysteries of the male god. And the experience seems one of acceptance, of the absence of fear and the acknowledgement that some things cannot be known.

For myself, looking back, the quality I associate most with Grandma is poignancy. Even as a child I knew she must be treated gently. I wish she had had more life, more zest. My grandfather's death is still piercingly sad to me, but that is a small part of his picture—he was vigorous, active, happy—fascinated almost to intoxication by the world he lived in. Grandma's death—after years of decline and sad confusion—was of a piece with her life. One evening she suddenly said to Eileen, 'The tide's going out.'

The next morning, she was dead.

I have Grandma's purse, entrusted to me by my cousin Alison, my uncle Jose's daughter. Jose and his wife Theo must have saved it as a relic from the great emptying of the old house at Marlborough. The purse is an old-fashioned brown leather one, with many pockets. It has photos of Grandma's parents, some vastly ancient coins, one so old it's completely smooth. But it also has a little folded piece of chamois leather. Unfolded it reveals a curl of golden hair, so fine it must be a baby's.

7

Voice Rehearsals and Personas in Sylvia's Letters to Aurelia

Adrianne Kalfopoulou

> *For a woman, the call of the mother is not only a call from beyond time, or beyond the socio-political battle ... this call troubles the words: it generates hallucinations, voices...*
> Julia Kristeva, "About Chinese Women"

"Both Sylvia and I were more at ease in writing words of appreciation, admiration, and love than in expressing these emotions verbally and, thank goodness, write them to each other we did!" says Aurelia Plath in the preface to her choices of Sylvia's letters home. The statement is indicative of the necessities language will serve for both mother and daughter. While Aurelia's selection represents a near-seamless expression of Sylvia, or more often Sivvy, as loving, devoted daughter, and omits, as Jacqueline Rose notes in *The Haunting of Sylvia Plath*, significant chunks of the "anger, illness, and left-wing politics", they give a sense of Plath's sheer need to voice herself in a cartography of growing ambitions, experiences, and challenges. They also provide a polyphony of selves that Plath in her various incarnations, as Sivvy-the-hardworking-many-faceted daughter, could inhabit. Here is a sampling:

© The Author(s) 2018
D. Salwak (ed.), *Writers and Their Mothers*,
https://doi.org/10.1007/978-3-319-68348-5_7

from October 21, 1951: "Can't wait to see you Friday. Your incorrigible Sivvy"

from April 30, 1952: "Your happy girl, Sivvy"

from June 2, 1952: "Your own Sivvy"

from November 19, 1952 [after a publication rejection]: "Love, your hollow girl, Sivvy"

from March 3, 1953: "Dearest one, Your busy loving, silvershod Sivvy"

from June 4, 1953 [while working as an intern for *Mademoiselle* in NYC] "Your managing ed, Syrilly"

from June 8, 1953 [still in NYC], "Your citystruck Sivvy"

from October 14, 1955 [in Cambridge on a Fulbright, having tried out for a play with the Dramatic Club], "Your loving daughter, Katherine Cornell"

from October 18, 1955 [after getting her driver's license] "Dearest Licensed Mother!!! ... Your happy Sivvy"

Sylvia writing to Aurelia is Sylvia addressing the source of what Aurelia called their "psychic osmosis". In a March 7, 1952 letter Sylvia writes: "Maybe your daughter is slightly crazy, maybe she just takes after her illustrious mother, but in spite of the fact she has three wicked writtens [sic] next week, she is just now feeling ... very virtuous because she refused three weekends this weekend—Frosh Prom at Yale Junior Prom at Princeton, and a blind date from MH ... ". This highlights a pattern in the content and style of the letters she wrote to Aurelia until her death, but particularly during her Smith College years. She will write of the goals, assignments, events, and encounters she is experiencing and will prioritize them around achievements she is hoping for or has accomplished; these are always worded to please and include Aurelia in her own sense of satisfaction. From an October 8, 1951 letter, there is this: "To have had you there in spirit! To have had you see me! I am sure you would have cried for joy. That is why I am spilling out at such a rate—to try to share as much as I can with you". To share as much as she can with Aurelia suggests more than a desire to include her in a *bildungsroman* of developing selfhood; it demonstrates what the letters as a whole testify to, which is Aurelia's role as a mirroring agent to Sylvia's efforts at forging a life. Aurelia as symbiotic extension to Plath's sense of herself, or in Aurelia's words, as "psychic osmosis", begged the question of what needs Aurelia's selfless devotion to her two children, Sylvia and Warren, after Otto Plath's death, were not fulfilling—what aspects of Sylvia's development did Aurelia's mothering not nurture. In the preface to the 1953 summer of Sylvia's first breakdown and suicide attempt when she learns that she did not get into Frank O'Connor's summer fiction writing workshop at Harvard, Aurelia writes:

> One unforgettable morning, I noticed some partially healed gashes on her legs. Upon my horrified questioning, she replied, 'I just wanted to see if I had the guts!' Then she grasped my hand—hers was burning hot to the touch—and cried passionately, 'Oh, Mother, the world is so rotten! I want to die! Let's die together!"

Not until October 23, 1961 does Plath write her poem "Mirror," but in it we see the darkly ambiguous role of the speaker whose purpose is to reflect the other "Just as it is, unmisted by love or dislike". As a mirror, the poem's speaker is dependent on what it reflects, whether it is "the opposite wall" that starts to feel like it is "a part of my heart," or "A woman" who "bends over me, /Searching my reaches for what she really is." This woman who " ... replaces the darkness" is a face which the poem keeps ambiguous; all we know is that in the mirror "she has drowned a young girl, and in me an old woman /Rises toward her day after day, like a terrible fish." What remains unclear is if the young girl and the old woman might be one and the same, and which of the two, if they are indeed separate, the other is mirroring. The poem's last four lines highlight the symbiosis: the mirror's ability to reflect what it "sees" is also what is being searched for in its reflection by the woman who "comes and goes. /Each morning ... " and whose face "replaces the darkness."

In the manner that Sylvia-as-Sivvy relays the days' demands and preoccupations in her letters, describing the highs and lows of rewards and failures, there is a tone of indebtedness to Aurelia. As with the journals, we see in the letters a testing of the parameters of her roles, whether it is that of the scholarship student or the aspiring writer or the young 1950s woman. In *Sylvia Plath and the Theatre of Mourning*, Christina Britzolakis notes her mastery of forms in the poems she wrote during her college years, that they "signal [her] precocious aspiration and professionalism. At the same time, these poems display an ironic self-reflexivity concerning their own status as a performance." That Sylvia is writing to Aurelia to please and entertain her as much as to update her on her forays and emphasize her ambitions and need for ever more discipline, is one of the constants in the letters. She says, in an October 13, 1954 letter (italics mine):

> Dearest Mother, ... Now I think it is the time for me to concentrate on the hard year ahead, ... I know that beneath the blazing jaunts in yellow convertibles to exquisite restaurants I am really regrettably unoriginal, conventional, and puritanical basically, but I *needed to practice* a certain healthy bohemianism for a while to swing away from the gray-clad, basically-dressed, brown haired, clock-regulated, responsible, salad-eating, water-drinking, bed-going, economical, practical girl that I had become –

We see Plath's "ironic self-reflexivity", as Britzolakis' has discussed it, in poems such as "Daddy", "Lady Lazarus", "Fever 103", "The Applicant", "The Jailer", and others, as a mechanism for both revealing and veiling anxieties that are only alluded to in the letters Aurelia has selected. In the poems we hear the voice that the unabridged journals make explicit. In the discussion of Plath's therapy sessions with Ruth Beuscher who had treated her at McLean Hospital after her first suicide attempt, Beuscher famously tells her, "I give you permission to hate your mother." Plath had resumed therapy from December 1958 to November 1959 when, married to Ted Hughes, she and Hughes moved to Boston. In a section titled "NOTES ON INTERVIEWS WITH RB: Friday, December 12th", Plath writes, "In a smarmy matriarchy of togetherness it is hard to get a sanction to hate one's mother especially a sanction one believes in. I believe in RB's because she is a clever woman who knows her business & I admire her. She is for me 'a permissive mother-figure'."

Despite her therapy Plath's ability to distance herself was complicated by her guilt and feeling of debt to Aurelia: "I have done practically everything she said I couldn't do and be happy at the same time and here I am, almost happy … Except when I feel guilty, feel I shouldn't be happy, because I'm not doing what all the mother figures in my life would have me do." In a May 12, 1953 letter to Warren (who is now at Harvard) she writes (italics mine), "You know, as I do, and it is a frightening thing, that mother would actually Kill herself for us if we calmly accepted all she wanted to do for us. She is an *abnormally* altruistic person." It is revealing that Plath uses the language of finance when she tells Warren (italics mine), "After extracting her life blood and care for 20 years, we should start bringing in big *dividends* of joy for her."

In Britzolakis' discussion of "the speaking subject" in Plath's work, she notes it is often "structurally incomplete, or 'jealous', dependent upon a loved/hated other: a lover, a father, a mother, a reader." Or in more quotidian terms, Plath's eagerness to please Aurelia is less dependent on the requirements of her audience than it is on a need for her own self-invention and self-affirmation. The letters are a method of writing herself into existence for Aurelia, but a method which becomes complicated by Plath's increasing and competing need to voice selves she felt Aurelia would not approve of. As late as October 18, 1962, she writes to Warren, "I fear I wrote two worrying letters to mother this week when I was desperate … Do try to convince mother I am cured. I am only in danger physically, mentally I am sound, fine, and writing the best ever, free from 4 a.m. to 8 a.m." It is another indicative moment, as the letter emphasizes the connection between the act of writing and being mentally sound. In a January 25, 1956 letter from Newnham, Cambridge she says to Aurelia: "When I say I must write, I don't mean I *must* publish … The important thing is the aesthetic form given to my chaotic experience, which is, as it was for James Joyce, my kind of religion … I think I *can* be competent and publish occasionally if I work. But I am dependent on the process of writing, not on the acceptance". While the italicized "must" and "can" emphasize the urgency of Plath's need to write, they also make the point of her differentiating between what it means to make that visible, public, an artifact or commodity, as something that can be possessed as in "big dividends" and what she is describing as something sacred, as "my kind of religion."

Widowed at 34 after Otto Plath dies on November 5, 1940, Aurelia is suddenly a single mother with two children (Sylvia, 8, and Warren, 5). Devoted, educated, and self-sacrificing, she also believes, like her own mother, that she is continuing the tradition of a love of literature with her own daughter. Aurelia writes in her introduction, "Fortunately, my mother was most sympathetic and when I was in college and read my literature books too, saying cheerily, 'More than one person can get a college education on one tuition'." She says this in the context of a love of literature passed down as a matrilineal gift from mother to daughter. It is uncanny because it is indeed language that is the means by which the young Sylvia learns to garner her mother's attention, but it is tied to a moment of anxiety when she feels unsure of it. There was "the one difficult period", says Aurelia, when she was nursing Warren, when Sylvia "wanted to get into my lap. Fortunately, around this time she discovered the alphabet from the capital letters on packaged goods on the pantry shelves. With great rapidity she learned the names of the letters and I taught her the separate sound of each"; already, from this early beginning, language provides succor and is the means by which Aurelia's attention is earned.

If Aurelia is the first to provide Sylvia with an enthusiasm for words, she is also the one whose nurturing, as her mother, will forever complicate that fact. In "The Disquieting Muses" (1957), which opens with a direct address to the mother, we get an early sense of what Aurelia's 1940s child rearing ethos, with its commitment to providing her children with opportunities and discipline, might have neglected: "When on tiptoe the schoolgirls danced, /Blinking flashlights like fireflies /And singing the glowworm song, I could /Not lift a foot in the twinkle-dress /But, heavy-footed, stood aside". The speaker's sense of her difference brings attention to the fact that a domesticity of "cookies and Ovaltine" and "witches always, always /... baked into gingerbread" did not console her; that "the piano lessons" and praise for "arabesques and trills" was not enough. She will learn, if reluctantly, from "muses unhired by you, dear mother":

> Although each teacher found my touch
> Oddly wooden in spite of scales
> And the hours of practicing, my ear
> Tone-deaf and yes, unteachable.
> I learned, I learned, I learned
>   elsewhere,
> From muses unhired by you, dear
>   mother.

In December 1958 when Plath is in therapy with Ruth Beuscher, she writes in her journal:

> I am experiencing a grief reaction for something I have only recently begun to admit isn't there: a mother's love. Nothing I do (marrying, saying 'I Have a husband so I really didn't want yours'; writing: 'here is a book for you, it is yours, like my toidy [sic] products and you can praise and love me now') can change her way of being with me which I experience as a total absence of love.

In that December 27, 1958 journal entry she quotes Beuscher as telling her that she was trying to do "two mutually incompatible things" that year: "(1) spite your mother. (2) write. To spite your mother, you don't write because you feel you have to give the stories to her, or that she will appropriate them …". Plath explains this to herself with the declaration, "And I hate her because my not writing plays into her hands and argues that she is right, I was foolish not to teach, or do something secure, when what I have renounced security for is nonexistent". The impasse between Aurelia's emotionally restrained example, and what Plath wishes for, is played out in the visceral kinds of language Plath will gradually make use of, language Aurelia is unable to give her. Plath writes in the same December entry: "I resent her too because she has given me only useless information about life in the world, and all the useful woman-wisdom I must seek elsewhere and make up for myself. Her information is based on a fear for security ... ".

Plath is not interested in the kinds of security that Aurelia's hard work and sacrifice has provided. What Sivvy-the-daughter-writing-home to Aurelia-the-mother is looking for is beyond Aurelia's cautionary tale of frugality; it is what Sylvia-the-poet will put into poems that allow the disquieting "witches" their voices. In a November 22, 1955 letter from Newnham, Cambridge she writes (italics mine), "I want to force myself again and again to *leave the warmth and security of static situations* and move into the world of growth and suffering where the real books are people's minds and souls". Ironically, as Jacqueline Rose has noted, the fact that Aurelia's selection of letters emphasizes Sylvia-as-loving-daughter while excluding qualities that developed the Medusa-writing poet, or the *Bell Jar*'s troubled Esther Greenwood, only foregrounds the subjectivity of Aurelia's choices. "What body, what psyche, is being constituted here?" asks Rose, as Aurelia's intention highlights the kinds of writing and language she the 1940s-self-sacrificing-mother approved of, which Sylvia-the-precociously-brilliant-daughter wanted very little to do with. The raw, declarative language and imagery of the late persona poems, such as "The stain on your /Gauze Ku Klux Klan/" from "Cut", Ariel's "Nigger-Eye", or Lady Lazarus' "eye pits" and "sour breath" was not the kind of language Aurelia probably had in mind when she wrote in her introduction to the letters, "we shared a love of words and considered them as a tool used to achieve precise expression ... ".

As part of 1940s America and a cult of domesticity that "The Disquieting Muses" ironizes, Aurelia comes to represent what is threatening. "I could draw no breath," the speaker says in "Medusa". In the December 27, 1958 journal entry Sylvia says explicitly of Aurelia: "I think I have always felt she uses me as an extension of herself". Reading through the letters with an eye to the complaints, if veiled, there are recurrences that express the constrictions she was feeling. Sylvia writes in a February 11, 1955 letter from Smith College, "I have always wanted to combine my creative urges with a kind of service to the world" and clarifies, she does not mean (italics mine):

a missionary in the narrow sense "but to fulfill her belief" in the potential of each man to learn and love and grow ... The important thing is
that the choice grows naturally out of my life *and is not imposed* on it by
well-meaning friends. Do consider what I say seriously. I hope you
understand.

Then in February 25, 1956 (italics mine): "I keep telling myself that I
have a vivid, vital, good life, and it is simply that I haven't learned to be
tough, and disciplined enough with the form I give it *in words which
limits me*, not the life itself". The words that limit her are those that
shortchange options for self-expression, the "working, sweating, heaving"
language she will use in her most famous poems. As Jacqueline Rose has
commented of Aurelia's selection, "decisions [are] being taken here as to
whether, and to what extent, Plath can be allowed to be low—low as in
nasty, low as in the degradation of culture." Low as in the ability to speak
"the emotional currents at war with these verbally expressed feelings", a
sentence from her December 27, 1958 journal entry, as in "The blood jet
of poetry", from "Kindness" rather than the "satisfactory letter-
relationship" of her correspondence with Aurelia because "both verbalize
our desired image of each ourselves in relation to each other."

In those last months of her life, separated from Ted Hughes and alone
with her two young children (Frieda 2 and a half, and Nicholas 9 months)
in the rented 23 Fitzroy Road flat, "writing the best ever", Sylvia tells
Aurelia of the kinds of worlds and language she admires; by October 21,
1962 while still at Court Green, North Tawton, she had written "Daddy"
(October 13), "Medusa" (October 16); also "The Jailer" (October 17),
"Lesbos" (October 18), "Stopped Dead" (October19), "Fever 103"
(October 20), "Amnesiac" and "Lyonnesse" (both written on October
21). In her letter she says:

I am doing a poem a morning, great things, and as soon as the nurse settles, shall try to draft this terrific second novel that I'm dying to do. Don't
talk to me about the world needing cheerful stuff! What the person out of

Belsen—physical or psychological—wants is nobody saying the birdies still go tweet-tweet, but the full knowledge that somebody else has been there and knows the worst, just what it is like. It is much more help for me, for example, to know that people are divorced and go through hell, than to hear about happy marriages. Let the *Ladies' Home Journal* blither about *those*.

The search for language to voice the darker ambivalences of the psyche are most often connected to instances of crisis in Plath, when the necessity of language, in Aurelia's words, was their "necessity for accuracy in describing our emotions". Clearly, as the therapy with Beuscher testifies to, Aurelia's and Sylvia's understanding of the necessities of language were mutually exclusive, or "mutually incompatible things". She says of Aurelia's influence: "How can I get rid of this depression: by refusing to believe she has any power over me, like the old witches for whom one sets out plates of milk and honey". Yet Plath gives Aurelia the unsent letter she wrote describing her suicide attempt that suggests she wished from Aurelia an acknowledgement of that self which had felt desperate enough to want to die. Aurelia tells the reader Sylvia gave her "*this following letter in the spring of 1954, saying 'I never sent this. However, I kept it as a record of how I felt about things at the time, looking back at last summer'*." It is addressed to Eddie Cohen and details the buildup to her breakdown, the "hectic month of June in the plushy air-conditioned offices of *Mlle* magazine" previous to her suicide attempt, when she "came home exhausted, fully prepared to begin my two courses at Harvard Summer School … " when "things started to happen." The crisis of self-confidence and emotional breakdown leads to her failed suicide attempt and stay at McLean Hospital where she gets insulin shots and "a series of shock treatments … ". Of this stay and her subsequent attempt at recovery Plath writes: "I need more than anything right now what is, of course, most impossible, someone to love me, to be with me at night when I wake up in shuddering horror and fear of the cement tunnels leading down to the shock room to comfort me with an assurance that no psychiatrist can manage to convey."

It seems noteworthy that Aurelia has juxtaposed this letter with one written to her, some three years later, on November 29, 1956, which gives advice to "S." who is the depressive son of a friend of Aurelia's. "I was most moved by your account of S … I suddenly 'felt myself into' his state where he must feel, as I felt … ". Plath gives this advice: "Try to give him a life perspective … and that, as you once wrote me, he must not let fear of marks blind him to the one real requirement of life: an openness to what is lovely among all the rest that isn't … show him that people will love and respect him without ever asking what *marks* he has gotten." What Aurelia has suggested in this ordering is that Sylvia has indeed recovered, and that the love Sylvia was in such need of has been provided in Aurelia's ongoing support. This is meant to undermine the suggestion that Sylvia's "shuddering horror and fear" remained unaddressed.

The myriad voices in the poems give us key instances of the ways Plath's speakers struggle at voicing "all the rest that isn't [lovely]" in life. Crucially, unlike Aurelia, Plath's relentless fight "not to be selfless" but to "develop a sense of self. A solidness that can't be attacked" is so often what makes for the crisis of vulnerability in poems like "Daddy" and "Medusa". That both poems are representative of parental authorities emphasizes, too, how intensely urgent the need for *self*-individuation and expression becomes. "Tremulous breath at the end of my line," ("Medusa"), suggests as Nephie Christodoulides writes in *Out of the Cradle Endlessly Rocking*, "not only the telephone line, but also the persona's reading and writing line which the Medusa wants to control and censor." In "Daddy" too there is a crisis of speech in the daughter-speaker's famously repeated, "Ich, ich, ich, ich, /I could hardly speak." It is as if Plath's personas, constructed to both veil and empower her speakers' fragilities, must confront those disquieting, finally terrifying muses which Aurelia's earnest security-mongering efficiencies sabotaged.

As Jacqueline Rose has written, the fact that Aurelia's selection of the letters overwrites the anxieties that begin to be expressed in a poem like "The Disquieting Muses" suggests what Plath's journal entries emphasize: that "the kingdom you bore me to" is one the maturing poet felt her mother was unable to protect her from. In "Medusa" she is the "Old barnacled umbilicus, Atlantic cable" that manages to keep itself "in a state of miraculous repair." She is the medusa who will not let go:

I didn't call you.
I didn't call you at all.
Nevertheless, nevertheless
You steamed to me over the sea,
Fat and red, a placenta

Medusa is, of course, the Gorgon that Perseus manages to kill by using Minerva's shield that will mirror the Medusa and so offset her gaze that turns people into stone. It is Minerva whose jealousy of the once beautiful girl turns her into a Gorgon because Neptune, her then suitor, was taken by Medusa's beauty; it is Minerva again who gives her shield to Perseus to help slay the Gorgon. Aurelia's name, etymologically tied to the moon jellyfish, *Aurelia aulita*, makes it impossible not to read the poem as an explicit critique of Aurelia's "umbilicus" hold. In Plath's rendering of the myth, the Medusa is "a placenta", an "unnerving head", an "old barnacled umbilicus", parts that remain "in a state of miraculous repair"—and "always there," clinging. The feeling is one of entrapment, psychic as much as physical as the speaker asks, "Did I escape, I wonder?" It is a question whose answer the poem leaves ambiguous. Minerva's ultimate revenge on Medusa is also one that keeps her image reflected on her shield. As Christodoulides notes, the reference in the poem to "Your stooges /Plying their wild cells in my keel's shadow", suggests that "the mother's stooges wish the daughter to speak the language the mother desires." The language Aurelia desires is what Sylvia repeatedly gives Aurelia in her "Dearest mother," letters which Aurelia has very carefully pulled together to emphasize.

In Danuta Kean's April 11, 2017 *Guardian* article on the new publication of Plath's unabridged correspondence between February 18, 1960 and February 4, 1963, Peter K. Steinberg, the volume's co-editor with Karen V. Kukil who edited the unabridged journals, notes the role that Ruth Barnhouse (Beuscher was her married name) continued to play in Plath's life. Barnstone remains "a permissive mother figure" as she put it in her journal, who gives her the courage to articulate what was unlovely in her life. There is a letter (Plath's estate has still not made available) "dated 21 October 1962, in which Plath claimed to Barnhouse that

Hughes told her directly that he wished she was dead." There is a description of Hughes' physical abuse two days before she miscarried their second child. Steinberg says, "It is possible that Plath found catharsis in writing out to Dr. Barnhouse and that in doing so it freed her to write those explosive, lasting poems."

In the next to last line of "Medusa", Plath's speaker is unapologetic— "Off, off, eely tentacle!" The Medusa's "eely" clutch, not unlike a phallus, and like Medusa's snake hair, suggests both the speaker's sense of oppression and the impossibility of getting away from what Plath called "a smarmy matriarchy of togetherness". In the enigmatic last line of the poem, there is the declaration that "There is nothing between us." The line can be read, and perhaps is meant to be read, both ways; it is after all the brilliance of the poem that it resists closure, which in a sense is what Plath's personas accomplish throughout her oeuvre. There is everything and there is nothing between herself and Aurelia.

In the second to last letter in the collection dated January 16, 1963, Sylvia tells Aurelia that she is "slowly pulling out of the flu." She also tells her that despite the poems she's been writing, the poems which she knew were going to make her name, there is this: "I haven't felt to have any identity under the steamroller of decisions and responsibility of this last half year, with the babies a constant demand." It is chilling to read this in light of the fact that it could not have been an infrequent, and terrifying, thought: This lack of identity under the press of responsibilities was also Aurelia's position after Otto Plath's death, but unlike Aurelia, Sylvia, like her speaker in "Stings", felt she had "a self to recover". These acts of self-salvage, when she managed them, are what we have in the brilliance of her late poems.

8

No Villainous Mother—The Life of Eva Larkin

Philip Pullen

Does your feeling imply a regret that you can't attach more significance to your childhood—no traumas, no villainous mother?
Well it would have been nice to have more technicolor, so to speak.
—Philip Larkin 'An Interview with John Haffenden' in Anthony Thwaite (ed.), *Further Requirements: Interviews, Broadcasts, Statements and Book Reviews 1952–1985*

Most of the biographical writing about Philip Larkin has drawn proper attention to the question of parental influence and has highlighted the extent to which his parents, Sydney and Eva, significantly shaped his life. In general, this acknowledges the complex duality of parental presence and tension which the young Larkin famously acknowledged when writing to his friend Jim Sutton in 1943: "I contain both [my mother and my father] and that … is the cause of my inertia, for in me they are incessantly opposed … Pray the lord that my mother is superior in me."

However, in biographical terms, it is Sydney Larkin who has generally occupied the superior position. Detailed examination of his background and notoriety, for example, his ardour for National Socialism during the

© The Author(s) 2018
D. Salwak (ed.), *Writers and Their Mothers*,
https://doi.org/10.1007/978-3-319-68348-5_8

1930s, and the impact that his adventurous admiration for English literature had on his son have taken centre stage. By comparison, Eva Larkin has been portrayed as a shadowy, background figure—subservient to her husband, nervous, continually whining, and contributing significantly to their unhappy pairing. Admittedly, in later life, her role is given more significance, for example, in providing a potential motive for Larkin not to marry and as a muse for some of his poetry but, overall, important aspects of her life and the experiences that shaped her character have been sadly neglected.

What, in particular, has been absent from the Larkin biographical accounts, is the first-hand voice of Eva Larkin herself. Most biographers have relied, instead, on a limited number of second-hand accounts, including those of her son who, on more than one occasion proves to be, at best, an ambiguous and, at worst, an unreliable witness. This leaves us with an incomplete, and in some respects, inaccurate picture of Eva as a person and the exact nature and extent of her influence over her son.

If Eva's voice is to be found anywhere it is in the thousands of letters she wrote throughout her lifetime to Philip and to other members of her family, together with other notes and personal diaries which are located in the Philip Larkin Archive at the Hull History Centre. Together, they provide a fascinating insight into the way she led her life, the challenges she experienced, and, most especially, the nature and importance of her relationship with her son. They help us to tell her story in her own words.

While there is more to say about Eva's childhood, married life and her relationship with her husband, the focus here will be on the final third of her life, from the point at which she became a widow. Arguably this represents the most definitive phase of Philip Larkin's relationship with his mother and the point at which her influence over his life was at its greatest. The impact of Sydney Larkin's death from cancer in 1948 at the relatively early age of 63 on both Eva and Philip and on their relationship was highly significant. They initially bought a house together in Leicester, where Philip was working in the University Library, but after he moved to Belfast in 1950 and subsequently to Hull in 1955, Eva lived alone in Loughborough, albeit for much of that time, only 100 yards or so away from her daughter Kitty and her family, who, for several years lived on the same road before moving to a larger house a few miles away. Despite her daughter's proximity, the communication Eva had with Philip, by letter and through the frequent visits he made, became the most vital part of her existence.

'Dearest Old Creature': The Shared Conversation

The activity of letter writing was crucial in forming an important commonality between mother and son, shaping and marking out the rhythm of their experiences. They wrote to each other very regularly, usually twice weekly, from the time when Philip went up to Oxford University in 1941 until the mid 1970s, when Eva's failing mental capacity meant that she could no longer reply to Philip's letters and postcards. No other collection of a writer's dialogue with his mother contains such a focus on the intimate and minute detail of each other's day-to-day life.

The style of Eva's letters, and even their content, often mirrors those of Philip. Both would typically write their letters with the other's previous correspondence in front of them; both would often start with some reference to the state of the weather; use the other's most recent letter as a means of structuring their own; and refer to an ocean of commonplace trivia and day-to-day detail (of faulty gas fires, difficult encounters with acquaintances, of neighbours). The language they use to address each other, not only the cosily intense greetings ('Dear Creature', 'Dearest Old Creature') but also particular colloquial expressions ('fancy that … ', 'I was interested to note that … '), is also strongly matched. They are remarkably similar in their thematic focus too. Often their gloomy, pessimistic attitude towards life becomes almost indistinct from one another. 'I listened to the Silver Lining [a popular radio programme of the 1950s aimed at disabled and housebound people] today,' Eva wrote in 1952, 'It was a talk to those of 40 and 50. He said that when one came to this age the outside world and work and even friends did not mean much—but our inner selves were more important—we were facing Death. Not very cheerful, and how about the sixty-sixes?' Philip could have, no doubt, described this more eloquently, but it was certainly a theme he could have warmed to.

Importantly, too, they acted as a 'listening point' for each other's woes and day-to-day concerns. There is nothing Philip does not write to his mother about: all the significant events in his life are referenced, albeit in a suitably veiled form. Most particularly he refers to all the important women in his life with whom he had romantic attachments. Comments about Monica Jones, Maeve Brennan, and Betty Mackereth occur frequently, sometimes even in the same letter, and Eva could not have been unaware of her son's close friendship with all of them. However, as any wise mother might do, she kept her own counsel, restricting herself merely to suitably mirrored comments where appropriate.

By the 1960s, after Eva had a telephone line installed, the weekly correspondence became supplemented by regular telephone conversations. While the ability to call one another provided more instant communication, it did nothing to stem the rhythm of letter writing on either side. Sometimes a preceding call had the effect of shortening a letter, but more often than not it generated an additional one, so that the writer could qualify some element of the previous conversation. In any case, both parties continued to take real joy from the physical receipt of each other's letters ('I love to see your blue envelope in the wire basket,' Philip wrote in March 1967) and both continued to find the act of sitting down to write immensely cathartic. Eva's comment in a letter from 1962 typifies this:

> I really don't know why am writing to you again this evening, when I might be cleaning the silver, or doing some sewing jobs which have been waiting to be done for ages. Perhaps I write because Tuesday night has been 'letter night' for years, or because it is more relaxing than the other jobs.

Surprisingly, given the biographical assumptions often made about her lack of intellectual gravitas, many of Eva's letters have a 'bookish' quality to them. She was well read and often adventurous in her choices and, like Philip, was a voracious reader. She writes in 1950, for example, having just moved to Loughborough:

> I have also joined the public library here. Of course I feel like a 'fish out of water' when I go to choose a book. I have put my name down for D H Lawrence's "The Woman who rode away" I can't get Dostoevsky's "The

Possessed". At present I have got five books out. E.M. Delafield's "Nothing Is Safe" and "The Optimist". Three books on psychology.

Eva's reading tastes were surprisingly broad and she found particular interest in books that reflected her own plight. 'At the weekend I got such an interesting book from Boots,' she wrote to Philip in 1953, 'It is called "All Passions Spent" by V. Sackville-West, and is about such a dear old creature who lost her husband who was a lord, and once Viceroy of India, when she was 85. She then plans her own life, what there is left of it and has such a peaceful, happy existence, to the surprise of her children and other relatives … I think you would like the book. I devoured it in a very short time.'

Moreover, Eva's responses to what she reads have a much more emotional, 'engaged' quality than those of her husband, Sydney, at least as expressed in his own letters to Philip. For Eva, reading seems to be an activity more closely associated with the heart, while for Sydney it is more a case of the mind or perhaps even of simply wanting to make an intellectual point. (In one letter, Eva remarks, rather tellingly, on Sydney's books being so clean 'that they appear never to have been opened'.) It is tempting, therefore, to attribute Philip's own emotional sensitivity directly to his mother's influence. Writing to his mother in 1955, he told her that he could never remember anything of the kind of letters his father used to write. 'They were very short and dry, weren't they? And slightly ironic.' Eva was quick to agree: 'Yes Daddy's letters were usually short and to the point. He never wasted words on non-essentials.'

There are tantalising glimpses too of some of Eva's views on married life. In 1952, for example, she warned Philip that 'Marriage would be no certain guarantee as to socks being always mended, or meals ready when they are wanted. Neither would it be wise to marry just for those comforts. There are other things just as important.' Again, in 1953, she draws upon George Bernard Shaw's views on marriage:

I have just finished reading "Love among the Artists" by G.B.S. in which occurs this passage "No: it is marriage that kills the heart and keeps it dead. Better starve the heart than overfeed it. Better still to feed it only on fine food, like music" In a way, I agree with him, but I think when one is old and left alone, it is then that one feeds on the love and romance of past years. Better to have lived a full life, I think.

These examples are typical of the way in which in many of her letters Eva chose not to express fully her underlying feelings or intentions or tackle dilemmas and anxieties head on but, instead, refer to them more obliquely, often using quotations from other people to address, or merely hint at, the issue at hand. As with her son, so much of the deeper meaning is left unresolved.

Eva's widowhood considerably exacerbated her inherent nervousness and led to periods of great anxiety throughout her life, culminating in a short stay in a psychiatric hospital in 1955, where she was subjected to electric shock treatment with no discernible improvement to her state of mind. The extent of her struggle surfaces regularly and painfully, both in her letters and in the notes she made in the small pocket diaries she received from Philip every Christmas. For the rest of her life, following Sydney's death, Eva did not sleep well, relying on sleeping tablets and other medicines to try to calm her nerves, which outwardly manifested themselves in a profound fear of thunderstorms. The early letters of widowhood painfully reveal some typical feelings of bereavement and particularly the emphasis on guilt and remorse. Extracts from three letters all written in May 1948, graphically illustrate the extent of Eva's grief:

Is there, do you think, any hope for a broken & remorseful heart? I know I ought not to burden Kitty and you with my worries, but it is the only way that I can keep my balance, and you have both done so much for me already that I am further filled with remorse and hope you will both forgive me.

I am still without the inward peace which I long to have ... I do hope you won't worry about me Philip, and perhaps in time I shall get more myself. I sincerely hope so.

I have read and thought a deal about what you wrote in your letter and I agree that my worry is not real guilt but—terrible remorse! If only you could help me with that ... I felt so extremely miserable yesterday— I do hope I shall get more at peace soon—else I do not know how I can keep going.

Childhood Memories

Perhaps as a way of staving off the sadness and despair of the present Eva often used her writing to remember happier days, particularly those of her childhood years spent in Essex. Shortly after Sydney's death she began to write what she hoped might turn into her biography and, although she returned to it on several occasions she never got beyond her childhood years. The recollections she left behind are full of carefree images and love of the countryside:

> On the whole I had a most happy childhood. Our house, which was semi-detached, had a lawn at the back separated from a large field owned by our butcher; and many, many happy summer days my brother and I spent there. Sometimes chasing butterflies with butterfly nets or gathering flowers from which we made peep-shows from the petals.

Philip's letters to his mother also contain some childhood memories and generally give lie to his protestation that his childhood had been 'a forgotten boredom'. I think so often about our days in Coventry,' he wrote in 1974, 'how the traffic used to go up and down St Patrick's Road, and I shd come in in the evening to find you 'picking fruit', with a cupful of water to put the maggots in—poor maggots! Do you remember how Daddy never liked <u>hot</u> pie, so his piece was always cut out and left to cool?'

Someone to Live With

A key feature of much of the early 1950s correspondence, particularly during Philip's time in Belfast, is Eva's concern over living alone and the question of whom she might live with and the hope and expectation that it might eventually be Philip. The dilemma this caused Philip is well documented in his letters to others, particularly Monica Jones, and it forms a major theme of his correspondence with his mother at this time.

The stress and anxiety Eva experienced through living alone are painfully obvious in her letters and involve her at one stage in advertising in the local newspaper as a widow looking for a live-in companion. Eva's accounts of the various personnel she encountered while searching in vain for a suitable person to share her house, undoubtedly the fate for many widowed women in the immediate post-war years, are both sad and amusing. It is easy to imagine the alarming effect they would have on her son:

> I expect you are wondering how I got on with Mrs Pell on Monday. I felt rather disappointed when she arrived, as she looked much older than me, and very countrified. Her husband was a gardener at one of the hostels of Loughborough College. Her age was 74 and I don't think she is quite what I am looking for. The two new 'persons' on the horizon are strangely both called 'Gamble'! One is a man, who wonders if I would kindly correspond with him regarding my advert, which correspondence he says must be private but is respectable!! I haven't answered because I definitely advertised for a <u>lady</u>.

The complicated and challenging dilemma this posed for Philip is clearly illustrated in a letter to Monica Jones in November 1950:

> I do sincerely think that life with a really sympathetic personality wd do her more <u>good</u> than life with myself or my sister, but there are very few chances of finding such a person, & many more of finding cadgers, bores, mean spirits, & so on who will be difficult to displace once they are installed.

A Search for Identity

What comes across most strongly from Eva's letters, particularly those of the 1950s, is an acute struggle to establish and cope with her new identity—that of a widow, at a time when that status was much more circumscribed than it is today. She turns to interests and activities that are probably not surprising for a middle-class 'elderly' woman living in a Midlands provincial town but, in the circumstances of the Larkin's previous family life, and the powerful controlling influences of both her husband and father, provide quite a challenge.

One further important element of her developing identity was that of being a grandmother. Kitty's daughter, Rosemary, had been born in April 1947 and Eva's proximity to Kitty's house meant that she was available to help out on a regular basis, often acting as baby sitter and assisting Kitty in the house from time to time, particularly when her husband, Walter, was away on business. (Because of Eva's unsettled, nervous disposition she would often stay the night at Kitty's long after she had moved into her own house.) Eva's letters kept Philip well appraised of Rosemary's development and achievements of which she was immensely proud. 'She comes bounding in usually when I am at breakfast and also after tea', Eva told him in 1951, shortly after she had moved to Loughborough. 'One day when she came in she said "Poor little Grandma, you do look lonely, are you 'miserable'?" Strange, because, to tell the truth, I <u>was</u> feeling a bit miserable.'

Eva's world in Loughborough, outside of her daily contact with her daughter's family, revolved around the local church and the various social organisations which it embodied, or which were related to it. She joined societies—the Sewing Club and Women's Friendly group—attended whist drives and church fêtes and met most of her friends through these activities.

For Eva, attending church services on a Sunday also became a regular activity for the first time since her teenage years. While the social aspects of this activity are important in their own right, there is no doubt that it was also combined with some form of spiritual significance for Eva, however vague or uncertain or even guilty she might feel about it. She would often take communion, something she had not done since childhood, and subscribed to the *Church Times*, frequently sending cuttings to Philip. Despite his own agnosticism it was not a feature of his mother's life that he sought in any way to challenge and would sometimes attend services with her when he visited Loughborough.

Practical Psychology

Alongside religion, Eva took a very deep interest in 'practical psychology', a popular movement that grew out of the rapid growth of interest in psychology in the aftermath of the First World War. With an emphasis on self-enlightenment, its aim was to make its scientific principles, particularly as applied to the human psyche, practically useful to ordinary citizens. Its proponents claimed that it held the key to a more fulfilling life.

Eva joined a psychology club in Loughborough, one of the many that had been established throughout the country, and regularly attended lectures, often detailing their content in letters to Philip. These events had some similarities with the church socials insofar as they provided a meeting place for social engagement—tea and cake mingled with inspirational talks designed to promote individual well-being and responsibility. The lectures had stirring titles such as: 'People, their differences, and why', 'Finding, freeing your real self', 'Personality and self-expression', 'How to get and maintain the positive outlook'.

Eva's participation in church activities and her sustained interest in psychology are closely combined insofar as the people and the activities overlapped. The driving force behind the psychology groups in Leicestershire, for example, was a Dr Edith Folwell, who lived in Leicester and was a very well-known 'practical psychologist'. Her son, Denis, was a local Leicestershire actor, famous for playing Jack Archer in the radio soap opera, *The Archers* a programme both Eva and Philip listened to regularly. As well as attending her lectures, Eva also visited Dr Folwell for private consultations, to help her to try to overcome her anxieties. These consultations had initially been suggested by Philip during the time he and Eva lived together in Leicester, and he had sought ways to help with her depression. In October 1949, Philip had told his friend Jim Sutton that he was 'thinking of sending her to a local psychologist: after twenty months she doesn't seem any better & it's grinding us all down.' Dr Folwell is undoubtedly the 'fake psychologist' referred to in Larkin's letter to Monica Jones in 1955 when he expressed concern about his mother's mental health: 'She goes from neighbour to daughter to fake psychologist to real psychiatrist & gets comfort from none, or not much. Very disturbing.'

Eva's appreciation of this type of psychological enlightenment, in turn, led to her recommending it to her son. In a nine-page letter, written in March 1951, Eva reflected on Philip's own disillusioned spirits (he had written to her from Belfast, bemoaning the scarcity of any good companions which had contributed to a feeling of 'clay-cold depression'). 'You know Philip,' she told him, 'I cannot help thinking that you would benefit from a course in psychology ... When one has reached the very depths of depression, psychology and religion are the last remaining props.'

Dr Folwell also led a spiritually orientated prayer group which Eva attended, called the 'Circle of Silent Ministry'. Eva described one of their meetings in a letter to Philip:

> There were ten of us there with Dr Folwell as leader. I must admit that it is something of an ordeal, for me, at least. A most solemn atmosphere prevails, even more than I have experienced in church (except at the communion service) and as we sit with closed eyes whilst prayers are said, I shouldn't be surprised if any one of us dropped off to sleep, in fact I noticed out of the corner of my eye one member who seemed to be that way inclined. We have 12 people this month to pray for.

Philip's response to her was typically kind and reflective:

> I laughed very much at the 'sleepers' in the Circle of Silent Ministry. Silent prayer is a difficult thing, I believe, wch is one reason why organised communal prayers are customary. It takes a good deal of training to concentrate on anything, particularly anything not of immediate personal concern.

This combination of religion and psychology unfortunately did little to improve Eva's overall sense of well-being, although it did, at least, provide her with supportive friendship groups. Ultimately, she felt trapped by memories of the past, aspects of her upbringing and no doubt her relationship with Sydney:

> I cannot get right. Although I go to the psychology lectures and to the church functions I always feel miserable about it and sort of half-hearted, and yet I think Psychology is a clever science and I like going to church and enjoy some of the social functions but somehow my past life stands between and prevents me from enjoying it to the full. (What would Daddy think?!!)

The Dutiful Son

Philip's equivocal responses to the predicament of his mother and what he should do about it, was often reflected in his letters to others. His most negative and hand-wringing accounts were reserved for letters to Monica Jones. This is perhaps not surprising, given the rivalry Eva posed for her in terms of Philip's time and attention. In 1954, Monica wrote a 20-page letter to Philip, begging him not to live with Eva. 'Don't be robbed! Don't be robbed of your soul!' she implored. Philip's response, while admitting to his mother's faults, was to defend her sympathetically. But, at the same time, he acknowledged her hold over him. 'You seem to suggest that I've yet to throw off my mother & grab myself primary emotional interest in a woman my own age. This may well be true—it sounds true—but it's not a thing one can do by will power.'

The correspondence between mother and son reveals that Philip's overwhelming attitude towards Eva was fundamentally one of duty, care and love, notwithstanding his strong determination to avoid living with her at any cost. Eva's letters often reveal the extent to which his actions supported her in various ways. He not only carried out practical tasks in her home, but also assisted her at a distance in managing her financial affairs. A letter from December 1952, following Philip's Christmas visit, captures some of the attentiveness he showed, as well as Eva's appreciation and desire for cosy domesticity:

I feel that I didn't thank you half enough for all you did when you were here. It is very comforting when I go into the coal shed to get the day's supply of coal and find such nice convenient pieces are ready to hand. Also the little box full of wood, already chopped is a great boon. I had recourse to it this morning when the dining room fire refused to go.

And there are many more nice things besides these—the 'teas' you got and the lovely biscuits and butter you bought, let alone the different atmosphere which you created, the conversation and the pleasant programmes you found on the radio, all so satisfying to a lonely creature. I thank you so much for it all.

Any tension in the relationship became more apparent during their face-to-face meetings. Philip kept up his regular visits 'home' throughout Eva's widowhood. They were usually over a weekend, starting with his arrival on a Friday evening and ending with him getting a Sunday afternoon train, either from Loughborough or Leicester if he had also visited Monica. They were never long enough for Eva, but she looked forward to them with a passion and held on to the moments of satisfying familial togetherness they generally contained. They would sometimes go for walks along the nearby canal or to the cinema. Occasionally they would travel further afield, particularly Lichfield, where the remnants of Sydney's relatives lived and where he was buried. It was a torturous journey in the 1950s and involved catching a total of eight different buses during the round trip.

Although the visits offered Eva much comfort they were not entirely free from anxiety for either party. Both mother and son were acutely aware of this and equally apologetic about it. 'I'm sorry I was not more sympathetic during my stay,' Philip wrote in February 1966, 'I'm not really unsympathetic, I just get mad with irritation. I suppose you really want someone who would live in, & do most of the work, organise things, & never go away, but it's a remote prospect, isn't it?' In a second note, written on the same day he returned to the theme: 'I am just about to set out for the University, a rather unhappy creature by reason of my impatience with you. Oh dear, I mean well, but when it comes to it my emotions get the upper hand.' Eva's response, as ever, was placatory and forgiving—'I am so sorry to think you were rather an unhappy creature. Please, please don't be miserable about me anymore. I know you mean well and have always been such a kind creature to me and I look forward to your visits so much and love having you here.'

Despite these difficulties, there is little doubt that Philip Larkin loved his mother more profoundly than anyone else in his life. There is even less doubt that he needed her; that, in truth, they *needed* each other. Their correspondence, in particular, suggests that the nature of their relationship was essentially symbiotic and so powerful in its reach that, in many ways it formed the underlying, day-to-day driving force for both of their lives especially during the 27 years when they lived apart. In some respects it is tempting to describe Eva as 'the other woman' in Philip's life, standing in the way of any total commitment to either of the two women who sought his hand in marriage. They, in turn, might be seen as interlopers or rivals for attention, demanding a level of commitment Philip could not give to anyone but his mother.

And then the Only End of Age ...

By the beginning of the 1970s Eva's capacity to cope with living on her own had decreased enormously and was a matter of great concern for Philip and his sister. They had begun to think about the need for her to have a visiting nurse, but before anything could be arranged, events took a dramatic turn. In January 1972, Eva fell and cracked a bone in her leg. After a brief spell in hospital she was admitted to Berrystead Nursing Home in Syston, just outside Leicester. She was to stay there until she died in November 1977. Sadly she quickly began to lose the capacity to write letters and those that survive are painful indicators of the growing struggle to communicate.

The nursing home owner had thought carefully about the residents' likely needs, even to the point of ensuring that the dressing tables in the bedrooms were made low enough to enable people in bed to see out of the window. He put effort into maintaining the pleasant gardens at the side and rear of the building too. But not everything worked so well. 'I wish all aspects of the place were as pleasant as the building,' Philip wrote to Kitty in April 1972. He was worried about his mother's deteriorating condition and wrote to the owner about his concerns: 'She now seems incapable of writing, to have occasional difficulty in articulation, and to be generally slower in understanding,' he told him. 'On a quite different and much smaller matter, I wonder if I might suggest that a lampshade be added to Mrs Larkin's room, Number 20? The absence of one spoils the appearance of an otherwise delightful room, and now that darker days are returning a naked bulb might very possibly be very trying.'

Philip would come to visit her regularly, right up until she died. Generally on a fortnightly basis he would continue to make the long journey down from Hull and spend a Saturday or Sunday afternoon with her. In between, he would write to her almost every day of the week, short, single sheet letters telling her of his doings. As the years moved on and her level of cognisance declined even further, he replaced them with an endless series of colourful picture postcards of animals and members of the Royal Family. The nurses put some of them into a scrapbook for her. The shared conversation, however, was no more. For the first time in her life, Eva Larkin was unable to reciprocate.

Eva was to survive for five years in the nursing home, buoyed up by the frequent weekend visits from Philip and the letters and postcards that arrived on an almost daily basis. In April 1977 Philip attended the wedding of his niece, Rosemary, in Loughborough and after the wedding reception went to visit his mother. He described the visit in a letter to Kitty:

> I took the flowers to Berrystead & the big stone vase. The girls were very kind & in the end mother had five flower arrangements in her room, looking delightful. Not that she really took them in. She was physically alright, and ate her sandwiches & cake, & I think she knew me & smiled & tried to talk, but as before something has gone and I'm afraid communication has broken down.

Eva died on 17 November 1977, aged 91. Her headstone lies directly underneath Sydney's in the churchyard of St Michael's Church in Lichfield, hard to find amongst the overgrown foliage of the abandoned burial ground. Her death left Philip bereft and attention has often been drawn to the fact that he wrote very little of note in the eight years left to him. His mother's superiority, it seems, had finally faded away.

9

Robert Lowell: Trapped in Charlotte's Web

Jeffrey Meyers

Robert Lowell's most formidable maternal relative was his grandfather Arthur Winslow. Born in Winston-Salem, North Carolina, the six-foot, self-made millionaire and mountain climber was educated at the University of Stuttgart and at MIT. A gold-and-silver mining engineer and geologist, he founded the Liberty Bell gold mine in Telluride, Colorado, and with Germanic efficiency tore the precious minerals out of the earth. When Lowell's father, Bob, was away on sea duty in the Pacific, the powerful Arthur Winslow, the only surviving grandfather, usurped his son-in-law's role in the family. After the death of his own son, Arthur became the surrogate father of the young Bobby Lowell, who became the Winslow Boy. When Arthur's farmer, his chauffeur and even his wife mentioned Bobby's father, they always meant his grandfather. In "Grandparents" Lowell openly cried out for the affection his mother failed to provide and parodied the marriage service by pleading, "Grandpa! Have me, hold me, cherish me!"

Lowell's parents united two grand Boston families, but were eminently unsuited to each other. His mother Charlotte (1894–1954) was born in Raleigh, North Carolina, her mother's home town. The one-time high school prom queen—with her tiny waist, dark eyes, rosy cheeks, strong

© The Author(s) 2018
D. Salwak (ed.), *Writers and Their Mothers*,
https://doi.org/10.1007/978-3-319-68348-5_9

chin, swanlike neck and pyramid of hair—looked like one of the handsome eighteenth-century aristocrats painted by Sir Joshua Reynolds. But
her expression was lifeless, her voice falsely dramatic. Lowell wrote that
"She had the lower jaw of a waterbuffalo /the weak intelligence, the iron
will." She never read anything and he thought she was rather stupid. Her
father's great wealth gave the spoiled darling—like Maggie Verver in
Henry James' *The Golden Bowl*—the best of everything: a small army of
servants, art-filled mansions, expansive summer "cottages," luxurious
cars, fashionable clothes and leisurely journeys to Europe. Lowell wrote
that his narcissistic mother, who lacked self-assurance, needed to feel
liked, admired and surrounded by familiar comforts. Her haughtiness
and chilliness derived from some deep apprehension.

In her unpublished autobiography Charlotte, prone to self-analysis,
criticized her own youthful character. She also shrewdly explained her
strangely mixed motives for accepting the patently mediocre Bob Lowell,
the tensions in her marriage and the mounting hostility to her husband:

> "As a child Miss B was self-conscious, introverted, aggressive and rather deceit-
> ful.... Miss B married because she thought it was time to. She was not at all
> in love with the man, nor did she really admire him. But he seemed the best
> that was offered.... After this marriage, having to live in constant companion-
> ship with this comparative stranger, whom she found neither agreeable, inter-
> esting nor admirable, was a terrible nervous strain. She became increasingly
> critical and unappreciative.... Her husband could not understand at all, was
> always kind, though irresponsible; and thought her half crazy."

Bob's aunt, in a caustic condemnation, agreed that he was indeed a hollow man: "Bob hasn't a mean bone, an original bone, a funny bone in his
body! That's why I can't get a word he says. If he were mine, I'd loboto-
mize him and stuff his brain with green peppers." Emphasizing Charlotte's
strong attachment to her powerful father, who could not be supplanted
by her weak husband, as well as the emotional emptiness of her marriage,
Lowell wrote in "During Fever":

> Terrible that old life of decency
> without unseemly intimacy
> or quarrels, when the unemancipated woman
> still had her Freudian papá and maids!

A martinet in the household, she inspected the furniture with white gloves and military efficiency to make sure the maids had not overlooked any dust.

There were, of course, endless bitter quarrels beneath the respectable Boston Brahmin façade and most of them focused on Bob's career. Lowell recalled that "Mother hated the Navy, hated naval society, naval pay, and the trip-hammer rote of settling and unsettling a house every other year when Father was transferred to a new station or ship."

Her status in the navy was based on her husband's relatively low rank. Bob's colleagues failed to recognize her own exalted social position and his superiors disapproved of her critical attitude and defiant behavior. Marshaling her arguments, "she would start talking like a *grande dame* and then stand back rigid and faltering, as if she feared being crushed by her own massively intimidating offensive." She particularly hated Bob's colorful friend Billy Harkness, who opposed her plots and glorified the navy.

Bob pulled strings in Washington and hurt his career to remain in Boston—building ships, then supplying, refitting, maintaining and repairing them—in order to please Charlotte. He also had to pay other penalties. After he'd flouted naval tradition and bought a house at 91 Revere Street in Beacon Hill, his outraged commandant, Admiral De Stahl, ordered him to spend every night in an official house in the Charlestown Navy Yard. This dispute continued until the end of Bob's career. In 1925 another admiral told Bob: "It is believed by the Commandant that the Engineer Officer should live in the Yard in his assigned quarters, and that he cannot properly carry out his duties if he lives out in town, due to lack of supervision."

Though Charlotte surrendered her husband, she won a small victory (no doubt at Bob's expense) by remaining in Revere Street. Charlotte also defeated Bob by insisting, after he'd come home to eat and changed from his dinner jacket (they always dressed formally in the evening), that he take the nightly trolley instead of his beloved car to the Yard. Alluding to Edward Gibbon's "I sighed as a lover; I obeyed as a son," when Gibbon's father insisted he break off his engagement to a Swiss girl, Lowell noted, "Father sighed and obeyed." Sunk in his berth on the base, Bob surrendered his son to his father-in-law and wife, and Charlotte's overwhelming presence filled the vacuum left by her husband. In his "Autobiographical Fragment," Lowell wrote that Bob gave him no paternal affection and disowned him by handing him over to the Winslows: "Always, he seemed to treat me as though I were some relation of Mother's who was visiting. He could remember my Christian name and even my nicknames, but somehow or other my surname had escaped. He would rather have had his fingernails pulled one by one than have said anything to me that was impolite, called for, or fatherly."

Bob was also deprived of marital bliss, which provoked Billy Harkness' sly remark, "I know why Young Bob is an only child." Charlotte, putting a burden on her young son and drawing him into her emotional whirlpool, exclaimed, "Oh Bobby, it's such a comfort to have a man in the house." Rejecting his role as surrogate husband, he replied, "I am not a man ... I am a boy." Charlotte first torpedoed, then terminated Bob's career and drove him from dry dock to shipwreck. His last real job was liaison between the Charlestown Navy Yard and MIT. In 1927 she delivered the fatal blow by persuading him to leave the navy. Noting Bob's public degradation, Billy bitterly observed, "Bob Lowell, our bright boy, our class baby, is now on a par with 'Rattle-Ass Rats' Richardson," who'd left the navy to become a press agent for a circus.

Cut adrift from the discipline and duties, the security and prestige of naval life, Bob felt like a deserter who'd jumped ship. He was anxious about his future prospects and soon got fired from his promising job as soap salesman. Then, stripped of his powers, he made a prolonged and desperate effort to fill up the empty hours of his life. Bob was completely dispossessed: the admiral took his home, Charlotte's lover took his wife, his wife took his career and his father-in-law took his son.

Lowell wrote that after Bob had been emasculated by Charlotte and stripped of his fatherhood, sexual life, profession and even identity, the apathetic, cuckolded man "treated even himself with the caution and uncertainty of one who had forgotten a name, in this case his own.... The strain brought about by his effort to make himself heroically nonexistent was extreme." None of the Winslows liked Bob, and Charlotte undermined Bobby by teaching him to despise his father.

Lowell's fury with his parents fueled his poems. The heroine of "The Mills of the Kavanaughs," partly based on Charlotte and speaking ironically, criticizes her husband's fateful decision: "My husband was a fool /To run out from the navy when disgrace /Still wanted zeal to look him in the face." *Life Studies* moves from Lowell's poems about his family to poems about his mental illness to show the clear connection between them. The title of his elegy "Commander Lowell" is also ironic: Charlotte was the real commander and Bob couldn't even command himself. The condescending portrait of paternal weakness and decline contrasts the promise of Bob's past with the hopelessness of his future. Bob sang "Anchors aweigh" in the bathtub when Lever Brothers offered to double his navy salary:

> I nagged for his dress sword with gold braid,
> and cringed because Mother, new
> caps on all her teeth, was born anew
> at forty. With seamanlike celerity,
> Father left the Navy,
> and deeded Mother his property.

Charlotte was revived as Bob, substituting bathtub for boat, surrendered his authority. By blackmailing him and threatening to leave with Bobby, Charlotte dominated the contentious house on Revere Street.

Many modern American writers—from Fitzgerald and Hemingway to Berryman and Jarrell—had strong, domineering mothers and weak, often absent, fathers. Lowell fit this pattern perfectly. There was universal agreement among Bobby's friends that Charlotte was a monster mom, the prototype of the cruel tyrants from Nero to Stalin who fascinated him throughout his life. Bobby was trapped in Charlotte's web and his relations with her were sometimes quite funny in a ghoulish sort of way. When Bob was stationed at Guantánamo and Charlotte was staying with his mother on Staten Island, she grieved over her pregnancy and rejected Bobby even before he was born.

In his last book, *Day by Day* (1977), published a month before his death, the unwanted son of a mother trapped in an unwanted marriage finally exposed the festering wound that had tormented him for a lifetime.

Lowell probed his psychological pain in his high-octane poem "Unwanted," in which Charlotte, heavy with child, laments, "I wish I were dead, I wish I were dead"—and by doing so also wished that he were dead. Lowell thought it was unforgivable for a mother to tell her child that she didn't want him to be born and give him the perpetual dread of not being wanted. Lowell's cousin recalled that his father also rejected Bobby. When Charlotte brought the infant to him Bob said, "Bring him back when he's three." Lowell tried to ease the pain with the extraordinary claim that "anyone is unwanted in a medical sense—lust [is] our only father." To Lowell, being unwanted was a source of deep-rooted guilt and misery. He said that Charlotte devoured him with her love, but lacked a truly affectionate nature. Unwilling to crease her dress, she never allowed him to sit in her lap. So he always wanted what he never had: a "mother to lift me in her arms."

Characteristically, Charlotte remained hysterical even in her calm. "She was not," Lowell wrote, "one whose hand was stayed from destruction by sentiment," and was merciless with both her husband and son. But Bobby's earliest memory offered a unique example of Charlotte's ability to exhibit sharp wit while observing the social proprieties. Fascinated by a cracked ivory elephant, no bigger than a molar, which a visitor wore on her necklace, he begged to have it. When his wish was granted, he promptly swallowed it. Comically exaggerating his Rabelaisian appetite, "Mother kept saying with Gargantuan suavity, 'Bobby has swallowed an elephant.'" After it was unmentionably ascertained that the elephant had passed through and been discharged from his body, Charlotte, sanitizing the offensive process, "managed to mention the chamber-pot, my movement and the marvelous elephant all in one pure, smirking breath."

Bobby felt drenched in his parents' passions. Ashamed of his father's humiliation yet mocking his weakness, he was determined to resist his mother's domination and as a small boy felt the first stirrings of revolt against her. Lowell's lifelong friend Blair Clark recalled her incessant nagging: "he was so clumsy, so sloppy, so ill-mannered. She would say things to him like 'See what nice manners Blair has.' And I played that role because it was helpful to him. I really think there was a psychological fixation on dominating Cal by that woman. And what does an only child do—with an obsessed mother and a weak father who goes along with that obsession? Bobby had two possibilities: he could rebel or escape, and he did both.

Lowell inherited his four dynastic names from his father, and was called the childish "Bobby" to distinguish him from the elder "Bob." But he changed his name to "Cal" in prep school and reveled in its negative associations, which also suggested calculating, callow and callous. Caligula was a Roman emperor and insane tyrant, known for his extravagance, sexual perversity and cruelty. Caliban, the son of a witch, was the brutal and evil monster in Shakespeare's *The Tempest*. "Cal" also hinted at the fanatical religious reformer John Calvin and, ironically, to the stodgy and boring Calvin Coolidge, American president when Cal was a boy in the 1920s. His first letter to his parents, in August 1936, was addressed to "Mother" (formal) and "Daddy" (familiar), and signed "Cal."

As a young man he quarreled with them about his plans to leave Harvard and ambition to become a poet (which Charlotte thought was a worthless pursuit), about his lack of employment and engagement to Anne Dick during his freshman year. He was clearly too young, inexperienced and unstable to get married, and all reasonable parents would have strongly disapproved. Knowing Bobby couldn't support himself, Charlotte resorted to a traditional ploy and threatened to cut off his funds if he disobeyed her.

Lowell was angry about their interfering in his life and roundly condemned their "false Back Bay morality and true sophistry." Always trying to mold him in their image, they had disloyally written to his friends and secretly sent his letters to Dr. Merrill Moore, Charlotte's psychiatrist. When Lowell punched and knocked down his father, the physical equivalent of Charlotte's verbal abuse, she wanted Dr. Moore to commit her son to an insane asylum.

Four years later, as these quarrels persisted, he again warned Charlotte to stop meddling in his affairs and seized the moral high ground by telling her: "I am not flattered by the remark that you do not know where I am heading or that my ways are not your ways.... One can hardly be ostracized for taking the intellect and aristocracy and family tradition seriously." Charlotte wanted him to be an obedient and conformist son, but he became defiant and rebellious. Bobby's parents never expected to have a gifted son and didn't know what to do with him.

Lowell's third wife, Caroline Blackwood, thought that Charlotte never recognized her son's outstanding qualities and hated everything he represented. In his mother's view, a successful son earned a Harvard degree, had a law career and membership in the best clubs, was a great tennis player and graceful dancer with debutantes. To counter her ideal image, Lowell rejected everything she wanted and walked (sometimes even talked) like a grumpy bear.

In the last years of their marriage Bob was ashamed of being oppressed by his wife and Charlotte dreaded the empty years that loomed ahead. She despised him for being less manly than her forceful father and for allowing himself to be enslaved. She expressed her lifelong dissatisfaction by taunting her hapless husband. She often called Bob a weakling whose only interests were steamships, radio and his former comrades. When visitors provided an appreciative audience she would say, "Don't you think Bob looks peaceful? They call him the undertaker at Lever Brothers. I think he is in love with his soap vat" or "Bob is the only man in America who really believes it is criminal to buy Ivory Soap instead of Lux." Ironically alluding to Ivory Soap's advertising slogan, Lowell slyly wrote that his father's (single) bedroom "was ninety-nine one-hundredths [percent] white." The biographer David Heymann defined the sterile atmosphere of the household: "although grievously unsuited for one another, both Lowells were traumatically formal and remote, Charlotte dreading any kind of lapse from the protocol of class, the Commander shirking all parental and social responsibility." Though weak, Bob deflected and absorbed some of Charlotte's antagonism to Bobby. She treated her son as a backward boy and felt obliged to remind him to put on his socks before his shoes.

Charlotte both denigrated Bobby and, after transferring her ambitions from her husband to her son, counted on him to restore the declining family fortunes. He had to resist her assaults or become emasculated like his father. In "Commander Lowell" he stressed his father's ineptitude by noting that sailor Bob was no good at sailing and took four shots to sink a putt. Elizabeth Hardwick, Lowell's second wife, recalled that in a similar fashion Grandfather Winslow also expressed intense disappointment at Bobby's ineptitude, and humiliated the boy by telling him: "One year thin and handsome and the next year bulky and brooding. Cannot shoot a gun, cannot ride a horse. What prizes have you won, except for collecting snakes and mismatched socks? On a sailboat, a menace." Lowell complained that Charlotte drilled home her father's disdain and thought his only practical accomplishment was fishing. It's scarcely surprising, as one critic noted, that the fierce, sinister and destructive "women in Lowell's poetry seem monster, [husband-murdering] Clytemnestra-projections" of his mother. He felt his generous cousin Harriet Winslow, who left his family her grand house in Castine, Maine, "was more to me than my mother."

In his late poem "Unwanted," Lowell agonized over his relations with both Charlotte and Merrill Moore. But when he was in college and still unaware of Charlotte's prenatal hostility, Moore deliberately undermined his precarious balance by informing him that he was an unwanted child. Moore even suggested that he and Charlotte collaborate on a case study of Bobby—just the thing to cheer him up. Her amateur diagnosis of Bobby's mental state was both cruel and wounding. Charlotte told Bobby that the authoritative Carl Jung (who'd unsuccessfully treated Zelda Fitzgerald and Joyce's daughter Lucia), had said, "If your son is as you have described him, /he is an incurable schizophrenic." Though nine years younger than Charlotte, Moore also became her lover. Lowell's friends described Moore as a charlatan and villain who oozed on to the scene.

Moore's behavior was unprofessional, unethical and perhaps even criminal. If the medical authorities had known about it, they would have revoked his license. He used Bobby to recruit wealthy patients; he slept with his own patient Charlotte; he let her, with no qualifications, take on some of his cases and the "doctor" (as Lowell called her) gave ill-informed advice to disturbed people. Moore simultaneously treated Charlotte and her teenaged son and wanted to treat Bobby's fiancée Anne Dick; he betrayed confidentiality by discussing Bobby's case with his mother (who then told Bobby what Moore had revealed about him); and he told Bobby that his mother had not wanted him to be born. The vulnerable Bobby, their prime target and victim, was caught in their emotional crossfire. The kindly John Crowe

Ransom thought Moore's "insensibility to Cal's sensibilities was so gross that I had to sit down and write him a very sharp letter."

Lowell was not the only one to criticize his mother. None of his close friends or wives had a kind word to say about her. Blair Clark saw her claws beneath the smooth façade: "Charlotte Lowell's white gloves sheathed steely hands determined to wrest victory from her strange, rebellious only child.... I think of her as a monstrous woman, clinically monstrous. I said to Cal in the last summer of his life, 'I think you spared your family.' And he said, 'I probably did—they were awful, quite awful.' " John Thompson, a Kenyon College friend, characterized her as the evil figure who lived in a land of permafrost in Hans Christian Andersen's fairy tale: "Charlotte was a Snow Queen who flirted coldly and shamelessly with her son [and his friends]. His father once ordered a half-bottle of wine for five at dinner." Allen Tate, even more caustic about Charlotte's rude behavior, declared that she had no peer "for stupidity, insensitivity, and ill-breeding."

Lowell's first wife, Jean Stafford, named her "Charlotte Hideous" and called her a neurotic with very little brain. Elizabeth Hardwick came from a poor family and had made a lucky escape from her background, but was not impressed by Lowell's aristocratic parents. After Charlotte had complacently said that she usually managed to make herself pretty comfortable, Hardwick satirized the parents' self-indulgent but empty way of life: "they were a knotty pair. They were in marvelous shape, very careful and prudent. And yet very sensual about fine bed linens, silk underwear, soft cushions, and the proper purring of household motors. The father's fine eyesight, healthy teeth, good tennis game did not keep him from an early death." Lowell's father was bald and had perfect vision; his son was hairy and myopic.

Though Charlotte constantly denigrated Lowell, she also criticized all his wives and lovers, who were not good enough for him—or her. Jean Stafford came from Colorado, where Lowell's grandfather Winslow had made his mining fortune, and both she and Winslow had studied in German universities. But nothing could staunch Charlotte's cataract of condemnation. It was all right to get rich in the West, but not to marry a woman who came from those parts. Charlotte was appalled by a daughter-in-law who was a writer, whose father wrote trashy westerns and whose mother ran a low-class boarding house. Dramatizing Charlotte's hysterical antagonism, Richard Eberhart imagined the scene in a satiric poem:

> Give up that wretched girl. You must!
> She is beneath you, not even in the [social] register.
> From the West, and her family is unthinkable....
> You must give her up, we are not of that kind....
>   It is an awful girl again.
> It is the same thing as it was last year [with Anne Dick],
> Only worse, for this one is an intellectual.

Furious that Bobby had rejected the inbred marriages of Boston, Charlotte subjected Stafford to snobbish criticism: "Your family is just a myth to me, Jean. In our little community here, we all marry our third cousins and know everyone." On awkward visits to her in-laws, Stafford was greeted with frosty politeness and offered unwelcome advice. When she mentioned their financial problems Charlotte, who seemed to be down to her last hundred thousand dollars, refused to help. Even her successful first novel, *Boston Adventure* (1944), was subject to censure. Stafford explained: "There are the same lectures and moral generalizations and refusals to countenance the way we live and the dredging up of all the mistakes of the past. I am more thoroughly, more icily, more deeply disliked than ever ... even though it is generally admitted that it's a damned good thing Bobby married someone who makes money writing." Though Stafford tried to control Lowell's behavior, Charlotte blamed her for his alcoholism and violence.

Charlotte typically zeroed in on the faults of one promising lover, the wealthy Washington socialite Carly Dawson. Anne Dick had psychological problems, Stafford was a low-class type from Colorado, Gertrude Buckman (another lover) was a Jew from New York—and Dawson was twice divorced. Lowell managed to extract a modicum of praise when his obsessively clean mother conceded that Dawson was excessively neat. But she also offered Dawson a dubious compliment by exclaiming that she "was a very <u>knowing</u> person, not a wise person, but a knowing person" who seemed to be acting.

When he married Elizabeth Hardwick, Charlotte expressed her usual hostility and asked Blair Clark "whether I thought Elizabeth was 'suitable' and would 'take good care of Bobby,' the same questions she had put to me about Jean." Charlotte felt Hardwick was opinionated (that is, didn't agree with everything Charlotte said), but conceded that she had good manners and played the role of dutiful daughter-in-law. Lowell and Hardwick both found the strain of Charlotte's criticism unbearable. Hardwick complained that "the horrid reality of Mrs. L. battered and crushed us."

In 1951, when Lowell and Hardwick were living in Europe, he made the mistake of touring with the recently widowed and impossibly demanding Charlotte, who brought out the worst in him and reinforced his infantile connection with her. He described her character, their mutual misunderstanding and their inexorably deteriorating relations in an amusing letter to Elizabeth Bishop: "She is a very competent, stubborn, uncurious, unBohemian woman with a genius for squeezing luxury out of rocks. That is, she has a long memory for pre-war and pre-first-world-war service; and thinks nothing of calling the American ambassador if there's no toilet-paper on the train etc. Well, under the best conditions, of course, I can't begin to make sense out of or to her. Each year since I was eighteen, it's gotten worse." Emphasizing her oppressive personality, he told Allen Tate, "we sat like stones on each other's heads— inhibiting and inhibited."

In February 1954 Charlotte suddenly suffered a cerebral hemorrhage in Rapallo, on the Italian Riviera. Teaching in Cincinnati at the time, Lowell flew there on a circuitous route to Boston, New York, London and Paris, where he stopped to see his old friend Blair Clark and spent the night drinking with him. He then flew on to Milan, couldn't find a taxi in the heavy rain, caught a tram to the Central Station, and finally took a train southwest to Genoa and another one twenty miles south to Rapallo.

Just after his arrival he wrote Hardwick that he blubbed for half an hour with the gray, bespectacled nurse, sharing their common language of hot tears. "Mother died very suddenly from a second attack just an hour before I arrived," he wrote. "She was quite wandering in her memory all the time and I don't think there was ever much chance. She didn't suffer and didn't altogether know where she was. They thought best not to announce my coming to her, and I don't think she suspected the need. Pretty rough—I spent the morning with her nurse who only speaks Italian, both of us weeping & weeping. I mean I spent it in the room with her body!" The doctors told him that Charlotte had had high blood pressure and arteriosclerosis, and couldn't have lived much longer even if she'd remained at home.

Lowell's claim that he arrived after a very long trip only an hour after her death exaggerated the truth for dramatic effect. In a prose draft of "Sailing Home from Rapallo," Charlotte was still alive when he got there: "Mother lay looking through the blacks and tans and flashings from her window. Her face was too formed and fresh to seem asleep. There was a bruise the size of an earlobe over her right eye." In fact, Charlotte died when Lowell was drinking with Blair Clark. He naturally felt guilty about dallying in Paris instead of hurrying on to Rapallo in time to see Charlotte and be with her when she died. But he was afraid to see her menacingly alive and felt it was better to reach the hospital after she was safely dead. Relieved but devastated, Lowell produced a flood of tears.

Charlotte's death released Lowell's deepest emotions and left him free to condemn her in his poems. Lowell's elegy on his mother, "Sailing Home from Rapallo," more emotionally charged than its satirical companion "Commander Lowell," reveals the contrast between the grief that Lowell was supposed to feel and the relief that he actually felt when he could no longer be tormented by her. It also has strong historical and mythical connotations. Lowell identified with oppressive Roman emperors and, like Nero, had created a kind of "death barge for his mother." By sailing home with his mother's corpse, he seemed like Charon ferrying the dead across the Styx to Hades. In "The Unbalanced Aquarium," his prose version of Charlotte's traumatic death, he said the Italians took advantage of his grief to overcharge him for her ugly casket, which had a huge brass crucifix attached to it. Though inappropriately Catholic, the coffin matched her queenly presence and extravagant taste. Since nothing was too good for his luxury-loving mother, she managed to make herself pretty comfortable, as if she were still alive, and traveled "first-class in the hold" while Lowell drank his way across the ocean.

In a letter to Blair Clark, Lowell said his mother's name on the casket had been misspelled *Charlotte Winslon*. His poem states, more convincingly,

> In the grandiloquent lettering on Mother's coffin,
> <u>Lowell</u> had been misspelled LOVEL.
> The corpse
> was wrapped like <u>panetone</u> in Italian tinfoil.

In any case, there's no letter W in Italian, which may account for the errors in Winslow or Lowell. He also confuses *panettone* with the flat, spicy fruitcake *panforte* which, like Charlotte, is wrapped in tinfoil to preserve it.

Writing to a friend, Hardwick asked if her apparently indestructible mother-in-law was "'*really* dead?' Not out of a sentimentality but from a genuine wonder that such a strange force could suddenly vanish. In my heart I do four times a day pay Mrs. Lowell the compliment of profound disbelief in this latest event." Charlotte had a formidable array of negative qualities. She was self-indulgent, perpetually dissatisfied and a dreadful traveling companion. She constantly mocked her weak husband, and provoked late night arguments that kept her young son anxious and awake. She victimized Bobby and devoured him with love. Unhappily married and with a complaisant husband, she flirted with her son's friends and took lovers. While working for a doctor, she pretended to have medical knowledge and advised his patients. She also alienated everyone who was close to her.

Though Charlotte's death doubled Lowell's income and gave him $50,000 in cash, her real legacy was catastrophic. When it seemed that his dead mother—silently sealed in her coffin, safely frozen and tinfoiled in the hold of the ship—could no longer torment him, she precipitated his next mental breakdown. Immediately after her death, he broke with Hardwick and became involved with an Italian woman he'd met while teaching at the Salzburg Seminar. "When Mother died," he wrote, quoting the *Book of Common Prayer*, "I began to feel tireless, madly sanguine, menaced, and menacing, I entered the Payne-Whitney Clinic [in New York] for 'all those afflicted in mind'." The mental illness that plagued him throughout his life did not come from his bland and boring father, but from his volatile and unstable mother.

Even in middle age, Lowell still felt disturbed about being unwanted by a mother who had never held or loved him. Again and again he sought compensatory love from other women. But his harsh treatment of these women was, in some ways, a form of revenge against his mother. He not only wanted to secure the love that Charlotte had denied him, but also was determined, by dominating them, to compensate for his father's submission and expunge the memory of his mother's oppression. Lowell suffered terribly, and poetry was his means of expressing and conquering his emotional turmoil. But as Robert Frost observed, "No tears in the writer, no tears in the reader."

Part II

Autobiographical

10

Mother Tongue: A Memoir

Ian McEwan

I don't write like my mother, but for many years I spoke like her, and her particular, timorous relationship with language has shaped my own. There are people who move confidently within their own horizons of speech; whether it is Cockney, Estuary, RP or Valley Girl, they stride with the unselfconscious ease of a landowner on his own turf. My mother was never like that. She never owned the language she spoke. Her displacement within the intricacies of English class, and the uncertainty that went with it, taught her to regard language as something that might go off in her face, like a letter bomb. A word bomb. I've inherited her wariness, or, more accurately, I learned it as a child. I used to think I would have to spend a lifetime shaking it off. Now I know that's impossible, and unnecessary, and that you have to work with what you've got.

"It's a lot of cars today, id'n it?"

I am driving Rose into the Chilterns to a nature reserve where we will stroll about and share our sandwiches and a flask of tea. It is 1994, still many years to go before the first signs of the vascular dementia that is currently emptying her mind. Her little remarks, both timid and intimate, do not necessarily require a response.

© The Author(s) 2018
D. Salwak (ed.), *Writers and Their Mothers*,
https://doi.org/10.1007/978-3-319-68348-5_10

"Look at all them cows." And then later, "Look at them cows and that black one. He looks daft, dud'n he?"

"Yes, he does."

When I was eighteen, on one of my infrequent visits home, resolving yet again to be less surly, less distant, repeated conversations of this kind would edge me towards silent despair, or irritation, and eventually to a state of such intense mental suffocation, that I would sometimes make excuses and cut my visit short.

"See them sheep up there. It's funny that they don't just fall off the hill, dud'n it?"

Perhaps it's a lack in me, a dwindling of the youthful fire, or perhaps it's a genuine spread of tolerance, but now I understand her to be saying simply that she is very happy for us to be out together seeing the same things. The content is irrelevant. The business is sharing.

I remember other journeys in the Home Counties we took together by train in the mid fifties. Typically, they would end on the station platform of our destination with my mother taking from her handbag a scented embroidered handkerchief, dabbing it on her tongue and screwing a wet corner into some portion of my face. The idea was to rid me of 'smuts', entities in which I had no faith at all. I was to be made fresh-faced for whichever aunt or friend of hers we were visiting.

The trains were of the old-fashioned sort, with corridors, and leather straps to hold the windows open, and dusty compartments in which it was common to hold polite conversations with strangers. On one occasion a lady got in who must have appeared to Rose to have considerable social standing. They began to talk and I remember being surprised by the change in my mother's voice. She measured out her sentences as she strained for her version of correct speech.

I was to hear the same transformation many years later, when my father was commissioned from the ranks. There were two tribes of officers; those who were drawn from the middle classes and had been to Sandhurst, and those who had risen from being ordinary soldiers and who never got much beyond the rank of Major. All my parents' friends belonged in the second group. Whenever some gathering in the Officers' Mess obliged my mother to hold a conversation with the Colonel's wife, the posh voice would creep in, with its distorted vowels—yais, naice—and aitches distributed generously to make up for the ones that were dropped else-where. But most significantly, Rose spoke very slowly on these occasions, almost lugubriously, aware of all the little language traps that lay ahead.

When I was eleven, I was sent from North Africa, where my father was stationed, to attend school in England. By any standards, Woolverstone Hall was a curious place, a rather successful experiment by a left wing local authority in old-fashioned embourgoisement. It had the trappings of a public school—Adam style country house, huge grounds, rugby pitches, a genially Philistine headmaster—and so on. But this ethos was rather stylishly undermined by the intake of mostly grammar school level working-class lads from central London. There were some Army brats like me (their fathers all commissioned from the ranks) as well as a tiny smattering of boys from bohemian middle-class backgrounds.

During my early teens, as my education progressed, I was purged of my mother's more obvious traits, usually by a kind of literary osmosis—when I was fourteen I was an entranced reader of the handful of novels Iris Murdoch had published. I was also reading Graham Greene. Slowly, *nothink, somethink, cestificate, skelington, chimley* all went, as well as the double negatives and mismatched plurals.

Sometimes I took myself in hand. I was in the first year of my sixth form when I arranged for my best friend, Mark Wing-Davey, a rare and genuine middle-class type, to say 'did' out loud every time I said 'done' in error. Very kindly, he done this for me. But he got into serious trouble one afternoon in a history lesson. I was earnestly delivering a prepared piece about the bold reforms of Pope Gregory the Seventh (how I loved to intone 'the extir-pation of simony') when Mark loyally murmured a 'did'. The history mas-ter, a kind Welshman, Mr Watts, whom we called Charlie because of his striking non-resemblance to the drummer, became incensed by what he considered to be a display of rudeness and snobbery. To prevent Mark being ordered from the room, I had to intervene and explain our agreement.

But these adjustments of speech and writing were superficial, and rela-tively easy. They formed part of that story, familiar in English biography, in which children who received the education their parents did not, were set on a path of cultural dislocation. What tends to get said is that the process is alienating and painful. But it seems to me now that there is more to it. There are gains as well as losses, at least for a writer. Exile from a homeland, though obviously a distressing experience, can bring a writer into a fruitful, or at least a usefully problematic, relationship with an adopted language. A weaker version of this, but still a version, is the internal exile of social mobility, particularly when it is through the layered linguistic density of English class.

When I started writing seriously in 1970, I may have dropped all or most of my mother's ways with words, but I still had her attitudes, her wariness, her unsureness of touch. Many writers let their sentences unfold experimentally on the page in order to find out what they are, where they are going, and how they can be shaped. I would sit without a pen in my hand, framing a sentence in my mind, often losing the beginning as I reached the end, and only when the thing was secure and complete would I set it down. I would stare at it suspiciously. Did it really say what I meant? Did it contain an error or an ambiguity that I could not see? Was it making a fool of me? Hours of effort produced very little, and very little satisfaction. From the outside, this slowness and hesitancy may have looked like artistic scrupulousness, and I was happy to present it that way, or let others do it for me. I was pleased when people spoke approvingly of the 'hard surface' of my prose; that was something I could hide behind. In fact, my method represented an uncertainty that was partly social: I was joining the great conversation of literature which generally was not conducted in the language of Rose or my not-so-distant younger self. The voices of giants were rumbling over my head as I piped up to begin, as it were, my own conversation on the train.

Of course, those remarks copied into a 1994 notebook after our visit to the nature reserve give no sense of Rose's warmth in conversation, her particular emotional tone. In the summer of 1970 I went with my father to collect her from the military hospital in Millbank where she was recovering from a stomach operation. It was customary for officers and their wives to occupy different wards from the other ranks and their wives. There was a noisy, tearful scene in the corridor outside Rose's ward as we were coming away. A dozen patients, the young wives of privates and corporals, had gathered to say goodbye and give presents to the woman who—so they said—had listened to their problems and given them her wise advice. In convalescence, she must have deserted her ward. She had been the wife of a sergeant, and before that, in her first marriage, of a private soldier. She would have felt more comfortable among the younger women in the other ranks' ward. And she was also in her element in a heart to heart. No language perils there.

I was six and we were living in Army quarters in Singapore I remember how I liked to loll unobtrusively on the floor behind the sofa when my mother had a friend round. I would listen to these roaming, intimate chats. Broadly, they fell into two categories—operations, and bad behaviour. How compelling and gory they were, these accounts of flesh under knife, and the aftermath. I'm sure they exerted their subliminal pull on my first short stories. And with so many bad people in the world, what a lucky six year old I thought I was, when my mother and her friends were always on the side of the good.

In my second term at Woolverstone I was sent on an errand to the Headmaster's secretary. The office was empty, and while I waited I saw on a desk a confidential report card with my name on it. 'Hopelessly shy', 'Can't get a word out of him', and worryingly, 'An intimate boy'. I half knew what the word meant. But surely you had to be intimate *with* someone. I looked the word up and saw in a secondary meaning the mention of secrets. I had none, but it was true that I only spoke freely on a one-to-one basis. I never acted in plays, I never spoke in class, I rarely spoke up when I was in a group of boys. Intimacy was what loosened my tongue, and I was always on the look out for the one true best friend.

My father, by contrast, loved to take control in a group of friends, especially if he could make them laugh, so I was far closer to my mother in conversational style. In my first stories I wanted to get as close as possible, put my lips to the reader's inner ear. These were almost parodies of artificial intimacy. Entering a public arena for the first time, I strove—too desperately, some said—to provide lurid secrets for a set of deranged narrators. Like men who had been alone too long, they had much to tell. Forcing them to confess at a couple of hundred words a day, and within a literary tradition, I thought I was freeing myself from my past. Writers who fictionalise their childhoods, I declared in my first interviews, bored me. The business is to invent. So I invented—intimately, with the embarrassed hesitancy of the inarticulate—in my mother tongue.

Rose Moore was born in 1915 in the village of Ash, near the military town of Aldershot. Her father was a painter decorator. One of my first memories is of visiting him in the larger of two upstairs bedrooms where he lay dying of tuberculosis. The house then, in the early fifties, was as it had been during my mother's childhood. A steep, unlit central stairway, gas lighting, a gloomy kitchen smelling of damp and gas, the brighter unused front parlour, the scullery with a copper under which a fire was lit every Monday for the weekly wash. In the garden, a plum tree and the wooden privy perched over its horrible pit. Beyond, Farmer Mayhew's meadows stretching away to a low ridge of hills known as the Hogs' Back.

Rose was the eldest of five. Her mother was a reluctant housewife, a chain smoker who liked to walk to Aldershot to window shop, leaving her first born to mind the younger ones. Granny Moore had come over from Ireland at the age of sixteen with a college education, according to my mother, who left school at fourteen. The age at which people went to college or left it meant little to her. She did not know where her mother grew up, or what her background was. My father, who grew up in Govan, Glasgow, also knew little about his family line. His parents were both tram drivers for the City Corporation, and their parents were agricultural labourers from the Stirling area. That was all he was told. This uncurious rootlessness characterises our family. I feel it myself, a complete lack of interest in family trees, or rooting around in parish registers. Two or three generations back is the land, and most certainly a hard life. But whose land, and precisely what kind of life are forgotten. Not even that—they were never known.

Rose developed rickets from malnutrition. In a photograph taken in 1918 with her parents—her father was just back from the war—she is wearing calipers on her legs. Poverty went for the bone. Like many of her generation and class, Rose lost all her teeth in her twenties. During my childhood her false sets—top and bottom, lurking at night like bear traps in a glass tumbler by her bedside—were always giving her trouble. Another impediment to easy speech.

In the mid 1930s Rose married Ernest Wort, also a house painter, and my half-brother Jim and my half-sister Margy were born. Rose often told this story to illustrate the 'ignorance of them times': when she was going into labour with her first child she believed and feared that 'it was going to come out of my bottom'. The astonished midwife set her straight. Ern was no great provider, though he clearly had charm. He often went missing for days or weeks on end—living under hedges, according to Rose, but she would only have known what he told her. Occasionally, the police would bring him back. Until then, she and the two children lived 'on the parish'—provisions made under the old Poor Laws, until the welfare system was founded in the next decade.

Ern died in 1944 from the stomach wounds he received after the D-Day landings. In 1947 Rose married Regimental Sergeant Major David McEwan, and the following year I was born. A wedding photograph shows her tense, uncertain smile. My father also left school at fourteen—the family's poverty forced him to abandon his scholarship, and four years later, unemployment on the Clyde forced him into the recruiting office. His lack of formal education sat unhappily all his life with his ferocious intelligence. There was always an air of frustration and boredom about him. He was a kindly man, but he was domineering too, with a Glaswegian working man's love of the pub—and the sergeants' mess.

The drunkenness distressed Rose but she never dared challenge him. She was always frightened of him, and so was I. When I came to early adolescence, I was like her, too tongue-tied to face down his iron certainties. I was at boarding school anyway, and in my mid teens began to spend my holidays abroad with friends. After that, I drifted away, and saved my darker thoughts for my fiction where fathers, especially the one in *The Cement Garden*—were not kindly presented. Our most serious clash came some years later when I was in my twenties and visiting my parents in Germany. Rose had nothing to do all day at home but polish the furniture. When she was offered an afternoon job running a tiny barracks library that lent out paperback thrillers to the troops, David turned the job down on her behalf. His firm view was that having a wife who went out to work would reflect badly on him. Two years after our row, the job came round again and, moving with the times, he relented.

In my twenties I was often defending, or trying to defend, Rose against David, or promote her cause somehow. The effect on my writing was fairly direct, though I think at the time I had no clear sense of the connection. I read *The Female Eunuch* in 1971 and thought it was a revelation. The feminism of the 1970s spoke directly to a knot of problems at the heart of our family's life. I developed a romantic notion that if the spirit of women was liberated, the world would be healed. My female characters became the repository of all the goodness that men fell short of. In other words, pen in hand, I was going to set my mother free.

It is spring, 2001 and I collect Rose from the nursing home to take her out to lunch. Sometimes she knows exactly who I am, and at others she simply knows that I am someone she knows well. It doesn't seem to bother her too much. In the restaurant she returns to her major theme; she has been down to the cottage in Ash to see her parents. Her father was looking so unwell. She's worried about him. Her mother is going to come up to see her in the nursing home, but doesn't have the bus fare and we should send it to her. There is no purpose in telling Rose that her father died in 1951, and her mother in 1967. It never makes any difference. Sometimes, she packs a plastic carrier bag of goodies—a pint of milk, a loaf, a bar of chocolate and some knickers from the laundry basket. She will put on her coat and announce that she is going to Ash, to Smith's cottages, to the home where she grew up and where her mother is waiting for her. This homecoming may seem like a preparation for death, but she is in earnest about the details and, lately, she has been convinced that she has already been, and must soon go again. Over lunch, she says that what she would really like is for her mother to come and see her room at the nursing home, and see for herself that her daughter is all right.

Afterwards, I drive her round the streets of suburban west London. This is what she wants, to sit and look and point things out as we cruise from Northolt, to North Harrow to Greenford.

"Oo, I really love doing this," she says. "I mean, look at me, riding about like Lady Muck!"

As we go along the A40 in a heavy rainstorm, past Northolt airport, she falls asleep. She was always so bird-like and nervous that sleeping in the day would once have been unthinkable. She was a worrier, an insomniac. Soon all her memories will be gone. Even the jumbled ones—her mother, the house in Ash with the plum tree in the garden. It's a creeping death. Soon she won't know me or Margy or Jim. As dementia empties her memory, it will begin to rob her of speech. Already there are simple nouns that elude her. The nouns will go, and then the verbs. And after her speech, her co-ordination, and the whole motor system. I must hang on to the things she says, the little turns, the phrases, for soon there will be no more. No more of the mother tongue I spent my early life unlearning. She was animated and cheerful over lunch, but for me it's been another one of those sad afternoons. Each time I visit, a little bit more of her has gone. But there's one small thing I'm grateful for. As she sleeps and the wipers toil to clear the windscreen, I can't help thinking of what she said—*riding about like Lady Muck*. I haven't heard that in years. Lady Muck. Where there's muck there's brass. It must have been in use in the 1930s, or 40s. I'll use it. It's right for the novel I'm finishing now. I'll have it. Then I'll always remember that she said it. I have a character just coming to life who can use her words. So thank you, Rose, for that—and all the rest.

11

'Persistent Ghost'

Anthony Thwaite

I was an only child. My memories of my mother seem to fall into two periods, before wartime evacuation to the U.S. in June 1940 and after my return to England in June 1944. In the first period, as an only child, I was very close to her: later, though very fond and certainly dutiful, I felt less close. She was a warm and intelligent woman, wholly centered on my father and myself, having been brought up in difficult circumstances, with a feckless drunken father and a weak mother.

My strongest feelings about my mother, perhaps disappointingly, are about an old woman, in her nineties; and these are the feelings caught in these poems, written in the time leading up to her death, aged almost ninety-seven, and soon afterwards.

THROES
Being with her now is a kind of boredom,
A dullness in which guilt and pain both ache,
When all my childish anguish after freedom
Has long since vanished. Now I wait to take

Her back to her own loneliness, where she
Can follow boredom of a different kind,

© The Author(s) 2018
D. Salwak (ed.), *Writers and Their Mothers*,
https://doi.org/10.1007/978-3-319-68348-5_11

Routine quite unresented, and set free
From all required constraints. She is resigned,

Stoic and still, to what is left to come:
First blindness, then a sequence no one knows –
Choked lungs, paralysis, delirium?
Each one may follow where the other goes.

We act out cheerfulness to one another,
Exchanging memories, recalling names:
Son in his sixties, ninety-year-old mother,
Playing our boring, life-sustaining games.

WATCHING
Old mothers, their time running out, when time doesn't matter,
Keep on consulting their watches, as if puzzled how time
Runs on, even when
Meals arrive on time, and each day a different carer
Arrives and takes over:
Even then
They look at their watches again and again and again.

Again and again and again they look at their watches,
As if puzzled how time runs on and on and on
Even when meals arrive
On time, and each day a different one
Arrives and is eaten:
Still alive,
Old mothers, when time doesn't matter, time running out.

WORST WORDS
The worst words, the words that hurt,
Are the words you don't use.
You are afraid to use them, because they hurt
And you know they will hurt.

So you go on using another sort of words.
They are the words that please, or at least get by.

They make life easier, they grease the wheels,
And no one notices them as they go by.

Until there comes a moment when the worst words
Are the ones you need, the words to do the trick,
The worst trick, to tell the terrible truth.
But it is too late. You have lost the trick of those words.

THE MESSAGE
I keep it in my pocket, take it out,
Read it again, then put it back, this scrap
Of envelope with those scratched and blurred
And urgent words I found stuffed in your bag –
A cry of rage, of misery, of mad
Incomprehension, just
Enough like your familiar hand to stun
The one you wrote it to: your son.

Now I have read the words so many times
I know them all by heart; but can't repeat
Or spell them out in my own writing. Grief
Blanks out their meaning, as your stroke blanked out
Whatever happened, and whatever followed.
I take the paper out and follow it
Again, once more, its deadened, endless shout:
Why have you done this to me? Take me out.

THE CRY
Not dead, not dead yet –
Like a cry curtailed
The words come back to me, and in her voice.
And it is terror that I feel at this
Impossible coming-back, the future filled
With that unstoppable presence night by night.

And yet I know she's dead, and wanted it
As I too wanted it. Why should she cry
Like this, persistent ghost

Asking to be missed
So strongly, plaintively, and nightly?
Not dead, not dead yet.

A CRACK OF AIR
'Would you let a crack of air in' – as I tucked
Your small frail body into bed
That early night, a week before you died,
You spoke those words I hear and recollect
Again and yet again.
They seemed like hope renewed, as if pain
Might still be turned away
By letting freshness in, till a new day
Brought light through opened windows, and the sun
Rose in its old way.

But that was habit speaking. You were old
And tired and far beyond a crack of air,
Or light, or anything to hold
The darkness back in bed as you lay there.

12

Living with Mother

Catherine Aird

I hadn't meant to live with mother—it was a case of force majeure. I had had every intention of leaving home at the age of eighteen—the earliest possible opportunity for me to do so in those days—and following in my father's footsteps to Edinburgh University. I was going to read medicine there on the way to becoming either a general medical practitioner or a physician—surgery never having appealed to me. To this end I was in the Lower Sixth form at school studying chemistry, physics and biology, as well as learning Latin as a subsidiary side-dish.

It was not to be. It has been said that 'If you want to make God laugh, tell him your plans' and this proved to be very true in my case. At the age of sixteen and a half I was found to be suffering from a very dangerous kidney disease—later, but not then, to be called the nephrotic syndrome. Then it was merely known as Ellis Type Two. At that time there was no treatment and a deep gloom prevailed among all the doctors I saw. Their talk centred on the management of the patient rather than its cure. This amounted only to a prolonged discussion on the merits of a high protein diet (to replace the protein lost by the kidney) versus a low protein diet (to put less strain on its processing by the affected organ).

© The Author(s) 2018
D. Salwak (ed.), *Writers and Their Mothers*,
https://doi.org/10.1007/978-3-319-68348-5_12

My mother thus had an ill daughter on her hands, then and for many years afterwards until I slowly recovered later in life. In fact until her death at the age of eighty-five I was to spend all of my life at home with her, and indeed with my father, too, until his death. She was no stranger to death and disease which must have helped a lot when I was ill. As well as being trained as a nurse, she had lost one brother in action in the First World War, another from a cerebral tumour (diagnosed by my father on the day of their engagement), yet another from tuberculosis at the age of four, a married sister from pneumonia and a father from septicaemia, these two both well before the advent of antibiotics.

In those far-off days doctors in general practice usually worked from home, the consulting room being part of the house. Living as we did 'over the shop' so to speak, the illnesses of patients, nearly all of them well known to the household, were thus part of everyday conversation. Clinical discussion at the dinner table was redolent of that between the two medical students—Bob Sawyer and Benjamin Allen—in Charles Dickens' *Pickwick Papers*, Mr Sawyer, if you remember, declaring that there was 'Nothing like dissecting to give one an appetite'. I was brought up so that talk of dissecting at mealtimes didn't take my appetite away—a very useful adjunct to being a crime-writer.

So was the steady stream of visitors to the house. All sorts of conditions of men and women and children in all states of health, wealth and happiness, could be found drinking tea at the kitchen table whatever the hour. My mother was immensely sociable but not particularly interested in a social life per se. What rubbed off from this was an awareness of where one's time and attention really mattered. There was definitely no ivory tower anywhere in the house, no space sacred to the act of composition. A valuable derivative of this state of domestic affairs was that I learnt to write however many times I was interrupted. Work laid aside as a consequence of what are euphemistically known as Life Events could be resumed as soon as circumstances permitted without resentment.

After so traumatic an upbringing, which had served to put everything else into perspective for her, the cardinal sin in my mother's book became making a fuss about lesser things. Added to this is the natural tendency of the entire medical profession to play down the sufferings of patients. This meant that any spectacularly dramatic response to events in my fiction had therefore to be imagined rather than replicated from observation. High drama was definitely out in real life whatever the demands of fiction.

It is important to stress that my long relationship with my mother was certainly not that of a dutiful daughter hog-tied to a demanding parent. There were no apron strings to be tied to in sight and certainly no suggestion ever that Mother Knows Best. I was no Princess Beatrice, the youngest daughter of Queen Victoria, locked into dancing constant attendance upon a Tiger mother determined to keep her last offspring at heel and much put-upon by her Royal mother.

My mother didn't need either an obedient scribe or a posthumous censor such as poor Princess Beatrice had been although she had written some moving verse on my birth. Nor did she need an amanuensis either, since she was perfectly healthy and capable herself—indeed, her help was invaluable to my father in his work. And, perish the thought, she might not even have wanted an unmarried daughter at home for life at all—she never said.

I was the one, bedridden for so long a time, who needed her. It was only much, much later when she was old and frail that our roles were reversed and I looked after her. An unexpected bonus of living and working at home with an Aged Parent is that becoming the carer is less traumatic than trying to cope as such at a distance and with other competing family demands.

What I think I gained most of all from this long relationship was an awareness of her understated sense of humour. This I am convinced is what took my writing so far in the direction of irony. Her influence was very subtle, her humour only discernible to an acute ear. While I was well aware of her almost invisible handling of my father—for some strange reason he always imagined that he was the head of the household and that what he said always went without question—he never even suspected that he wasn't and it didn't.

What I was less sure about then and now was her thinking on a vast array of subjects since she seldom voiced a direct opinion. She disliked debate and would never engage in argument, however theoretical. Serenely downgrading the many important "matters of principle" so dear to my father's heart, she would insist that they weren't at all important in the long run, always declining to give a view on anything that smacked of the confrontational. She was equally unperturbed by his constant assertion that there was too much hope about.

While this was very comforting to live with it was naturally no help whatsoever to the seeker after good controversial dialogue to emulate in her work as a crime writer. It is, after all, the essence of much detective writing that characters disagree both with each other and with the law, the conflict providing clues for the constabulary, *quae* detective hero, to unpick.

Fortunately for this aspect of my writing my father was at hand, ready for discussion on anything one cared to mention—but especially medical matters and physics as well as physic. (Isaac Newton was a man dear to his heart.) After all, someone has to do the verbal conflict and she never would. In fact the only matter on which we seriously disagreed was the number of books I brought into the house: she insisted that the sitting-room at least remained unencumbered by them and in her lifetime it always was. (You should see it now.)

Living as I did with someone who was intuitive by nature for so very long, I was nevertheless always surprised when my mother was found to be right against all the odds. In a later life of writing I therefore had to be very careful that the actions of my fictional characters were strictly logical and that their conclusions were not achieved by instinct or intuition alone. I also had to be quite sure that their reactions and behaviour were not abnormally restrained as I came in later life to think hers had been.

Listening to the wireless on 3 September 1939, as did the whole nation, to the Prime Minister, Mr Neville Chamberlain, announcing that we were at war, we heard the air-raid sirens go off almost immediately afterwards. My father promptly disappeared to a medical aid post leaving my mother with myself, aged nine, and my brother then seven. We children, not particularly interested or alarmed, said we wanted to go out into the garden to play. My mother reached for her sewing basket and told us she was going to sew name tapes onto our vests first in case she had to identify our bodies if we were bombed. She had, after all, seen bodies mangled in war. We waited impatiently while she did this and then scampered out to play.

Neither of my parents, though, believed in the over-protection of children and when later on in the war we had a patient's dead baby in the house we children were shown the body so that, we were told, we would know that death was nothing to be afraid of. Her reaction to some other events too proved unexpected and therefore not a lot of use to a budding author keen to glean what she could about normal human behaviour for her writing.

There was, for instance, the occasion when she was out shopping in the local market town when she saw a woman, not known to her, walking towards her dressed from head to foot in clothes from her own wardrobe. There are those people who might have challenged the wearer, gone for the police, displayed outrage or even doubted their own sanity but she waited until she got home for an explanation.

There was one. A couple had fallen off a local ferry into the river and my father had brought the woman home so she could get dried and dressed to go into the town to buy new clothes for the pair of them. My mother's decidedly low-key response to this was an example of her complete self-assurance and confidence in there being a reasonable explanation. And in not making a fuss, of course.

Less predictable was her reaction to a birthday gift from my father. He once gave her a blank cheque and said she could fill it in for any amount she chose, even up to all his worldly goods. This, she declared, posed a problem—should she make it out for a large sum he might think her greedy and if only for a small amount he might think she had everything she wanted. In the end, after much amusing wrangling, she tore it up.

One thing I definitely did learn at my mother's knee was deviousness—needless to say a very valuable concomitant indeed to detective writing. Determined to keep me out of the kitchen, though the subject was never mentioned, ingredients would be hidden and no cooking implement ever kept in the same place twice. In later life when I was once complimented on my handling of a delicate situation in the wider world with "a fine Italian hand" I knew exactly who to thank for that.

As well as understanding my father so well, I have to concede that she understood me and the way I thought, too. Better than I did her, certainly. Holding firmly as I did to the dictum in the crime-writing canon that enough clues to the identity of the murderer should appear in the first three chapters of the story she would first read these and only these. Then she would write the name of the murderer on a piece of paper and seal it, unseen by me, in an envelope. The end of the manuscript duly reached by me months later, we would ceremoniously open the envelope together to find that she had invariably named the villain correctly. It was something that I missed a lot after she died.

13

'Bring Her Again to Me ... '

Ann Thwaite

My title, from W.E. Henley, is part of the epigraph to a book my mother sent to me when I was a child. The book was *A Child's Garland* 'gathered' by Jane Carton and published by Faber and Faber in 1942. When I received it for Christmas that year, my mother and I were 12,000 miles apart.

I was about to write that this was an obscure, long-forgotten book, but thought I had better check on my iPad. It turns out not only that it is, as I write, readily available from Amazon, with jacket, for £5.49 (postage in the UK £2.80), but also, jacketless, it can be had for rather less on eBay.

Jane Carton, a *Times* journalist, had collected the poems, and some passages from the Bible (including Psalm 23), for her daughter, Polly, aged eight. Polly and her brother had gone to Canada in the summer of 1940, at just the time I had gone, with my brother and my mother, on the much longer journey to New Zealand, our parents' homeland. We had left England not just to escape the bombing, but because, in that dangerous summer, invasion seemed imminent.

I had over the seventy-five years wondered from time to time about Polly and her mother; and now, thanks to the Internet, I have, amazingly, heard their stilted, self-conscious voices, talking to each other across the

© The Author(s) 2018
D. Salwak (ed.), *Writers and Their Mothers*,
https://doi.org/10.1007/978-3-319-68348-5_13

Atlantic, on a BBC WWII archive, linked to a blog from someone called 60goingon16. The blogger had come across a copy of *A Child's Garland* in a charity shop and had pursued her curiosity.

My copy of this book is inscribed in my mother's hand 'Ann Barbara Harrop, Marsden School, Wellington 1942', with the word 'Christmas' added by my father. Underneath a teacher had scribbled her initials, indicating that the book was considered suitable reading for my young eyes. I was ten years old and it was nearly a year since my mother had left us in New Zealand to make the perilous return journey on a troopship, to go back to my father in London. She had left a letter with her sister to be given to us only if she had drowned. Her ship crossed the Pacific, passed through the Panama Canal, hugged the eastern shore of the United States and joined a convoy in Canada for the last lap across the Atlantic. It had been a brave and difficult decision to make. It would be another three and a half years before I saw my mother again, after the war was over.

It was the fact that in our family we all write easily that made us able to survive the separation without lasting damage. It was a bond with my husband, Anthony, who, as a child in America, also did not see his mother for years. We both think these separations made us strong and independent. During the five years the war lasted, hundreds of letters (and later airgraphs) crossed the world, and many parcels of books, some inevitably sunk at sea.

A Child's Garland has a particular significance for me. Unlike the stories I loved so much (many by M.E. Atkinson) this book (I think I realised) was an introduction to English literature. In it I read some familiar poems and Bible stories, but I was also reading many of the writers who would mean so much to me throughout my life: Edward Lear, Alfred Tennyson, Blake and Browning and T.S. Eliot, even Shakespeare.

Jane Carton's notes in italics made everything easier for the child reader and my mother had added some notes of her own. They were in pencil, still clear to this day, and emphasising that you should never write in books in ink—except at the front. Often there were questions: 'What do you think of this?' or 'Would you like to learn this?' By Blake's 'Jerusalem' she wrote, 'There is a lovely tune to this.' There were reminders too. After E. Nesbit's name she added 'who wrote all those books D. collected.' My brother David had had them all on his bookshelf at home in England. So

I can truly say that my mother, like so many mothers, introduced me to and encouraged in me a love of reading and the need for writing.

There is one other great gift my mother gave me, which stood me in good stead as a biographer. She put me in touch with the Victorians, so that I always saw them as people like us, not remote distant inhabitants of history books. She was herself less than seven months old when Queen Victoria died in 1901, but both her father (born in 1863) and her favourite Aunt Win (born in 1886) had written memoirs, and my mother was steeped in family history. This went with her when she left New Zealand in 1923 and found herself on the same side of the world as all those Victorians who had featured in the stories: the English inn-keeper, baker and goods guard, and the Scottish tailor, sailor and farmer. (It was only on my father's side there was anyone described in the records as a 'gentleman'.)

My mother's own father, to whom she was devoted, was, like all my grandparents, born in New Zealand. It was the earlier generation who had been the adventurous emigrants. When my mother was a child, her father was headmaster of her primary school, which was difficult for all his children. That must have been the origin of her perpetual need to be *good*, which she passed on to me. At sixteen, she wanted to be 'humble, helpful and holy', as she wrote in her diary. It was not enough to be good, Hilda had to try to be the *best* at everything. For Christmas 1914 her Aunt Win had given her *Pollyanna*, published the previous year. It impressed her immensely, so life wasn't just about being good, or at least the best, but about making the best of everything.

Fortunately 'School is lovely' she wrote a little later, 'And so is Miss Watson', a new tennis-playing teacher. 'I wish *she* would love me.' Love for girls and women teachers could cause pain, but absolutely no guilt. Hilda had no idea that there could be any latent sexuality in such devotion. She was good at female friendship, making a large number of women friends, both at high school and university, she would always keep, maintaining close relationships by letter over many years from the other side of the world, refreshed by occasional meetings in either England or New Zealand.

A devoted Christian all her life, my adolescent mother wrote that she was 'beastly dissatisfied' with herself. She felt she should be doing more for other people and not worrying (as so many in her church did) about dividing the population into sheep and goats. She wrote: 'Do not worldly people want to be straight and true and clean and brave and pleasant to those around?' She felt that the difference between churchgoers and other people was 'not always noticeable'. The fact that Hilda was reading George Eliot, that acknowledged agnostic, at the time, may have had something to do with this. Many of my mother's closest friends through-out her life were not Christians. Yet she herself felt that it was only with God's help that she could become the sort of woman she wanted to be: 'gracious, kind, large-hearted, generous-natured (to give much because I have so much), sincere, unself-conscious, wide in views, sunny-tempered, sweet, loyal, true, noble, unassuming'.

It was quite a list, but there were many, writing to me after her death, who suggested that she was indeed the sort of woman she had wanted to be when she was sixteen, with many emphasising the huge interest she had in other people's lives and the zest with which she lived her own.

In her first year at university she tried to curb that curiosity and zest. Relationships with men were much more complicated than with women. She wrote a list of rules for herself:

> I must not act on impulse—I must think of what I'm saying.
>
> I must not be keen on anything proposed by men.
>
> I must not be very friendly—that is, I must be quiescent and stationary and let them move *all* the way towards me—if they want to, they will, and if they don't, then I mustn't want them to.
>
> I mustn't let them know my views on matters without their seeking them: make them curious!
>
> Keep self-control perfect.
>
> Don't respond at once to overtures.
>
> Keep conversation strictly impersonal.
>
> Don't let men ask questions—change the subject.
>
> Don't tell them what you're thinking even tho' you want to.
>
> Don't think of what *you* want—self-gratification is often at the expense of the other's interest.
>
> Don't let them be sure of you—keep them guessing.
>
> Don't take them into your confidence.
>
> Don't discuss other people. Don't even mention other girls or men.
>
> Don't discuss rules of conduct.

Confine yourself to general topics—work, sport, books, music.
If you do get excited, don't show it.

What strange conversations Hilda must have had as she whirled round
the dance floor in 1919 with Mr Luke, Mr Gray, Mr Park, Mr Petrie and
a dozen others. My father, who had been playing tennis with Hilda since
they were sixteen and would marry her seven years later, was not a dancer.

I have told their story in *Passageways, the Story of a New Zealand Family*,
published by Otago University Press in 2009. Now I must think more
about my own relationship with my mother. I know how much I was
wanted. In 1928 my parents were visited in their north London home by
her mother and father. On the night before they returned to New Zealand,
Hilda wrote: 'Mother taught me to crochet edges for Ann Barbara's shawl.'
It gave me a shock, reading my mother's diaries for the first time, to see my
own name four years before I was born, when Hilda had felt confident she
was expecting a daughter. It seemed some sort of compliment to the particularly close relationship she had that year with her own beloved mother.
But seven months later that child was stillborn, a son they named John.

Hilda told the sad story in the memoirs my brother published after her
death. 'In those days I wasn't even allowed to see him and my poor Angus
had to take the little white box to the nearest cemetery in West Hampstead,
in a taxi, by himself.' She added 'But I was so fortunate to have David and
then Ann Barbara within the next four years—so I do realise I was very
blessed in the end.' Even sixty years later it must have been hard to maintain that Pollyanna tone.

Hilda called her memoirs *A Privileged Life*, introducing the '30,000
words of random memories' she wrote over eighteen years from 1969 until
she gave up in 1987, three years before her death at ninety. I was of course
particularly interested in what she had written about that momentous decision to leave us in New Zealand in 1942 to return to my father. I see now
that he undoubtedly needed her far more than we did. ('I decided I couldn't
be away from Angus any longer', she wrote.) I don't believe I could have
made such a choice myself, but I can see it was a wise one. David and I
flourished in that peaceful country, writing our long weekly letters home.

We arrived back in England on July 5th, 1945, election day. My mother
skated over the problems: 'As may be imagined we had some difficult times

readjusting to normal family life again.' I was nearly thirteen and considered myself entirely grown up, though there was plenty of evidence to suggest that this was not the case. I did however publish my first story (outside a school magazine), written when I was fourteen, in the *Empire Youth Annual*, 1948: 'Meet you at the station'. It is a story of stolen Maori treasure and was illustrated rather splendidly by F.H. Coventry, who had produced a striking jacket for my father's *England and the Maori Wars*. I was paid a proper professional fee and the publisher, P.R. Gawthorn Ltd, had offices in Russell Square, not far from Faber, who published *A Child's Garland* and who would eventually be my own publisher for over twenty years.

In the following year, 1949, my mother wrote her only book, *The Young Traveller in New Zealand*, one of a series published by Phoenix House. I am not sure how she came to get the commission, but she was an experienced journalist and it was lucky for me that she did. It was a long series (ten countries had already been covered), but they had not yet included Japan. When, after Oxford, we knew we were going there for Anthony's first job, my mother arranged for me to meet her editor. It was suggested that I submit a couple of chapters when we had been there six months. If Phoenix House liked them, I would get a contract.

The Young Traveller in Japan, my first book, was published in 1958, the year after we returned to England and dedicated to our first daughter: 'For Emily Jane, who was born in Japan and will read about it one day.' It was the first of many books.

It now seems that after that my mother put aside any ambitions she might have had of her own and did everything in her power to encourage me and support me as a writer—helping with child care, reading my manuscripts, making it much easier for me to be a writer. I owe her a lot.

Hilda was widowed for many years. In her old age (younger than I am now) she moved into an Abbeyfield house in the Cathedral Close in Norwich, not far from our home in south Norfolk. She worked on her memoirs and, looking back on her life, realised how privileged she had always been to live the sort of life she wanted, a life full of writing and reading, gardens, music, travel, and friends and family on both sides of the world.

In 1990 for one reason and another I had to cross the Atlantic six times. I particularly remember how much it helped me to have in my head my mother's words: 'I've had my life; now you must make the most of yours.' In that last year of her life, *A.A. Milne: His Life* was published. It was dedicated

> In memory of my devoted parents
> A.J. and H.M. Harrop,
> particularly because he gave
> *Winnie-the-Pooh* to her
> when it was first published
> and read it to me years later
> at just the right moment.

In this essay I have tried to bring my mother back into my mind as the vibrant energetic person she had been. She had a stroke at eighty-seven and life was increasingly difficult. We both longed for her to die and, at her request, I would read Psalm 23 to her over and over again, as she walked through the valley of the shadow of death, fearing no evil. It was the psalm I had first got to know long before in *A Child's Garland*. My mother died on my birthday, October 4th, 1990.

14

My Mother, and Friends

Reeve Lindbergh

Although it is the words that remain, it is not exactly, or not entirely, the words that I remember. I have read them all many times, in her diaries and letters, in her poetry, in the early accounts of her flights as a pioneer aviator in partnership with my father, in the bestselling *Gift from the Sea* and in her one or two semi-autobiographical novels, though she generally avoided that form. I did too, years later. Writing fiction was not the most comfortable literary activity for either one of us, perhaps because whatever we wrote was always so close to our own lives that fiction seemed needlessly deceitful.

No, it is not the words that I remember about my mother, though I am very familiar with the words. It is instead a sense of her unconditional loving presence, a kind of surrounding that remains one of the strongest elements in my life.

It was forever strange to me that my father was the object of interest for most people, when she, not he, was the real center of my own world. For those who were fascinated by the Lindberghs as a couple, though, he was the Hero, the Great Man, the shining star, or by contrast the pariah, the political target, and in some eyes the anti-Semite, though not in mine. What I thought was that at the time he made anti-interventionist speeches before World War II and was accused of anti-Semitism, he didn't even know what that meant, "Anti-Semitism." In some way characteristic of the man, he didn't have a clue. My mother did. She told him, but he was not able to hear what she was saying, or truly understand. This happened to him sometimes. What she told me about my father was that at certain times in his life "he only listened to himself." That's what made him successful in his flight across the Atlantic in 1927, and that's what caused him to make those controversial speeches before the War.

I listened to my mother, and thought I could hear and understand her. I loved her voice, as well as the words she used. She was the only person in my daily life who regularly referred to herself using the word "one," as in "One never knows … " or "One often feels …." She pronounced the word "God" unusually, too, with a breathy reverence, not "Gahhd" but "Gaud." I knew she didn't sound like the other mothers in our suburban Connecticut neighborhood. Her voice was low and pleasant, without nasality. Some of my friends at school claimed that my mother had "an English accent," but I knew they were wrong. This was the uninflected voice of truth, clear as water, answering all my questions and quenching every thirst.

Beyond her talking to me and to our family, I learned to know her through her conversations with other women, year after year. These conversations were at first mysterious and tantalizing to me, discussions I witnessed but could not fully grasp. They took place over the teacups in the living room of the house in Connecticut, with two or more women looking out toward Long Island Sound, drinking Earl Grey or Lapsang Souchong tea and nibbling tiny triangles of buttered toast as they shared thoughts across the tea table, talking about men and children and books and work, their discussions punctuated now and then with laughter, or sometimes with sighs.

I had my favorites among these women. One was my mother's editor, Helen Wolff, who had escaped from Nazi Germany with her husband, Kurt in the 1930s. Kurt Wolff had been Franz Kafka's first publisher at his company, Kurt Wolff Verlag. After leaving Germany, the Wolffs lived in Italy and in France before coming to the United States in 1941 with their son, Christian Wolff, now a noted modern composer. Together Helen and Kurt Wolff founded Pantheon Books, where they published both Pasternak's *Doctor Zhivago* and my mother's best loved book, *Gift from the Sea*. Helen Wolff and my mother became close friends.

Mrs. Wolff, as I always called her, had a real accent, not English but German. She too spoke in a low voice, full of warmth and humor and wisdom, and she had a kind of steadiness that appealed to everyone she addressed, including children and dogs. When we had a young German Shepherd who showed all the sensitivity characteristic of the breed, he was not nervous around Helen Wolff.

"I don't go to animals," she told me. "I let them come to me." And they did, like the writers who wrote in different languages and came from many countries of the world. As she worked with them, I imagine that she expected the best in them to emerge, not because she imposed her opinions upon them but by offering the depth of her intelligence and the nourishment of her attention. There is a quote of hers in her *NY Times* obituary: "You have to keep yourself open to the creative efforts of authors; you must be totally receptive."

For my mother she was the perfect editor, a friend who loved her writing but did not hesitate to offer criticism when criticism was called for. Once, my mother said, Helen Wolff remarked of an early letter from my mother to my grandmother, "This is a letter that only a mother could love!" and they removed it from a projected volume of diaries and letters.

For me it was restful simply to be in their combined presence. Even though my mother and Mrs. Wolff said things to one another that I did not understand, not knowing the people they talked about or the books and writers they referenced—Pasternak, Rilke, Günter Grass—the conversation itself washed over me with peacefulness, as if I were playing in the warm and gentle shallows of an ocean where these two women swam together not far away, the two of them easily buoyant in an element in which I had yet to be immersed.

Another, very different friend was Ernestine Stodelle, or as my sister and I called her, "Miss Stodelle," a respectful name that I pronounced as a slurred, mysterious single word, "Mistadelle," befitting such a magical person. She taught after-school ballet classes at the "DCA House," the Darien Community Association's large, Regency-style building on Middlesex Road. I remember her as beautiful in a fairy tale way—a princess, a Fairy Godmother in a leotard, with long gauzy pastel scarves tied around her head. She offered her students music and dance and her delighted laughter, along with endless kindness to each and every one of us, however young or awkward we might be.

Though I knew only the local classes for children which I attended, Ernestine Stodelle also taught dance criticism at New York University and had her own dance studio in Cheshire, Connecticut. She had been a pioneering modern dancer, had performed with José Limon and Doris Humphrey, and wrote reviews in dance journals and books about the dance technique of Doris Humphrey and Martha Graham.

She was originally married to a Russian theatrical director, Theodore Komisarjevsky, and had a daughter and two sons: Tanya, Christopher and Benedict. Christopher was about my age. I thought he was very handsome, and for a while I had a secret crush on him, but I did not see him often enough to suffer over it, which was ideal.

Mr. Komisarjevaky died in 1954. A few years later Miss Stodelle married John Chamberlain, a writer and conservative columnist whose wife had also died and whose two daughters had studied dance with Miss Stodelle. Together John and Ernestine Chamberlain had a son, John, who became a close friend of my mother's oldest grandson, Lars Lindbergh.

Even at the very end of my mother's life, when she was in her nineties and quite fragile and Ernestine and John were not much younger or stronger, the three of them still met for tea at my mother's house in Connecticut. It was good to see them together, old friends conversing as always, though at that time my mother did not say very much at all, and nobody knew what she was thinking. John, too, was quiet, but Ernestine filled the room with brightness and beauty and her extraordinary energy, which she lavished generously upon all those around her. She made everything seem possible. At one of these meetings she turned to me affectionately and said, as if sharing a wonderful secret, "John and I are thinking of taking your mother to Europe!"

Even though I knew this plan was completely unrealistic, absolutely unworkable—at that time my mother's life had begun to be a matter of "work," for me and for others: working out the schedule of her hours and her days, working with caregivers who were with her, now, around the clock—my heart leapt with hope—a mental jeté at the very idea of the three of them, Ernestine and John and my mother, traveling freely abroad together. For one lovely moment, at a time when I would not have believed it possible, Ernestine again showed me what it meant to dance.

Then there were the aunts: Aunt Con and Aunt Margot, my mother's sister and sister-in-law, respectively. Aunt Con, Constance Morrow Morgan, was seven years younger than my mother and the youngest of the three daughters in the Morrow family: Elisabeth, Anne, and Constance. Constance, or Con, was a brilliant student and graduated Summa Cum Laude from Smith College. Later she served on Smith's Board of Trustees for fifteen years, four of them as Chair. In her diaries my mother always deferred to her younger sister in matters of knowledge, intellect, or any kind of scholarship. She told my father just before the first time he took her flying, "I think Con ought to have this [experience] instead of me—she is so much more intelligent about planes than I am."

This was my mother's attitude toward both of her sisters. She compared herself unfavorably to them, sure that Con was more intelligent than she was, more practical, more effective and much more up-to-date in political and intellectual matters. Elisabeth, on the other hand, was more beautiful and more sophisticated, wittier, more poised and far more successful with men. My mother wrote gloomily in her diary after she met my father that he, like all other men, surely must have been drawn to Elisabeth when he first met the three Morrow girls in Mexico in December of 1927.

In fact, he was not. He was attracted to Anne, not Elisabeth, and later it was Anne, not Con, he invited to go for a plane ride. It must have been strange for my mother, a real shock to her system, to realize that for once she was the one preferred.

I wish I had known her older sister, Elisabeth Morrow, a teacher of young children and an early proponent of Montessori-style education. She married a Welsh-born diplomat, Aubrey Morgan, but she died in 1934 at the age of 30, from a heart condition complicated by pneumonia. Some years later Aubrey married Con, Elisabeth's much younger sister, and Con became the mother of their four children and his companion and collaborator in working for the British Information Service during the Second World War. They gathered and surveyed material from the American media for British officials in Washington DC and London. After the war, Con and Aubrey settled down in Ridgefield, Washington, raising dairy cattle and harvesting timber on their land. They called the farm "Plas Newydd," Welsh for "New Place."

I visited them in the summer once or twice, and I remember that my Aunt Con would feed what seemed to be dozens of young men and women, college students and friends of the family, who came to the farm to help bring in hay and perform other needed chores of the season.

"If you can read, you can cook," she cheerfully told the admiring young women—nieces, college roommates and classmates of her daughters—who came to help her in the kitchen while the young men were working with Aubrey in the fields. This division of labor was still standard at the time: men labored outdoors, women indoors. I was a few years younger than these farm workers of both sexes, visiting Plas Newydd only as a guest and witness to all the activity. It was a household in which hard work was done all day long while the evenings were devoted to good food and good conversation, covering anything from literature to philosophy to international affairs. For one week during these summers the whole group would travel to Ashland, Oregon, to attend the Shakespeare Festival and, by day, to go rubber-tubing on the Rogue River. I had the time of my life in the company of all these people; above all, I admired and adored my Aunt Con.

Each year she would travel "East," as my mother put it (meaning New England rather than Asia). She would stay with us in Connecticut for some of the time during these trips, often associated with her work for Smith College. Her older children remained at home or in boarding school, but she brought her youngest daughter, Margaret Eiluned Morgan, called "Eiluned" by those who knew her well (a Welsh name, pronounced "Eee-lin-ned," with the accent on the second syllable). At the age of five my cousin Eiluned, five years younger than I was, astonished me with her understanding and execution of intricate ballet steps, and by her ability to recite from memory entire librettos of Gilbert and Sullivan operettas.

Meanwhile our mothers would sit together at the end of a long day of committee meetings (Aunt Con) or struggling with a book (my mother). They talked and they sipped from glasses of amber sherry, usually Pedro

Domecq, usually dry rather than sweet. If my cousin and I came down-stairs at this time we could share the food, though not the sherry. There were little plates of crackers—Carrs Wafers or Ry-Crisp or Wheat Thins or Triscuits, and dainty wedges of Gouda cheese, or sometimes a small brown ceramic crock of spreadable wine-cheddar. In later years a favorite cheese was Saga Blue, which I loved, or Boursin with herbs, which seemed mild, but not bad. I sometimes wonder how much cheese I ate, growing up, just because of being raised in my mother's household.

The talk of children and husbands and books and work would move on into issues of higher education or current events or international affairs. Names would be invoked, perhaps President Mendenhall of Smith College, or Dag Hammarsköld of the United Nations, or Democratic statesman Adlai Stevenson II, whom my mother admired so much that she influenced my father to vote for Stevenson when he ran for president in 1952. My father tended to vote Republican, and up to that time had never voted for a Democrat in a presidential election. However, my mother left a book of Stevenson's essays on my father's bedside table the night before the election, and urged him to read it. He did so, then cast his vote for Stevenson in the morning. He later said that after reading Stevenson's book he was convinced that the man could effectively lead the county. I heard this story from my father himself, and it was clear to me, not for the first time or the last, that my mother was a very powerful woman.

My mother and her sister Con were both physically small, neither one of them much above five feet in height. They were often described as "petite," or "charming," or some other term designating diminutiveness and implying, too, the diminished status that most women, however admired, occupied at the time. In my mother's own diaries she referred to herself as "the youngest, shiest, most self-conscious adolescent that—I believe—ever lived," and many of her writings are peppered with self-deprecation. A careless reader could be forgiven for forming an impression of her character as retiring and reticent, even weak. Nothing could be further from the truth.

The Morrow daughters were well educated and had been brought up with very good manners, so that they never put themselves forward unbe-comingly, or claimed territory that seemed rightly to belong to someone else, especially someone male and of substance in the world, such as one of their husbands. Still, my mother and my Aunt Con nonetheless were, as one of my cousins described them in their later years, "Tiny Titans."

Born at a time when women in this country did not yet have the right to vote, each in her own way was a passionate champion of the advancement of women, my mother in her pioneering aviation adventures and her writing, my aunt through her deep lifelong commitment to higher education for women. They were two of the strongest people I have ever known.

Another titan in all of our lives was my Aunt Margot, who had been married to my uncle, Dwight Morrow Junior. She'd met him when she and Aunt Con, a close friend, were both young actors, and together had started the Brattleboro Summer Theater in Vermont. Aunt Margot and Uncle Dwight had three children, Stephen, Faith and another Constance, before they were divorced in 1946. Margot remained close to the Morrow family for the rest of her life, an intimate both of Aunt Con and my mother.

A lifelong Buddhist, Margot had grown up with her sister in a family of Theosophists in the Ojai Valley in California. She and her second husband, John Wilkie, had a home with their combined family of seven children in Katonah, New York, less than an hour's drive from where my family lived in Connecticut. Later they had an apartment in New York City, too, on East 66th street, with a doorman to greet us when we entered the building and an elevator whose doors opened directly into Margot's apartment. When it finished its ascent Margot would be waiting for us in the hallway every time, beaming with joy at our arrival.

Margot's apartment was full of light, and beautiful furniture, and paintings and books. It was the place where my mother met on Thursdays with what she called "My Group," a gathering of women who read books and talked about them together. I wasn't a witness to those conversations, but my mother told me about them afterwards. Some of the names I associate with their weekly meetings are Krishnamurti, Thomas Merton, Brother David Steindl-Rast, and Nancy Wilson Ross, all representing to me religion and spirituality and the wisdom of the East (Asia, not New England). The Group may have started each meeting with a period of meditation. I know that Margot meditated. She had a shrine in one small room through which I would pass, feeling respectful but uneasy, on the way to the bathroom. There was a cushion and a vase of flowers on the floor in front of a tapestry on the wall, bearing an image of the Buddha, or maybe not. It could have been Ganesh, the Hindu god with the elephant head, also known as the Lord of Good Fortune. Margot was fond of Ganesh, and a few years before she died she brought me a little statue of him which I treasure.

The women in The Group were all very intelligent, well-mannered and well dressed. They smelled good, too, especially my Aunt Margot. She was not tiny, like Aunt Con and my mother, but she was magnificent and, I thought, delicious. I remember her in her nineties, wearing a deep pink silk blouse over elegant white trousers, and wafting the scent of Chanel no. 5. She always wore bright, wet-looking lipstick, which didn't stop her from kissing people enthusiastically in greeting. As a child, I would wear Aunt Margot's lipstick mark on my cheek proudly all day.

She knew everybody. From New York Society leaders of all generations to theater personalities to spiritual leaders from around the world, everyone was an intimate friend. Once an old friend of mine, also a friend of Margot's, called to tell me a story about her. The two of them had gone together to hear the Dalai Lama speak in New York City, and had just settled into their seats before the program. The Dalai Lama appeared on stage smiling, looked over the assembled crowd benevolently before beginning to speak, and then said to the audience, "Wait—I need to greet somebody." He left the stage, walked down the aisle to where my Aunt Margot was sitting and embraced her affectionately before turning to go back up the aisle and back on the stage again to deliver his talk. When my friend looked over at her in awe and astonishment, Margot laughed and said dismissively, "Oh, it's nothing, I've known him since he was a little boy."

These were the women I knew best in my mother's life, though of course there were many others, and there were men as well, old friends and new ones who would come and visit her, especially when my father was away, which was a frequent occurrence. These male visitors included a British pilot from the old days and a young doctor introduced to my mother by a woman who had dated him while working as a secretary for my parents. Sometimes they were the husbands of women friends, but they arrived unaccompanied by their spouses. They all seemed very respectable to me. I thought of them as sedate "admirers," though my mother told me many years later that the British pilot, whom she and my father had gotten to know in the early 1930s during a stopover in Greenland on a survey flight, had told her on one of these later visits, "You must know that I've always adored you." She seemed flustered when she told me this story, and claimed that she hadn't known of his devotion, not at all, not ever. I wasn't so sure. My mother was always very pretty, and so often alone.

Of all the men who came to see her, the one I liked best was her doctor, Dana Atchley, of Columbia Presbyterian Medical Center in New York. He was a friend of both my parents, and treated my father with great skill and sensitivity during his last illness. Dr. Atchley had twinkling eyes and white, white hair. He laughed quite a bit, but not too much, when he was talking to children, and he seemed to be very fond of my mother without worshipping her. This pleased me.

I learned as an adult that Dana Atchley, whose wife I never met and thought of as an invalid, and my mother, whose husband was so often away from home, almost certainly had a love affair sometime in the 1950s. If I had been told about this at the time it was going on, or even a few years later in my teens, I wouldn't have believed it, probably because I could not imagine people of their age making love at all, with their legal spouses or with one another or anybody else. Now, when I think about it, I do believe it, and I am inclined to be pleased for both my mother and Dr. Atchley. Having learned in recent years that my father had several relationships with women other than my mother during this period, I can quite easily accept her loving friendship, in whatever form it took, with a man whose affection for my mother I had appreciated from the time I was a child.

I can see them all, the circles of women (and sometimes men) who surrounded my mother, listened to her and talked with her, strengthened her with their affection and were privy to her thoughts over the years. They showed me who she was in a way that I would not have seen by myself, not even as her daughter. They offered me a view of her truer than a biographer's, truer even than the view available to me or any other reader of her words. Close friends do not see you as readers do, or scholars do, or even as your admirers or detractors do, if you have them. Close friends simply are with you in friendship, moment after moment throughout your lifetime, however joyful or anguishing or simply mundane the moments may be.

When my mother could no longer drive to New York to see Aunt Margot, Margot would send a car and driver to pick her up and take her home again. When she arrived at Helen Wolff's apartment building one day and did not know where she was or who she was visiting, the doorman recognized her and brought her directly to Helen's door. She and Aunt Con had telephone conversations at the very end of their lives, when my mother was literally, uncharacteristically, "at a loss for words," and barely spoke at all. I could hear the same phrases I'd heard all my life, "No, Dear," and "Yes, Dear," and sometimes my favorite, which was "Oh Dear." These were immensely comforting.

I now meet regularly with my own friends, including my own "Group" of women who discuss books, another group of writers who meet once a month to share whatever we are working on, and a third, smaller group that meets now and then for a drink, having started doing this when all of us had husbands with serious illnesses. In most cases our husbands are better now, but we still meet now and then. We talk about husbands and children and sometimes grandchildren, about work, and about books. The talk is punctuated with laughter, and sometimes with sighs. It bears truthful, easy witness to our being here together and caring about one another. With sympathy and interest we gather together, as my mother and her friends gathered long ago, and without even knowing we are doing it we tell each other gently who we are.

15

My Mother's Desk

Martha Oliver-Smith

My mother Martha Bacon wrote sitting upright, back straight at a desk. It wasn't always the same desk because my family moved so many times, zigzagging across the country from Rhode Island to California and back, with stints in Boston and New York City. Wherever we lived, a desk, borrowed or bought second-hand, stood in a room without a door but that still provided my mother a modicum of privacy to write. Covered with her papers and notebooks in tidy stacks, her desk nestled in its semi-private space was a sign that we had settled in one place, at least for the time being.

From 1953 to 1958 the family moved back and forth three times between Peace Dale, Rhode Island where my grandmother lived and New York where my mother found work writing and editing copy for magazines. Our migrations depended on whether she had work as a writer and the state of her marriage, first to my father, Philip Oliver-Smith, a struggling artist and graduate student and then to our first step-father, Carlton McKinney, a struggling writer.

If our mother was out of work or separated from a husband, she, my older brother Tony, my younger sister, Pippa, and I moved back to Rhode

© The Author(s) 2018
D. Salwak (ed.), *Writers and Their Mothers*,
https://doi.org/10.1007/978-3-319-68348-5_15

Island to live with our grandmother in her large run-down Victorian mansion called The Acorns. Built by our grandfather's wealthy parents for him when he married our grandmother, the house was our haven away from the city. We children were happy to move back full time to the place where we spent our summers.

Our grandfather, Leonard Bacon, was a poet, translator and literary figure of the 1930s and 40s who won a Pulitzer Prize for poetry in 1941. His reputation faded with the growing Modernist movement, but in his prime, he was the lord of the manor, the center of his small universe. The Acorns, a dependable haven for family and friends, had once been a site of frequent literary gatherings and parties. Before the Depression, there had been money and energy to keep the place going in style, but by the time of my grandfather's death in 1954, the house had fallen into disrepair and money was scarce as the family trust fund slowly but inexorably diminished.

We loved the place with its surrounding woods and fields and barely noticed its perpetual state of disrepair. Our kind and gentle grandmother, also named Martha Bacon or MayMay as we called her, quietly presided over its four attic to basement floors, its dozens of rambling rooms, narrow hallways and odd angular spaces. She allowed us to roam inside and out as we wished. We considered the place our real home where we were free to hide, ride our bikes to town or get lost and found in the woods.

Released from the constraints and reminders that we were on scholarships at our exclusive private schools in the city, we happily went to the local public schools with the rest of the children from town. This was exactly what we wanted, though our mother, who disdained public schools, was deeply disappointed that all her efforts to keep us in our New York schools were wasted once again.

I imagine packing up and moving back to Peace Dale probably felt like defeat to our mother. She could never make enough money to survive in the city on her own, so she was dependent on her widowed mother for a roof over her head. We would stay in Peace Dale only until she found a new job or a solution to her marital troubles—possibly a new husband. Then we'd move back to the limitations and grit of the city. At her desk, wherever we lived, no matter what was going on, my mother wrote. If there was no freelance work she worked at her novels, poetry, articles, reviews and children's books. When and wherever she was writing, her desk was her home.

The Acorns, 1956: Scarred for Life

My mother's desk is an old-fashioned wooden secretary desk with a drop front that is always open. Tucked into a corner at the far end of the living room, it is obscured by a large wing chair that serves as a screen. Here she can hide from the constant traffic of children running in and out of the front door and through the hall next to the living room. Out of sight in her corner, the general commotion of daily life in the house barely touches her, yet she can break away if absolutely necessary. That seldom happens.

Though we are not supposed to touch anything on the desk, my sister and I are attracted to it. When Mum is elsewhere doing chores or running errands, we like to explore its contents. The desk has a top shelf where photographs of her parents and the three of us perch and gaze upon our mother as she writes.

A lower shelf is fitted with slots for papers and envelopes and several narrow drawers, including a secret one full of odds and ends: old letters from a relative in Savannah during the Civil War, metal buttons from my grandfather's World War I army uniform, his sacred bird caller that often floats to other drawers in other rooms and back again, fountain pen nibs, paper clips, a tiny, red leather Italian ring box with no ring, several of my grandmother's tortoise shell hairpins.

When she is at her desk, we all know not to interrupt Mum while she writes her first drafts in long hand followed by many other drafts over hours, days or weeks of incessant typing. We are used to her tuning us out and have learned, for the most part, how to navigate the varying degrees of her tenacious attention span.

Sometimes I try to talk to her about writing. I am ten years old and have discovered a perfect word to describe the sky, a word with soft sounds and an undulating rhythm. I have even written a poem so that I could use the word; it is not a common word one would hear in ordinary conversation. I'm so delighted with my poem that I risk interrupting her at her desk to show it to her. She turns away from her typewriter, taking a moment to focus on the scrap of lined notebook paper I've thrust at her.

Taking it, she stares at my words as if looking at a map of the ancient world written in runic script. When her eyes focus, she reads quickly while I wait for her praise. She looks at me, shakes her head a little and says in the unwavering British accent she acquired in her days as an actress: "Patty Dahling—never use the word 'cerulean' in a poem about the sky." Except for that rhythmic blue word, I don't remember anything else about the sky poem, which I immediately lost or threw away.

Decades later, however, I clearly remember my mother at her desk, typing, completely absorbed. On a particular afternoon, I imagine she is working on one of the novels it took me until just a few years ago to read. She sits upright, her slender fingers poised on the typewriter keys.

In her stillness, she stares at a half page of print, backed by carbon paper in the roller. I say her name three times, at first softly, then almost shouting.

"MUM?"

"Mmmm?"

She turns to look at me. For some minutes I have been standing patiently right next to her, but she hasn't even sensed my presence let alone seen me. Despite the urgency of my need—I am bleeding rather profusely—I wait to penetrate the thick membrane of her concentration. I like watching her, like to look at her because she's pretty, and because I don't see her that often. She is elusive and often away, on trips back to New York or Boston to meet with a publisher or to do research in a city library for one of her books or articles.

When her eyes finally focus on my face, she seems not to recognize me. She still doesn't notice my bleeding finger. I know I shouldn't bother her when she's writing. The rule is that we are not to disturb her at her desk unless we are bleeding from the mouth or ears. I hope my wounded finger qualifies. I have stabbed it with a pair of open library scissors, trying to force a cork down into a bottle of Rose's Limewater with one of the long blades. My sister and I are making a concoction, a witch's brew of various mixers and alcoholic liquids we've discovered in the pantry. A steady stream of blood drips, forming a small pool on the parquet floor.

"What is it Dahling?"

"I'm bleeding."

"Oh—so you are—What a nuisance!"

Should I ask her now if she'll take me to the bathroom to clean and bandage my wound? I wait, silent. She eyes my dripping finger.

"You'll live—Run along now and find a Band-Aid."

Apparently my gory finger does not qualify for her undivided attention. Before she turns back to her typewriter, she throws me a vague though friendly glance from her cerulean blue eyes.

As I type this, almost sixty years later, my right index finger with its fine, white crescent of a scar hits the "U" in cerulean.

When we lived in New York my mother's desk was a small rectangular writing table, its surface covered with stacks of manuscripts, flat boxes of carbon paper, yellow legal pads on which she wrote her longhand drafts, and, of course, her typewriter. At the far end of our living room, set beneath a window looking out on the grey shaft of 116th street between Riverside Drive and Broadway, the desk, stripped down and utilitarian, served its purpose as one of the tools of her trade.

There, in her writing trance, she would often labor nights after work and weekends on assignments she brought home from the office or the occasional freelance job. Family traffic flowed through the living room, but an invisible, impermeable shield seemed to protect her from our intrusions and even our presence in the room. I now know that I was being imprinted, conditioned to what it means to be a writer and a mother—no matter how I resisted the model.

New York, 1958: On the Banks of the River Garigliano

Early on weekday mornings, my mother moves around in the kitchen in our New York apartment, two paces from my closed bedroom door. Running water and clanking plates merge with my morning dreams as she washes last night's dishes and makes coffee. When she opens my door, Chanel #5 laced with coffee drifts into the room displacing its persistent dank odor. I breathe in my mother's essence, my eyes still closed. Every day she dabs a little perfume behind her ears. It follows her around all day like a faint, sweet ghost. "Wake up Dahling," she chirps, "Up you get!"

The fake British accent, I notice, is more crisp this morning than usual. Lately her "biscuits," "petrol" and "shedules" annoy me. Her way of speaking never used to bother me. When one of my friends would ask, having noticed that nobody else in the family speaks with an accent, I'd shrug and say that's just how she likes to talk. Now I find it embarrassing—find her embarrassing. She always laughs and tosses off her answer when someone inquires about her accent: "Pure Affectation–dahling."

Competing with coffee and perfume, a garbage odor wafts from the narrow hallway—the week's trash hunkering behind the door to the service elevator. The stink often wafts into my room, a cell once intended as a maid's bedroom. Completing my private sanctuary is a miniscule bathroom with a toilet and a tiny square tub that swarms at night with roaches traveling through the wall from the water pipes shared with the kitchen sink. I don't care about the roaches or the smell because the room is mine. Mum allowed me to move in here when I turned twelve and my brother left for boarding school. I no longer have to share a room with my younger sister.

I open my eyes. Mum stands in the doorway, her office mask painted on for the day, eyebrows plucked even, bright red lipstick, perfect. She wears a beige "sack" dress from the clearance rack at Bloomingdales, one of last year's latest styles touted by *Harper's Bazaar*, the magazine where she works as a copywriter and editor. She has to dress stylishly even though she's not in the fashion department. The skirt of the sack dress is so narrow that she has to take very short steps, like a Geisha girl.

I am still in bed when she reappears in the doorway. She's about to leave to take my sister to her bus stop before going to work.

"We're leaving now Precious. Giulietta will be here tonight to work with me on her book. And don't wake Carlton. He's had a dreadful night—poor dahling. Don't turn your radio on or he'll have a nervous breakdown."

Carlton, my stepfather, has "bad nerves" and insomnia. He stays up all night smoking, drinking bourbon, and writing his novel. I don't think he's making much progress, judging from all the paper balls on the floor. Usually he's still at home when I get back from school, though lately he hasn't been here much at all. Recently he was out all night and came home with a black eye and a swollen lip.

So as not to muss her lipstick, Mum blows a kiss off her fingertips. After she and my sister leave, I turn on the radio: "To know, know, know him is to love love, love him ... " Lying on my back, arms stiff and straight, I pretend I am in a sarcophagus at the Metropolitan Museum. I would prefer to go there today instead of Miss Hewitt's Classes For Young Ladies, a girls school where I am on scholarship. It is a place where I feel I don't belong, full of girls from wealthy families who live near the school between Madison and Park Avenues. Except for the other girls on scholarship, I don't have much to talk about with my classmates who vacation in Bermuda and go to Barclay's Dancing School on Wednesday nights.

Since I stopped trying to pass math, I dread school. I dread the girls whose uniforms are starched and new while mine are limp and worn, purchased from the second-hand sale in the school's basement. I also dread the long, lurching bus ride from our apartment on Riverside Drive as my breakfast of scalded café au-lait and stale French bread that I fix for myself, churns in my stomach. I always think about getting off the bus at the Metropolitan on 88th street, but I haven't—so far.

My morning bus ride makes me wonder if my mother feels the same queasy way about her job at *Harper's Bazaar* as I do about school. She has written and published two novels and several books of poetry, so she complains that the magazine work is very boring for her. She gets little pay and no credit for the skimpy, gossipy writing she has to do. Since she married Carlton and has to work full time while he writes his book at home, Mum hasn't written any of her own work.

Lately she's been spending most weekends and evenings translating an Italian World War II memoir called *The Child across the River*. She learned Italian as a girl when she lived in Florence. My grandfather moved the family to Italy so that he could be a writer there. They loved Italy but left when Mussolini came into power in 1932. My mother has told me she was very sad to leave. She has never forgotten her Italian, which now comes in handy so she can make some extra cash.

She works beneath a window looking out onto the dark side street. Even on sunny days, soot and shadows filter speckled light over her desk and the pages of the memoir manuscript. I know the story well from what my mother tells me of each chapter.

In 1943, when the Allies invaded Italy, the author, Giulietta d'Alessandro, was separated from her young daughter Anna for two years. Anna was visiting her grandmother across the River Garigliano when the territory on that side of the river fell to American troops. Giulietta was stranded on the German side but climbed mountains, braved the German Army, minefields, the SS and Allied bombs, then waded and swam across the river to find her Anna.

When Giulietta comes to our apartment to work on the memoir translation, I stare at her, fascinated by this brave and pretty woman. I try to picture my mother crawling under barbed wire in cold mud and frozen fields full of land mines to find her way back to me. I envision myself as Anna, who was reading in a library when Giulietta finally found her. Anna looked up from her book to see her mother, arms outstretched. I imagine my own mother standing before me—arms outstretched.

Most days when I get home from school, Carlton is home sitting in the old wing chair in the living room, still in his sour-smelling pajamas, smoking a cigarette in a long black holder, and clinking the ice cubes in his glass of bourbon. This afternoon, when I let myself into the apartment, there's no sign of him. He's still not back when Mum arrives home at 6:00 or when Giulietta comes to work on the translation.

Mum puts on her bright face even though I can tell she's upset. She tells my sister and me to "Run along now," but I linger, quietly pretending to do my math homework. She forgets all about me as she and Giulietta sit together on our uncomfortable old blue silk couch with the hard scrolled arms, the manuscript's pages spread out on the coffee table.

They speak only Italian as they leaf through the manuscript of *The Child across the River*. Their fluid syllables tumble over me. I don't understand a word, but I love the music of the language. Sometimes serious, sometimes laughing and gesturing, they pore over the pages, reminding me of two schoolgirls sharing stories about their day.

After Giulietta leaves, my mother quickly switches into high worry gear. Her voice shakes when she calls the West End Bar where Carlton sometimes spends his afternoons. I can hear how close she is to the edge of losing control. The bartender tells her he left hours ago with some young man. My mother, the actress, sighs, shakes her head, and forces a fake little laugh: "What a relief—that naughty boy! He's going to feel like the wrath of God tomorrow."

Her strained cheerfulness is not convincing. If he's not home in the morning, she'll call the police like she did last time. She forgets to ask about my homework before sending me off to bed.

From my room I can hear faint but frantic typing. In spite of her worry about Carlton, she is writing, probably working on the memoir. I wonder how she can switch so easily from the edge of hysterics to concentrate on work. Maybe it helps to think about someone else's story.

There's music on the phonograph—Bach, the Cello Suites, Pablo Casals. I hate her classical music. It seeps under my door and gives me a headache. I especially hate the Cello Suites because when the bow meets the strings, it sounds like someone sobbing. I feel as though I could get caught up in that sound and start to cry without knowing why or how to stop it.

I don't know why, but recently I have begun to hate whatever my mother loves: Bach, opera, whole wheat bread and dry Italian cookies that taste like dust, George Eliot. My mother gave me a copy of *Mill on the Floss* for my ninth birthday. I was interested to know that George Eliot was a woman who took a man's name in order to get published, but I couldn't get through the book. I tried, started to read it, but never got past page five.

For months Mum would ask me how I liked the book. I would shrug stupidly until finally I skipped to the last chapter to find out that some girl named Maggie Tulliver drowned in a river with her brother. That thick book full of tiny print, long words and no pictures defeated me.

These days, except for homework reading for school, I read what Mum calls "rubbish." I have become addicted to magazines like *Modern Screen* and *True Confessions* that I buy with my babysitting money and keep stashed under my mattress. I gravitate to all things she despises: bologna sandwiches on wonder bread, chewing gum, rock and roll: "To know, know, know him is to love, love, love him, and I do … " Carlton is still out when I fall asleep.

I wake to an odd, faint noise, more sensation than sound that filters through the darkness and silence of the night. The typing and music have stopped, but there is something. I get up, step into the hallway and pass into Carlton's empty office. Careful not to knock over a whiskey glass full of cigarette butts on the floor, I move toward the French doors leading to the living room. One door is ajar. I can see my mother sitting in the dark, on the couch, holding a yellow cushion in her lap.

The streetlights on 116th Street stream a wan shaft of light across her desk, surrounding her in a pale, thin aura. She pulls the cushion up to her face, sobbing into it—the muffled sound that awakened me. I've witnessed her dramatic tantrums and theatrical hysterics for the benefit of an audience, but I have never seen her weep like this. I watch her breaking apart, understand that her world is collapsing. She can't pretend away the catastrophe that is Carlton.

I want to throw the doors open, go to her, put my arms around her. I want to keep her company, to tell her it will be all right, to rescue her from her sadness. But I am afraid. Her mask is off. I am afraid she will push me away and say, "Run along now, Dahling." Her grief floods the room. I can't find my way across its distance to get to her. I turn around, sneaking back in the dark to my little hole of a room, leaving her stranded.

When I was very young, I vowed that I would certainly not be a writer, nor would I be like my mother as a mother. I judged her on both counts and without realizing it, declared a sentence on myself. In my determination to show her how it was done, I dropped out of college after my freshman year, married when I was still a teenager, and had three children. I divorced in my late 20s, remarried and had a fourth child. At some point in the intensity of those child bearing and raising years, I recognized that the false and flimsy self-satisfaction of assuming I was a better parent than my own mother was not enough to fill my life.

When my children were still quite young, I decided to finish my undergraduate degree. I then went on to graduate school on a teaching fellowship for a master's degree in English literature. I had to prepare and teach freshman composition classes, and, of course, I had to write, but that kind of writing didn't count, I rationalized. As far as I was concerned, academic writing wasn't the same as writing poetry or fiction. I wasn't doing what my mother did.

As a working mother, I was determined to stay close enough to keep an eye on my children and to always be available for their small needs and major emergencies. I got used to constant interruptions and was somehow able to retrieve a lost sentence or disrupted train of thought. I still prided myself at being "not my mother."

My children tell me now, without any particular rancor, about their difficulties in getting my attention when I had a paper due and remind me of the summer I was slaving to finish my thesis. Somehow I managed to get them to swimming lessons, soccer and drama classes, but I was indeed distracted.

Ironically, I did my master's thesis on George Eliot's *Middlemarch*, having read many of her novels in one of my graduate courses. I never had a chance to talk about *Mill on the Floss* with my mother. We lived on opposite sides of the country then, and by the time I was writing my thesis she was ill with the cancer that would kill her. Our phone calls were limited to discussions of the children and elaborate, dramatic and somehow amusing stories she would tell me about her adventures in the hospital. She died a year after I finished my degree.

Long after my children were grown, and I was about to retire from teaching, I came to the realization that I was going to write, that I was, that I am, a writer. Though I had let go of my early resentment against my mother for her parental sins, I still judged her and would not commute my self-imposed sentence. I refused to call myself a writer. I still punished myself, while blaming my mother for being herself, and now it was time to stop. I opened the gate—just a crack at first. I wrote a poem.

For several years I gave myself permission to write poetry. Then I wrote a book, a memoir about my grandmother who was an artist. Now another is in the works—about my mother, the writer and mother. In order to write this book, I've had to do something I'd never done before: read her books. I also read her poetry, articles, essays and reviews as well as her four children's books. And her letters—the few she'd written to me that I saved, and many more to and from others preserved in various Rhode Island institutions.

I avoided reading most of my mother's writing until I was in my 60s because I couldn't bear hearing the sound of her voice, her many voices which live and emanate powerfully in her written words. Now as I have plunged into the work, I find myself exclaiming aloud when I read a letter or savor a sentence. I admire and criticize her novels, her style, laugh at her clever self-deprecating humor, react at how oblivious she can be in her letters. These days we are in an ongoing conversation, speaking across the years on the page, more to one another than we ever did when she was alive.

Unlike my mother, I do not work at a desk. Most of my writing happens either at the kitchen table or in bed. In my kitchen, I am surrounded by whatever collects and disperses on the surface of the table—books, piles of junk mail, magazines that share space with the salt and pepper shakers, binoculars, the sugar bowl, keys, a vase of withering flowers.

As I write, I am oblivious to the clutter, to my husband, the cats and dog wandering in and out, the radio announcing the news or playing music. In between bouts of writing, I interrupt myself to do laundry and other minimal house chores that involve running up and downstairs for exercise. The kitchen table as desk has been my choice of writing space for many years since my children were young. This is where I am most at home writing.

The indulgence of writing in bed comes from another old habit of pretending to myself that I wasn't hiding from my family in order to go deep into my thoughts and ideas without constant interruption. I would take to my bed and still do, when necessary. This occurs in the early drafting stages of a writing project.

After my husband goes downstairs to make coffee and start his work day, I prop myself against stacks of pillows, knees bent to hold a large book as backing for the plain white copier paper on which I write in long hand with a black or blue roller ball pen. Sweating in my nightgown, I write hard, channeling Edith Wharton as sheets of paper slide off the bed to the floor, until I run out of time or hit a wall.

I could if I wanted to, write in my study up on the second floor of the house away from noise and distractions. The space is fully equipped with multiple writing surfaces, drawers full of office supplies, plenty of electrical outlets, good lighting, a pleasant view of apple trees, our dirt road and beautiful woods beyond our driveway. But somehow I have never been able to concentrate on my work sitting at a real writing desk. This is one of a few ways that I am not like my mother.

16

Mater Sagax

Rachel Hadas

Who was my mother? I'll quote two paragraphs from my sister Beth's Afterword to *Ferdinandus Taurus,* our mother's 1964 translation into Latin of Munro Leaf's 1936 classic. *Ferdinandus* was reissued by David R. Godine in 2000; my sister and I each contributed a kind of postscript. Beth writes:

Elizabeth Chamberlayne Hadas (1915–1992) was a teacher, a reader, a translator, a mother. Those activities were not separate parts of her life. She was the most bookish person I have ever known [which, I might add, is saying quite a lot; Beth has been an editor for about half a century]. She read aloud to my sister and me long before we could possibly understand what she was reading to us, and it is not an accident that both of us have devoted our lives to books, one of us as an author and the other as a publisher....

Elizabeth Hadas was brought up to teach. Her father, Lewis Chamberlayne, a professor of classics, died when she was a very small child. Faced with raising two daughters, her mother, Bessie, took a job teaching at St. Catherine's School in Richmond, Virginia. Bessie and her little girls lived on campus, presumably in exchange for supervising the boarding students. From St. Catherine's, Elizabeth went to Bryn Mawr, and after graduation she went on to teach Latin at St. Timothy's School. Eventually she devel-

© The Author(s) 2018
D. Salwak (ed.), *Writers and Their Mothers,*
https://doi.org/10.1007/978-3-319-68348-5_16

oped an interest in seeing the world beyond girls' schools. She moved to New York during the war years, married Moses Hadas, had two daughters, and stayed at home with us until 1959, when she went back to teaching Latin at Spence, another girls' school. She spent the rest of her career there.

Beth covers the main points deftly and crisply; her very concision means that much has been elided. There's a great deal that could be said about the distinguished men, both professors of classics, in my mother's life: her father Lewis Parke Chamberlayne (1879–1917), and my father Moses Hadas (1900–1966). (Can a father who dies when his child is two years old be said to be in that child's life? Yes and no.) But I want to try to stick with my mother.

The dead keep their own counsel. But my mother was exceptionally good at keeping her own counsel even during her lifetime. Furthermore, although, as my sister notes, our mother was one of the most bookish people imaginable, nevertheless Elizabeth Chamberlayne Hadas didn't leave much of a paper trail. That's not quite true; think of the dozens of detailed report cards (more like essays) she wrote over the course of a quarter of a century for her Spence students. Think of the letters she wrote (now mostly lost). Still, for such a supremely articulate woman, it's a meager record.

What are books, I ask my students, if not a person talking to you who is no longer able to talk to you? When my father died in 1966, I turned to his books to hear his voice. There was nothing terribly personal there, but as my memories of him in life receded, the written record was precious. More than forty years later, partly because I was now the age my father had been when he died and partly because my new love and I found ourselves comparing notes on our departed fathers—their shared affection, for example, for bow ties, Groucho Marx, Gilbert and Sullivan—I returned to my father's writings. But here I am writing about Moses again. As my old friend Lydia Davis notes, "of course it was your father who received more attention, who seemed to collect the energy in the room into himself. Not that she seemed fazed by that— she seemed very accepting, very unruffled." But today, Mother's Day 2017, a week before the twenty-fifth anniversary of my mother's death, I am turning my thoughts to her, and she is more elusive.

In addition to the lack of a paper trail, there's a deadline. And there are numerous alarming, yawning gaps in my memory; indeed, almost any specific memories of my mother turn out to be the exception. Another challenge is that when it comes to evoking and celebrating my beloved dead, or indeed trying to capture and express any emotion or idea, I turn naturally to poetry, not prose. It would be possible to assemble a little anthology of elegies I've written, though there too Moses gets more air time than Elizabeth. But though I'll end by smuggling a little poetry in, my mode here is prose.

As my sister's account suggests, it is possible to see the twenty-one years of my mother's marriage to Moses Hadas—they were married in 1945—as a kind of island in the midst of various girls' schools. (It should be added that Elizabeth put in two stints as a librarian, first at the Library of Congress and then at the New York Public Library.) When she retired from the last of these schools, Spence, in 1984, my mother became a pretty much full-time grandmother to my son Jonathan, her only grandchild, who had been born earlier that year. She died when Jon was eight years old. What does he remember? He writes:

> My memories of Lizzie are sparse: her presence in the house in Vermont (making "great speckled pancakes" or bacon in the even-then ancient electric frying pan), her reading Tolkien to me on the sofa in the Riverside Drive apartment, or feeding me cube steak and milk. I remember the apartment with its grandfather clock (unless I'm making that up?) and exercise bike. Her cats ... Meanwhile Lizzie's own presence seems to have been so discreet as to be vanishing—light footprint indeed.

Some aspects of that somber, first-floor Riverside Drive apartment are captured by Lydia Davis in her 1986 story "Five Signs of Disturbance." Lydia and her family were friends of my family; Lydia spent some time in the apartment in the summer of, I think, 1982:

> In the dining room she pushes upright the heavy books that have been leaning far over to one side on the shelves and sprawling open for so long now that their covers are warped out of shape. There is another bookcase in the living room, with glass doors, and on top of it a clock that hisses every

time the second hand passes a certain point. [Can this be the grandfather clock Jonathan thought he remembered?] Now she walks down the hall, straightening more books as she comes to them. The hall is long and dark, with many angles, so that around every bend more hallway opens out and this hallway seems to her, sometimes, infinitely long.

Cindy Quimby, whose friendship with me dates back to summers in Vermont in the 1950s, writes, "It's interesting what images stay fixed in memory, isn't it?" The feeding and the reading Jonathan recalls, the food and the book: these (unlike that grandfather clock, which was a figment) ring true. Later Jonathan said that he thought he remembered his grandmother reading him the chapter about Beorn in *The Hobbit*. One of my own (vanishingly few) memories of my mother's mother, Elizabeth Mann Chamberlayne, is her reading me Edward Lear's "The Owl and the Pussycat" in her Virginia accent and a wonderfully growly voice.

When I think about my mother and my son together, I remember her carrying him as a baby around the garden in Vermont and naming flowers. A little later, I remember walking down the dirt road with her, Jon on my shoulders or on hers—he ruffled her white hair. "Amma's hair," he said. Or, touching her glasses, "Amma's asses." Earlier still, I think it was when she was carrying him down the long hall of our West End Avenue apartment (hers also had a long hall) that Jonathan, looking up over his grandmother's shoulder at the light fixture on the ceiling, said his first word: Ite! Ite! Jon inherited my mother's flawless spelling, her interest in gardening, and her love—the family love—of books. Books! There's no end to the memories here. *Ferdinand*; *The Princess and the Goblin*; *The Young Visiters*; *The Hobbit*; *A Little Princess*; *Racketty-Packetty House*. Books she didn't read me but loved, and that I came to love too: *Kim*. Books she read me that I later read and reread: *Pride and Prejudice*. Beth remembers being read *Alice in Wonderland*; I don't. It was our father, not our mother, who especially enjoyed performing Dickens's fairy tale *The Magic Fishbone*. But books were the lingua franca of the household.

My mother was primarily a reader of books, not a writer. After translating *Ferdinand the Bull*, she spent some time translating some of *Aesop's Fables* into Latin. That this project was never finished may mean that it was interrupted by my father's death in 1966. Earlier, in 1960, she edited *The Life of Christ*, a rich little book (it really should have been a capacious coffee table tome) which combined Gospel passages and works of art to tell the story. I wish my mother had written more. Given the right prompt and within her range of subject matter, chiefly literature (not only the classics) and art history, Elizabeth was extremely knowledgeable. She always seemed to know the answer to every question. My sister Beth inherited this trait—it's no accident that Beth aspires to go on *Jeopardy*, where everyone in the family is sure she would perform brilliantly and where, in many categories, Elizabeth would have done very well too.

Reminiscing about my mother, Cindy Quimby brings up her salient quality of being able to answer questions: "to me it seemed that [Elizabeth] always offered innately sound, informed, and logical answers to any and all questions. She seemed to be an oasis of calm and competence." (Cindy adds "and her light southern accent was calming, too.") I think of the charming line in *Ferdinandus*: "*Quod erat mater sagax, etsi vacca.*" Sagacious: a good word for Elizabeth. Debbie Hadas, Elizabeth's stepson David's daughter, unknowingly echoes this adjective: "If I had a problem, [Elizabeth] would offer sage (and confidential) advice."

The conversations Cindy is recalling took place in the summers of the late 1950s and early 1960s, in the cramped kitchen of our house in Vermont, where my mother would be making dinner for our family of four, for her stepson David's family of four, and for our friends the Quimbys, another family of four. "Cooking for twelve is no easy thing!" Cindy notes. My mother wasn't brought up to cook; I think my father taught her. I seem to remember a running joke between them about the initials S.C.; she had been born in South Carolina, but Moses, as I recall, insisted that S.C. stood for sour cream.

To be cooking for twelve people, six of them children and two of those very small children, with both one's stepdaughter-in-law (David's wife Hannah) and my mother's beloved friend Mary Jo, Cindy's mother, in and out of the small kitchen, and simultaneously to carry on any kind of conversation at all, let alone a calm and logical one—this feat (as complicated as this sentence is becoming) may not have been exactly what I had in mind when I wrote, in my Afterword to *Ferdinandus Taurus*, that "my mother never made heavy weather of any task." But it's the same kind of accomplishment. Lydia Davis calls Elizabeth "calm and quiet"; but she was also indefatigable and focused even in the midst of multi-tasking. That multi-tasking included, for most of my childhood, not only running a household and raising two daughters, but also teaching Latin at an excellent school. My mother's scores of students over the years could and probably would like to write their own tributes to her. It's as a teacher that she touched the most lives; but it's also true that most of the younger people she encountered outside the classroom—that is, her family—learned from her. Debbie writes that Elizabeth "didn't hesitate to encourage me to improve my spelling, or my character. I remember a letter pointing out I'd misspelled the word 'tomorrow,' and also her pointed missives reminding me of the importance of thank you letters."

Part of my mother's sagacity lay in her unerring sense of which book to give a child, and at what age. (I like to think I have inherited this gift, though in a much diluted form.) Among the books she gave me that made a lasting impression were two poetry anthologies: Louis Untermeyer's *The Magic Circle* and John Hollander and Harold Bloom's *The Wind and the Rain*. I was then around eleven or twelve. Did my mother know I liked poetry? Clearly. That I was on my way to becoming a poet? Possibly. But these were also books, or poems, she had enjoyed herself and thought I'd like too. The luminous figure of the (great great great) grandmother in *The Princess and the Goblin* explains to little Princess Irene, her namesake, that a name is one of those things you can give away and keep at the same time. The same is true of books. It occurs to me now that as Robert Frost wrote in "The Figure a Poem Makes," "the figure is the same as for love." You give it; you pass it on; you also get to keep it.

It may be that Elizabeth's sense for precisely which books to give children only applied when those children were girls. Her father had died when she was two; she had no brothers. Her world, as Beth suggested, was largely one of girls' schools. Beth recalls our mother saying "I don't know what I would have done if you all had been boys." (I'd amend this to "youall," a southernism that better captures her inflection.) Our father, fifteen years my mother's senior, had no appetite for throwing balls or for active sports, and I knew he was glad Beth and I were girls. But our mother was relieved too. Edward writes: "[Elizabeth] did not really know what to do with boys—my father [Elizabeth's stepson David] suggested that, and it made sense."

But whether she knew what to do with boys or not, it was to Elizabeth that Edward turned at a difficult juncture of his boyhood:

> When my parents split up, I wrote a long letter to her. I don't remember at all what I said, but I remember I put my heart into it, whatever was in my little boy, would-be man heart. I somehow thought she was the most upright and unconfused person in the world, and that was somehow a comfort. She had that effect on me for as long as I was in contact with her. In retrospect, that judgment seems vastly exaggerated. She was as baffled by the problems of life as anyone, I suspect. But she wasn't like anyone in my life then. She wasn't Jewish, she wasn't tormented, she wasn't crude or excited. She wrote me back something polite and calm. I remember being a little comforted and a little hurt that she didn't seem to understand what I was saying (whatever it was). But calm was something she did very well.

Eddie's sister Debbie writes in a similar vein: "Lizzie was my grandmother who somehow seemed to understand me when no one else did. Her kindness to me in my teens and twenties cushioned me through those difficult years."

Edward was Elizabeth's step-grandson; Debbie her step-granddaughter. And now that I too am a step-grandmother, I realize that the latest child who can be thought of as my mother's heir is my step-granddaughter. This little girl, born in January 2017, is named Camilla. I suggested the name; we knew that the child would be a girl and that the name had to begin with C, since her mother's name does—a custom of the country in her father's native Guyana. The suggestion met with approval. Camilla, now four months old, has been repaying me ever since I suggested her name. She has sent me back to the *Aeneid*, where there's a warrior maiden named Camilla; and ever since, I've been reaping the rewards of close attention (I've been on sabbatical and have had the time) to this timeless poem, whose darker reaches I hadn't properly plumbed. To date, I've written twenty-seven poems that all refer to lines from the *Aeneid*. I'm going to call the resulting little book *Poems for Camilla*. Catullus writes *cui dono lepidum novum libellum*—"To whom shall I give this pretty little booklet?" To Camilla, that's who. Our time together may be brief; she may not remember much about me; but she'll be able to read the poems.

I wish my mother could read them too. But part of growing into a writer is coming to terms with the fact that you're no longer writing for your parents. I wish my father and mother could read the verse translations of Euripides' Iphigenia plays I recently completed. But although I may have undertaken these translations in my father's shadow, in his tradition, through him, or my Camilla poems in the tradition, in the lineage, of my Latin teacher mother, through my mother, through isn't the same thing as for.

Mother, grandmother, stepmother. The latter term comes with cultural baggage attached. At my mother's memorial service in 1992, David, my half-brother and my mother's stepson, recalled that when he first met my mother, he was prepared to dislike her because he knew she had made his own mother unhappy. But it proved impossible for him to dislike his father's second wife: "As a wicked stepmother, Lizzie was a miserable flop."

Elizabeth excelled at giving books or answering questions, but she rarely volunteered opinions or information unless she was asked. Edward recalls Elizabeth correcting his sister Debbie "about some phrase which D. had used wrongly—Lizzie looked very frustrated—that surprised me. She usually had great equanimity." But what was the wrongly used phrase? For that matter, when Cindy Quimby recalls my mother's sound, informed, and logical answers, what were the questions (is this a game of Jeopardy?)? What were those conversations in the crowded Vermont kitchen about? What did those letters in what Debbie accurately calls Elizabeth's "beautiful neat handwriting" say? Gone with the snows of yesteryear.

Still, a couple of answers my mother gave me do remain etched in my memory. In both cases, I'd been overhearing her talking on the phone and badgered her with questions afterwards. The easier question (though still not all that easy) came when I'd heard her make some excuse for not being able to attend a social event with my father. I didn't know that they had other plans for that evening, and as soon as she got off the phone, I asked her about this. A thoughtful pause; and then my mother told me the truth: "Honey, it was a social lie." My much harder question, after I'd heard my mother talking, perhaps in hushed tones, to her brother-in-law, my Uncle Clinker, was "Mommy, what happened to Aunt Mary?" Again that pause; again the truth. "She hanged herself," answered my mother. I might have been twelve years old. What stands out here: the honesty; the clarity; the lapidary concision.

My mother never said much that I recall about her feelings for her troubled older sister Mary—or she didn't say much to me. And when her beloved husband died, she didn't say much about her grief. Edward remembers "seeing her cry discreetly once shortly after Moses died." And he tries to imagine his way back to a much younger Elizabeth, when she and Moses (who had been her Latin prose composition teacher at Columbia Summer School in 1942) were first together: "I often think now what she must have been like with Moses when she was young and he was married [to his first wife]—not all that reserved, I presume."

Unreserved: among Cindy Quimby's memories of Elizabeth is an unexpected and intimate, almost dreamlike vignette from about 1963. Only three years before my father's death, my mother retains some of her youthful glow: "I can still picture her with long braids wrapped around her head. I once saw her and your father in bed at your apartment on Riverside Drive. They were reading the newspaper and drinking coffee, and she looked radiant—it was the only time I saw her with long hair flowing freely. The two of them presented such a beautiful domestic image."

I can remember playing paper dolls with Beth on the floor of our shared room on Sunday mornings while our parents slept in. But coffee in bed? Did she make the coffee and then take it to Moses in bed and climb back in? Hard to imagine, but that's how it must have happened. As often happens with memories from our childhood, my sister may recall this scene more clearly than I do. I'll have to ask her. On the other hand, it may be something Cindy witnessed and never forgot, and that Beth and I, absorbed in our paper dolls or later our homework, simply never noticed.

Elizabeth lived for twenty-six years after Moses died: teaching Latin, summering in Vermont, a kind and hospitable hostess to Eddie when he was a student at Columbia, always welcoming Debbie on visits, in touch with both their father and his new wife and with their mother; and finally, a devoted grandmother to Jonathan for the eight brief years she and he coincided. I like to think her stoical equanimity was a constant resource over what must often have been lonely years. She and I spent lots of time together during these years; I and my family lived only a mile or so south of 460 Riverside Drive. But my most poignant memories of her are earlier ones—not only from my childhood, but from the time of my father's death. Not surprisingly, one of these memories is connected to a text.

Soon after my father died, my mother sent me a passage, in both Latin and English, from Tacitus's *Agricola*, a tribute to the historian's father-in-law. I am struck, rereading Tacitus's wise and consoling words all these years later, by several things. First, that my mother was in need of consolation herself; she offered me something that had helped her, but she didn't advertise her own emotions at all. Second, that it is probably pretty unusual for a mother to send her seventeen-year-old daughter a passage from a Roman historian. And third, that this passage is now at least as applicable to my mother as it was to my father. She was a role model I'm happy to try to emulate. As I near the age of seventy, and now that I'm a grandmother (or step-grandmother), I have much more in common with Elizabeth in her later years than did the anguished adolescent to whom she sent these words.

In Latin and then in English, with a few adjustments for gender, here is the passage.

> Si quis piorum minibus locus, si, ut sapientibus placet, non cum corpore extinguuntur magnae animae, placide qiescas, nosque domum tuum ab infirmo desiderio et muliebribus lamentis ad contemplationem virtutem tuarum voces, quas neque lugeri neque plangi fas est. Admiratione te potius et immortalibus laudibus et, si natura suppeditet, similitudine colamus: is verus honos, ea coniunctissime cuiusque pietas. Id filiae quoque uxori praeceperim, sic patris, sic mariti memoriam venerari, ut omnia facta dictaque eius secum revolvant, formamque ac figuram animi magis quam corporis complectantur; non quia intercedendum putem imaginibus quae marmore aut aere finguntur, sed, ut vultus hominum, Its simulacra vultus imbecilla ac mortalia sunt, forma mentis aeterna, quam tenere et exprimere non per alienam materiem et artem, sed tuis ipse moribus possis. –Agricola 46

If there is any mansion for the spirits of the just, if, as the wise aver, great souls do not perish with the body, quiet, O Mother, be your rest! May you call us, your household, from feeble regrets and unmanly mourning to contemplate your virtues, in presence of which sorrow and lamentation become a sin. May we honor you in better ways—by our admiration, by our undying praise, even, if our powers permit, by following your example. That is the true honor, the true affection of souls knit close to yours. To your daughter ... I would suggest that she revere the memory of a mother by continually pondering her deeds and sayings, and by cherishing her spiritual, above her physical, presence ... The image of the human face, like that face itself, is feeble and perishable, whereas the essence of the soul is eternal, never to be caught and expressed by the material and skill of a stranger, but only by you in your own living.

When I began to feel I was coming into my own as a poet, I sometimes had the sense that the profound familiarity with and love of literature my mother instilled in me was analogous to some superior ingredients which I, a chef, had been provided with, and which I then somehow processed into poetry. This notion of the raw and the cooked now seems condescending and presumptuous to me. The essential qualities of my mother's soul—her patience and discretion, her generosity and, yes, her sagacity—weren't raw ingredients. Rather they are traits I'm fortunate to have inherited, to the very incomplete degree that I have indeed inherited any of them (the patience not so much). I didn't cook them—I, or nature, recombined them somewhat differently. (Isn't that what DNA does?)

I like Tacitus's reminder that images of the physical presence, like that presence itself, are "feeble and perishable." In a poem written not long after my mother's death, here is how I expressed this idea of the tangible versus the imperishable parts of what we inherit:

As for my mother's legacy,
it can't be told as quantity,
piled up or counted or assessed.
If right this moment I should divest
myself of all that can be seen

in what she left me, there'd remain
hours upon hours of gentleness:
her reading voice's calm caress,
the realm of books she opened to
my young attention as I grew
and let me roam in, safe and free,
with a whole world for company
of voices I can always hear
whenever no one else is near
or when I'm reading to my son
and so can hand affection on
in the same shape as what I took
so happily from her: a book.

– from "The Double Legacy," in *The Empty Bed*
(Wesleyan University Press, 1995)

17

My Wicked Stepmother

Martin Amis

'You know your father's got a fancy woman in London,' said Eva Garcia, with her thick Welsh accent ('Ewe gnaw ewe father') and her thick Welsh schadenfreude (the simple pleasure of relaying bad news). Eva had served as our nanny-housekeeper during the family's years in Swansea; and she was summoned down to Cambridge to help alleviate an opaque domestic crisis.

My father Kingsley was elsewhere, and no one had told me why. I was 13; I found Eva's words completely unabsorbable, and I cancelled them from my mind.

A week later, as my mother Hilly dropped me off at school, she said that she and my father were embarking on 'a trial separation' (due to incompatibility). All I remember feeling at the time was numbness. I didn't know then, of course, that trial separations were nearly always a great success.

When the summer holiday began Hilly took her three children (Philip, Martin, Sally, fifteen, fourteen, ten) to Soller, Majorca, for an indefinite stay. My brother and I were enrolled at the International School in Palma, while Sally attended classes, in Spanish, at a local nunnery.

By November we were missing our father so acutely that we spent an hour every morning waiting for the postman to stop by on his motorbike;

© The Author(s) 2018
D. Salwak (ed.), *Writers and Their Mothers*,
https://doi.org/10.1007/978-3-319-68348-5_17

and once in a while we received a brief and uninformative letter. When half-term came Hilly put Philip and me on a plane to Heathrow. All we had was the address of Kingsley's 'bachelor flat' in Knightsbridge.

The flight was delayed, and it was past midnight when we rang the designated bell in Basil Mansions. My father, wearing pyjamas, opened the door and rocked back in astonishment (Hilly's telegram had not arrived). These were his first words: 'You know I'm not alone here.' We shrugged coolly, but we were as astonished as he was. Silently the three of us filed into the kitchen. Then Jane appeared.

A modern youth would have thought, simply, Wow. But this was 1963, and what I thought was more like Cor (with the reluctant rider, Dad can't half pull). Tall, calm, fine-boned, and with the queenly bearing of the fashion model she once was, in a spotless white bathrobe and with a yard of rich blonde hair extending to her waist, Jane straightforwardly introduced herself and set about making us bacon and eggs.

Our five-day visit was a saturnalia of treats and sprees—Harrods' fruit-juice bar, restaurants, record shops, West End cinemas (*55 Days at Peking*, with Kingsley lying down on the cinema floor every single time Ava Gardner appeared on screen), punctuated by several agonising and tearful heart-to-hearts between father and sons (during one of which Philip— very impressively, I thought—called Kingsley a c***).

But there it was: He had made up his mind and he wasn't coming back. On the last night, in the middle of a small dinner party, the telephone rang and my father answered; he listened for a moment, and shouted out, 'No!' Then he hung up and said four words. Jane wept. And one of the guests, journalist George Gale (or, as *Private Eye* called him, George G. Ale) grimly fetched his overcoat and headed off to Fleet Street and the *Daily Express*. It was November 22. Kennedy had been assassinated.

Howard met her third husband Sir Kingsley Amis in 1962 while the two were each having problems in their respective marriages. Over the next three or four years my lovelorn mother's household in Fulham Road—lax, bohemian, chaotic—steadily disintegrated; and, by the time Philip and I went to live with Kingsley and Jane, I was a semiliterate truant and waster whose main interest was hanging around in betting shops (where, tellingly, my speciality was reversible forecasts on the dogs).

The move was Jane's initiative. She always had a pronounced philanthropic bent, and was strongly drawn to losers and lame ducks—to those who, as she put it, 'led such terrible lives'.

She liked goals, tasks, projects; unlike both of my parents, she was organised. Philip was far bolder and far more rebellious than I was; he didn't last very long in the elegant and mannerly house in Maida Vale (and by his own efforts he went on to the Camberwell College of Arts). But I felt fearful and confused, and I responded.

When Jane took me on I was averaging an O-level a year, and read nothing but comics, plus the occasional Harold Robbins and (for example) the dirty bits in *Lady Chatterley's Lover*; I had recently sat an A-level in English—the only subject in which I showed the slightest promise—and I failed.

After just over a year of Jane's tutelage (much of it spent in a last-ditch boarding crammer in Brighton), I had another half-dozen Os (including Latin, from scratch), three As, and a second-tier scholarship to Oxford. None of this would have happened without Jane's energy and determination.

The process also had its intimacies. One day, early on, she presented me with a reading list: Austen, Dickens, Scott Fitzgerald, Waugh, Greene, Golding. I started, leerily, with *Pride and Prejudice*. After an hour or so I went and knocked on the door of Jane's study. 'Yes?' she said, leaning back from her desk. 'I've got to know,' I said. 'Does Elizabeth marry Mr Darcy?' She hesitated, looking stern, and I expected her to say, 'Well you'll have to finish it and find out'. But she relented (and in addition she put my troubled mind at rest about Jane Bennet and Mr Bingley).

Not long afterwards we agreed that this was the simple secret of Austen's narrative force, and of the reader's abnormally fierce desire for a happy ending: With all her intelligence and art, Austen created heroes and heroines who were literally made for each other.

In the early years at least, Kingsley and Jane seemed made for each other. It was an unusual, and unusually stimulating, ménage: two passionately dedicated novelists who were also passionately in love. Their approach to the daily business of writing formed a sharp contrast, one from which I derived a tentative theory about the difference between male and female fiction. Kingsley was a grinder; no matter how he was feeling (hungover, sickly, clogged, loth), he trudged off to his desk after breakfast, and that was that until it was time for evening drinks.

Jane was far more erratic and mercurial. She would wander from room to room, she would do some cooking or gardening, she would stare out of the window smoking a cigarette with an air of anxious preoccupation. Then she would suddenly hasten to her study, and you'd hear the feverish clatter of her typewriter keys. Very soon she would cheerfully emerge, having written more in an hour than my father would write in a day.

The great critic Northrop Frye, in a discussion of Milton's elegy *Lycidas*, made the distinction between real sincerity and literary sincerity. When told of the death of a friend, the poet can burst into tears, but he cannot burst into song. I would very cautiously suggest that there is more 'song' in women's fiction—more real sincerity, and less tradition-conscious artifice. This is certainly true of Elizabeth Jane Howard. She was an instinctivist, with a freakishly metaphorical eye and a sure ear for rhythmically fast-moving prose.

Kingsley once 'corrected' one of Jane's short stories, regularising her grammar. All his changes were, strictly speaking, technically sound; and all of them, in my view, were marked disimprovements.

By this time mutual hostility was clearly looming; and an attentive reader of Kingsley's novel, *Girl, 20* (1971), could feel pretty sure that all hope was already lost. At the outset, one of the qualities that attracted my father to Jane was her worldliness, her social poise, her sophistication—her class, in a word. England in the Sixties and Seventies was stratified to an extent that now seems barely credible; and it is naïve to expect artists or intellectuals to be immune to the stock responses, the emotional clichés, of their time. The daughter of a prosperous timber merchant, Jane was educated by governesses and grew up in a large house full of servants. The son of a clerk at a mustard manufacturers, Kingsley was a Clapham scholarship boy and the first Amis to attend university (he was also a card-carrying Communist until the ridiculously advanced age of 35).

That gulf in status was part of the attraction, on both sides; there is bathos as well as pathos in the fact that in the end it proved insurmountable. Kingsley would later write that many marriages adhere to a familiar pattern: the wife regards the husband as slightly uncouth and ill-bred, and the husband regards the wife as slightly over-refined and stuck-up. And it was as if Kingsley set himself the task of broadening that divide.

To take a relatively trivial example (while remembering that marriages are measured by trivialities), among her other accomplishments Jane was a culinary expert who expended a lot of time and trouble in the kitchen; Kingsley did not go so far as to smother her soufflés with HP sauce, but with increasing frequency he reached for the pickles and the jams, muttering that he had to make this or that terrine or smoked-fish mousse 'taste of something'.

In a good marriage the principals soon identify each other's irritabilities and seek to appease them. Jane, and especially Kingsley, did the opposite. As he became coarser, she could not but seem snootier. The infection proliferated and ramified; it became a cold war.

Jane was a self-confessed 'bolter', and no one was even mildly surprised when, in 1980, she did a runner on Kingsley. My brother called me and said, 'Mart. It's happened'; and I knew at once what he meant.

Her disappearance seemed harsh, and certainly gave rise to many complications, due to my father's lavish array of phobias (he couldn't drive, he couldn't fly, he couldn't be alone after dark). That last complication necessitated a system of 'Dadsitting' by his three children—until we hit upon an unlikely arrangement involving my mother and her third husband, which endured until Kingsley's death in 1995.

A man who abandons his first wife and is then himself abandoned by her successor loses everything: He becomes an amatory zero. But as soon as Kingsley was reunited with Hilly (if only platonically) he stopped 'feeling cut-up' about Jane. And thereafter, I'm sorry to say, he never had a civil word to say for her.

After 1980 I naturally saw far less of Jane. She wanted more from me—more than I felt I was able to give. It was always that way. From the very start I sensed emanations of love from her. I was always deeply fond and deeply grateful. But your father's 'other woman', I fear, is doomed to love her stepson without full requital. The blood loyalty to the blood mother is simply too deep and too powerful.

'I'm your wicked stepmother,' Jane said to me after she and Kingsley got married in 1965. And it was true: she was wicked in the sense of 'exceptionally and satisfyingly good'. In my last letter to her, written in December 2013 after a long telephone call of condolence, I congratulated Jane on her artistic longevity; and I cited the example of Herman Wouk, who had recently completed a novel in his late 90s.

I half expected her to duplicate that feat. But she died barely a month after her younger brother Colin, an unsung hero of this saga (charming, witty, not very happily gay, universally adored, and one of the most sweet-natured people I have ever known), who lived with Jane before Kingsley and through the lion's share of the Kingsley years.

For reasons that no doubt go back to a dismal childhood, Jane was elementally desperate for affection; and at the same time she remained a disastrous chooser of men. Indeed, my father—by any standards a mixed blessing—was probably the pick of the bunch, standing out from a ghastly galère of frauds, bullies, and scoundrels. So maybe in the end it is Colin who will have to serve, and serve honourably, as the love of Elizabeth Jane Howard's life.

18

About 'My Mother Enters the Work Force'

Rita Dove

When I was growing up, my mother taught me a number of skills relating to clothing—how to iron, how to mend and sew my own clothes. She started me out ironing handkerchiefs, then pillowcases; when I had mastered the flat heat-resistant surfaces of cotton percale, she introduced me to gathered skirts and synthetic fibers; the crowning triumph were sleeves. Then on to sewing—from reattaching buttons and marking hems to choosing the right fabric for the project at hand—a circle skirt, a spring coat, puffed-sleeved blouses and their pinafores—and then the efficient laying out of pattern pieces on the ping pong table in the basement (regulation size, built by my father), followed by cutting and pinning and—at last!—the keenly awaited initiation into the mysteries of the Singer sewing machine. My siblings and I were always spectacularly well-dressed, compliments of my mother's miracle work; she could conjure an Easter dress from the lining of an old coat, while the coat itself was subdivided into tiny blazers and vests. As I grew into adolescence, I was gradually permitted to apply my own variations (hot pants and Nehru-collared maxi vests) to the Simplicity patterns at my disposal. I was extremely proud of these creations—especially when my friends thought I had acquired them from someplace exotic, like Detroit.

© The Author(s) 2018
D. Salwak (ed.), *Writers and Their Mothers*,
https://doi.org/10.1007/978-3-319-68348-5_18

My mother, Elvira Elizabeth Dove (*née* Hord), was born in 1924 in Akron, Ohio. Her parents were working class, products of the Great Migration that swept thousands of Americans out of the impoverished rural South to seek the American Dream in the factories strewn along the blistered lips of the Great Lakes; they worked hard, with few aspirations beyond putting food on the table and clothes on the backs of their family, leading the way for generations to come with no expectation of seeing the mountaintop themselves. They were not bitter, just realistic: They had, in their definition, a good life.

The first born of four, my mother went through the public school system, skipping two grades to end up with a high school diploma and full scholarship to Howard University at the age of sixteen. But her astonishing precocity, ironically, led her right up to an insurmountable wall: A girl of sixteen on her own, navigating the sin-soaked streets of our nation's capital? Not a chance! My otherwise kind and open-minded grandparents feared the worst for their firstborn and formed a united front. She was too young, and female to boot. Elvira had to turn the scholarship down.

When I first heard this story, I was a high school junior, contemplating colleges—the same age as my mother when her adventure was thwarted. I was appalled; how could they have denied her such a unique opportunity? At the very least, she would have been a credit to her race! In my self-righteous teenage mind, even the home-taught skills she then fell back on for economic survival—working as a seamstress to pay for business school, which supplied her secretarial skills necessary for attaining the next rung on the ladder—seemed tainted. My cherished dressmaking skills became a reminder of the future she had had to give up because of her gender. And yet (as she gently reminded me, dimples showing her amusement at my discomfiture), had she left Akron for Washington, D.C., this pretty dark-skinned girl would not have met my father, who was also dazzled by her intelligence—plus the fact that she could beat him at ping pong.

And so, as a budding feminist in the early seventies, I had to come to terms with this paradox: I was a product of her lost opportunity; now it was my turn to climb the next rungs on the ladder in the ongoing quest to transcend the struggles of my race, my grandparents' lower class, the fetters of gender ... I couldn't mess this up by becoming a writer, could I? Could I?

MY MOTHER ENTERS THE WORK FORCE
The path to ABC Business School
was paid for by a lucky sign:
Alterations, Qualified Seamstress Inquire Within.
Tested on Sleeves, hers
never puckered—puffed or sleek,
Leg o' Mutton or Raglan –
they barely needed the damp cloth
to steam them perfect.

Those were the afternoons. Evenings
she took in piecework, the treadle machine
with its locomotive whir
traveling the lit path of the needle
through quicksand taffeta
or velvet deep as a forest.
And now and now sang the treadle,
I know, I know....

And then it was day again, all morning
at the office machines, their clack and chatter
another journey—rougher,
that would go on forever
until she could break a hundred words
with no errors—ah, and then

no more postponed groceries,
and that blue pair of shoes!

19

A Shadow in the Grass

Andrew Motion

My father Richard was a brewer and his office was in Smithfield; he commuted to London every day from our home in north Essex. But he thought of himself as a countryman, with good reason. He lived for country things—for 'peace and quiet', for seclusion, for doing the old things in the old ways—and he distrusted or despised their opposites. My mother Gillian, who was the daughter of a GP in Beaconsfield, was less emphatic. Although her parents were old-school (they sent her brother to university, but decided she needed nothing more in the way of higher education than a trip to visit relatives in South Africa), they couldn't or wouldn't deny her a glimpse of faster and more metropolitan life. A generation later, she would easily have found it: she was clever and amusing and spirited, she made friends easily, and she was pretty. But things being as they were, when she married my father aged twenty-two she settled for doing things his way. She sank into country customs. She walked the dogs. She learned to fly fish (my father was a very good fisherman). She began riding again: ponies had been a small part of her childhood. She took up hunting, which was my father's passion. And what else? So much of our parents' lives remain mysteries to us their children. All I know for sure is that she taught me to read, she sang me to sleep, she spoiled me

© The Author(s) 2018
D. Salwak (ed.), *Writers and Their Mothers*,
https://doi.org/10.1007/978-3-319-68348-5_19

rotten. My brother, too, when he was born two and a half years later. Then there was my father. She 'did the house' for him. She put his supper on the table when he came home from work. She exercised his horse. Did she flirt with the puce-faced and randy local farmers who lived round-about? Probably. Did she have affairs with them? I doubt it. In all sorts of ways my mother had surrendered her young and inexperienced life to suit my father's wishes, but so far as I can tell they were happy together.

And yet my mother was ill a great deal, so something must not have been right. When my brother Kit was born she contracted brucellosis and stayed in bed for a year. Kit and I were looked after by Ruby, my grand-mother's housekeeper, who back in the day had been my mother's own nanny. I have no memory of this, which is not to say that it had no effect on me. As she recovered, and I became dimly conscious of her as an inde-pendent character, I could see why everyone said her illness had 'knocked the stuffing out of her'. She was fun, but she was 'delicate'. Not faint-hearted. Frail. Easily tired (resting for an hour after lunch every day), taking a lot of pills for this and that, being told by my father (affably enough) to finish her food at meals so as not to 'waste away'. Perhaps this was partly why I cultivated a slightly 'delicate' identity myself. My father was always on at me and Kit to 'toughen up', but my mother's way of liv-ing—alluring because it was mildly alarming—seemed preferable.

All the more so, after my parents packed me off to prep school at the age of seven. I've no doubt my father took the lead on this, as he did on everything, and while it was clear that my mother supported him, I also knew that she hated me leaving home almost as much as I did: our part-ings were equally tearful. As a way of toughening me up it was a disaster. The school was a vortex of horrors: pederastic old bores, routine beatings and beastliness, pederastic younger bores, unkindness, tedium and stu-pidity. Instead of growing an extra layer of skin I felt that I lost several. I learned next to nothing. I switched from thinking life was pleasure inter-rupted by unhappiness into thinking it was unhappiness interrupted by pleasure. When my five-year sentence was up, I had changed from a cau-tious and shy child into an anxious and melancholy one.

After another two years of education, at my much more enlightened public school, the lights in my mind finally began to flicker on. I grew more confident. I began to read books. And although reading smacked of school, I found that my mother liked it too—found, in fact, that she liked a whole range of new things that were beginning to appeal to me. She didn't mind when I said I wanted to give up riding. She took me to see the Nutcracker. She gave me records of Julius Katchen playing Beethoven. She wondered whether I'd like to read Iris Murdoch's *The Bell*, which had been sent to her by the Book Club she'd recently joined. She gave me poems to read by Francis Thompson and Rupert Brooke, because she had enjoyed them herself at my age. She even, when I sent her a long letter that pompously paraphrased some early Fabian writing I'd been looking at (thanks to the crush I'd now developed on Rupert Brooke), sent me an equally long reply that felt as though it came from a friend.

By the Spring and Summer of 1968, when cobblestones were flying through the air in Paris, I felt sure that my mother was on my side about everything important. My father, who had fought in the war to keep the old structures intact, was not. Rock and roll, long hair, effeminate clothes, revolting students, left-wing politics: all these things were anathema to him—not to the extent of forcing us into a permanent confrontation, he was too retiring a man for that, but enough to make us feel continually at odds. Enough to convince me that my mother and I were now a team of two, floating in a bubble of art-life across the country-life created by my father.

But my mother inside the bubble was still delicate. Very delicate, in fact: for the last three summers, exactly as Kit and I left school to begin our long holidays, she was diagnosed with glandular fever, and took to her bed. It meant that we spent a large part of every day sitting quietly in her bedroom, while the yellow of her illness bloomed and faded. Then, when she got better for the third time, it was my turn to be delicate. I developed arthritis, which kept me in plaster for a while, put me in hospital for two operations, and finally kept me home for a long stretch when I should have been at school. It was painful and tedious in all sorts of ways, but it was wonderful as well. For months on end I had my mother to myself, and time to myself. I listened to music. I read and read and read. I began writing poems. At the time I never considered there might be a psychological dimension to any this: I was too ignorant/innocent to imagine such a thing, and no doubt too self-absorbed as well. But with hindsight it seems perfectly clear what was happening. I had to be ill to break with my inheritance in general and my father in particular. And my mother had to be ill to get more attention than any of us gave her when she was well.

Those months of illness—hers, and mine—were the most formative of my life. Not just because I started to write in earnest, and so to set my life on the track it has followed ever since, but also because everything I thought and said was quickened by things my mother thought and said. This wouldn't have happened without our 'bad luck', so we thanked our unlucky stars. They cast a light that felt oddly privileged. They made us seem like conspirators, treasuring 'our things' while the rest of the world—the healthy world—got on with other business.

In the summer of 1969 I went back to school. I was healed in body and felt transformed in my mind. When that term ended we all flew off to Portugal for our annual family holiday. My father sat on a boulder and complained loudly about the Pope. My mother and I—of course—fell ill with food poisoning. Then I went back to school again and began the second of my A level years, plunging into my English course as though my life depended on it. Then home for the holidays again. Then….

Because I was staying with a friend when my mother had her accident, and my father was at work, I had some difficulty in piecing together exactly what happened. On the Thursday morning between Christmas and the New Year, my mother and Kit went fox hunting. At some point around midday my mother was riding through a wood then had to jump a ditch to get out. Her horse (its name was Serenade) stumbled. She clung on while galloping across a ploughed field, then finally tumbled to the ground as she crossed a cement track. Her hard hat came off and she hit her head, suffering a serious brain injury. Serenade galloped on past Kit, my mother's empty stirrups banging against her empty saddle. This was the first he knew of any mishap.

I've written a great deal about my mother's accident—there are poems about it in every one of my books, which I began to publish in 1976; I describe the day it happened in my childhood memoir, *In the Blood*; and in the spring of 2018 I'll publish a long poem that tells the story of her slow death, as well as the story of my father's death many years later.

The facts of the matter are these. After the accident, my mother lay unconscious for three years, then spent the next six in limbo. Eventually she was able to speak a little, and turn her head a little, and lift her right hand a little. She remembered some things from the distant past, but not much from any nearer time. She was moved from hospital to hospital as doctors looked for a way to help, and eventually settled in an annex to one of the Chelmsford hospitals called 'The Links', which specialised in the care of incurable patients. She got pneumonia several times a year, and whenever this happened my father and Kit and I would tell ourselves that this was it, she was going to die. But she didn't die—not until nine years after the accident, when her chin sank at last onto her chest, pressed down by the weight of her monolithic depression, and pneumonia returned to take pity on her.

Was there a psychosomatic element to my mother's accident, as I suspect there was to her previous illnesses? Was it another and much more dangerous unconscious bid for the attention she felt was missing? These questions have formed a part of my thinking throughout the years following her fall. At the time it was simply the facts of the matter that seized my attention. The bruise engulfing my mother's face like a flame. Her shaved head (before the operation to remove a blood clot from her brain, she had beautiful yellow hair). Her nimbleness and her skinniness slowly vanishing into a body fattened by drugs. The violation of her privacy—the oxygen mask, the tube poking into her throat, the other tubes with their bags attached, that wormed beneath her blanket. The well-meant banality of nurse-talk (which was never quite talk, but always a half-shout). The fug and stink and racket of her ward.

I often wanted to look away. But that would have been unforgiveable. Besides, for the first three years at least we lived in the hope that my mother might suddenly open her eyes and be herself again. So day by day during the school holidays, on the week-ends we were allowed home during term-time, through most of my gap year before I went to university, and then through my university vacations and term-time visits, my brother and I sat beside her bed and held her hand, talking to her and wondering whether she could hear us. My father did the same every evening, on his way back from work in London: in the whole nine years he only missed a handful of days. I thought then and I think now that he was saintly in his devotion.

When my mother's eyes did finally open, which was early in my time at university, I felt like the prince in the fairy story, watching Sleeping Beauty come to life. Except it wasn't a rapid change like that. It was a slow and difficult climb from wooziness and forgetfulness into brighter wakefulness and better remembering. But never complete remembering. And it was complicated in other ways as well. On the one hand my mother was glad to be alive, and to share what she could of our existence. On the other hand, she was dismayed to discover how little was now possible for her, and would never be possible again.

Hoping for the best, my father bought a Ford transit van and had it adapted into a kind of ambulance, with a tail-lift and space in the back to take my mother on her stretcher. He added a small wing to the house, thinking my mother might live there with a full-time carer. But the doctors would never allow it. She was too damaged. She needed more nearly full-time nursing than a carer could provide. The best she could expect was a trip home at week-ends for Sunday lunch. The worst, which she dreaded so much it overshadowed almost the whole of every visit, was having to return to the hospital at the end of the day. I shall never forget the expression on her face when Sunday afternoons turned into evening, and she gazed up from the stretcher into my father's eyes and begged him to let her stay.

When my mother died, several family friends told us it was 'a merciful release'. We knew what they meant of course, but I deplored the idea and still do. The phrase seems to devalue the love we poured into my mother, trying to fill up the enormous deep cave of her distress. And it doesn't give enough credit to the beautiful and brave person that she remained until the end of her life. Even when she was completely unconscious, even during the bleakest moments of her posthumous existence, she was still my mother and my brother's mother; she was still my father's wife.

This means, among other things, that when I ask myself what her influence has been on my own life, I find myself answering under two headings. One has to do with the influence of her life before the accident, when along with my A level English teacher, and my best friend at my secondary school, she led me towards my immersion in poetry. The other has to do with the influence of her life after the accident, and of her death, which gave me subjects that will preoccupy me until I die myself.

Subjects I see by the light of certain lucky stars I gratefully acknowledge, and also see by the light of unlucky stars that convince me I'm alone, and bound to succeed or fail by my own efforts, if I succeed at all.

Two years ago I'd have ended there, conscious that I have once again failed to say everything there is to say about the effects of the accident, but feeling at least that the broad shape of its narrative was settled. Then, in the Spring of 2015 when I was about to leave England and start a new life in America, an email arrived that told me something I didn't know. It was sent by a gamekeeper now living in the north of Scotland. He said he'd been reading my childhood memoir *In the Blood*, and was surprised that I'd got the details of my mother's accident wrong. I replied explaining that I hadn't been there, and had relied on what others had told me: how did he know any better? He wrote back and said that he had seen her fall: would I like to hear more? I told him I would, and asked him not to spare me any details. I wanted to know exactly.

It was a lawn meet, at a house where he was then employed; his job that morning had been to take round a tray of drinks for those on horseback, so they could fortify themselves against the cold morning before hounds moved off. When this happened, and the riders began to follow, he stood to one side, and noticed my mother's horse shy at something—a shadow in the grass, he thought, perhaps the shallow dip where a ha-ha had been filled in. Serenade reared up and my mother, who was a good horsewoman, was caught off guard. She toppled backwards. As she fell to the ground Serenade kicked out, catching her with her iron shoe on the left side of her head just below her hat. The gamekeeper ran towards her and knelt down. My mother was unconscious, lying on her back, with blood coming out of her ears. He stayed kneeling, and took off her hat. A doctor appeared from nowhere (he'd been among the foot-followers of the hunt) opening his oblong bag. But there was nothing to be done except ring for an ambulance. It arrived very quickly, and took my mother to hospital in Chelmsford.

Does knowing all this make any difference? It does to me. Facts are facts, for one thing, and it's always good to know them. For another, knowing the truth deepens still further my sense that what happened to my mother was simply bad luck. The sort of thing that might happen to anyone, and often does. The sort of thing that comprises the only reliable law of life: its randomness. My mother wasn't galloping wildly through the countryside, taking outlandish risks. Serenade was just walking dully along. There was no great obstacle threatening her. There was just a shadow in the grass.

20

Mrs. Gabbet's Desk

David Updike

My mother is alone in the house, a couple of hundred yards from where I now sit, in a structure we call 'the barn', which in truth is more of a loft—a single, large room with a small kitchen, a bathroom, a wood burning stove, many windows that look out onto the road and the marshes beyond. Over the years it has been rented out to tenants, and before that housed family members in various states of transition, and now holds a lot of personal effects and photographs that we do not know what to do with. It is early morning, and my mother is waiting for my older sister to arrive, for lunch, and then the two of them will drive north, up into Vermont, to the summer house halfway up a mountain road that her parents bought during the Depression for two hundred dollars. "Two thousand?" I asked, but she stuck to her figure. It is a lovely old farm house, still with no hot water, and minimal heat, and she has been coming here in the summers since she was a child, then teenager, then the wife of a young Harvard senior, then the mother of a girl, then boy, then four of us, arriving each summer for a week in whatever station wagon we owned at the time.

But here on the coast, for the rest of the year, she lives in this large white house on a salt water, tidal estuary alone, and she would rather live here than in one of the residential complexes that some of her friends

© The Author(s) 2018
D. Salwak (ed.), *Writers and Their Mothers*,
https://doi.org/10.1007/978-3-319-68348-5_20

have migrated to in town. Her husband Bob 'passed' a year and a half ago in the bedroom they shared for more than thirty years. At the time, she was still recovering from her own infirmity, a cracked pelvis, but none the less, soon after his death, she dismissed all of the home health aides and other medical visitors, aside for one or two who would come once a week to give her physical therapy. As it happened, the winter of 2015 would be the worst winter in decades, one large storm followed by another, and several times she had been picked up and moved to my sister's house, in town, until the storm has passed, the driveway plowed, the walk shoveled, the electricity back on, all more or less safe for her return.

She was eighty-five then, and is eighty-seven now, survived another fall about a year ago, and a broken hip, and returned to the house after a month or two in a hospital, then rehab. But she no longer drives, and is dependent on her children and others for shopping, and some work around the house, but otherwise does most of her cooking and cleaning for herself. The vacuum cleaner is heavy, and so when I visit one of my tasks is to move it from one floor to the other. She has friends in town, of her own generation, some in good health, others not, and she often has them over for 'drinks'—cheese and crackers and olives and a drink or two. In this way, she and her friends are still looking after each other, providing a social life beyond their houses.

Once or twice a week or so, I drive the thirty-five miles out from the city and spend the day with her, or half a day, or sometimes the night, help her with errands, shopping, do a little 'work around the place' as my father would say, and otherwise try to be useful, including, simply, keeping her company. Loneliness is one of her quiet battles, and when I leave, generally after lunch, I am moved by the sight of her in the doorway, waving, thanking me for whatever small help I have been, and then I am off, and back to my life in the city. I once thought I could live here, spend half the week here and the other half in the city where I live, but now have my doubts, and feel I need to be in a busier, more cosmopolitan world— to be 'where the people are', as my father wrote somewhere. For as lovely as the town is, it remains a fact that it is not at all diverse, or cosmopolitan, and so it seems a little unreal to me, not the world I wish to live in.

Inside, the house is lovely and elegant, and on the walls are many of her paintings, which are also beautiful, interiors and landscapes, and sometime both: a landscape framed by a window—the marsh and the edge of woods and the water beyond. She painted in college, and then for a year afterwards at the Ruskin School of Drawing in Oxford England, where she and her newly married husband had a year's scholarship after college, drawing and painting and studying art. But her young and brilliant husband John began, increasingly, to publish in magazines across the ocean, in *The New Yorker*, poems and stories, and later Talk of the Town pieces; in April of that year a baby was born, my sister Elizabeth, and two years later, back in New York, another child, myself, and so her own artistic life took a back seat to being a mother, and to her husband's rising career. They left New York and its stilted, overly self-conscious and competitive literary scene, and moved to the small pleasant town north of Boston where they had spent their honeymoon some years before. Two more children were born, my father became steadily well known, and although she would sometimes take a drawing or painting class, she did not have the time or the energy or the psychological space in which to paint. Years later she said to me, as in explanation, "How could I compete with a talent like that?" And although I am sure my father had encouraged her to paint or draw or take a class, he was also preoccupied with his own writing life, 'getting the words out', as he put it, as well as being the provider for his wife and four children.

There was a busy social life, too—young couples like themselves, with many children: cocktail parties, dinners, sports to learn and practice—tennis, skiing, golf for my father, Sunday afternoon volleyball games, followed by cocktails at someone else's house. In February there was a group ski trip to a mountain in Maine, and in summer week-long trips to Pennsylvania and Vermont where my grandparents lived.

How adventurous they were, it seems to me now! When I was only two or three, we went to a small island in the Caribbean to live for a winter month, or two, in part so that the Caribbean sun could work its magic on my father's psoriasis, in part because a change of scene was good for a writer. There were no hotels on Anguilla at that time, few cars or Caucasian people, and we lived on the second floor of a wood frame building with a porch on all sides, and two young local women named Daisy and Selma, who cooked and helped my parents with us, the children. We took long slow walks on the beach while my father stayed behind and wrote. Behind the house was a large pond from which salt was harvested, and on the other side of the road a long flat beach full of shells. I got a large splinter on the bottom of my foot, from the lovely but weathered porch, which my father skillfully but painfully cut out of my foot with a razor blade. How brave and daring they were, to take us to this small island between the Atlantic and the Caribbean Sea—three small children, no hospital to speak of. When I asked my mother, recently, how they had chosen Anguilla, she said it had been referred to them by a friend, and it was the cheapest place they could find.

Two years later, also in winter, we made another family journey to the south of France, only this time there were four of us, my younger sister having been born a year or so before. We travelled on an ocean liner, the Leonardo da Vinci, from the deck of which we could see both Gibraltar and Tangiers, Europe and Africa; men in small, bobbing boats appeared in the sea below us, selling scarves and souvenirs that via ropes somehow conveyed money and merchandise along a swaying, diagonal path. We rented a house high on a hillside above Antibes, where my father wrote on the second floor, and we played in the garden below, and my mother did paint, this time, pastels and a lovely oil painting she keeps in a closet in the house on Labor-in-Vain Road. When I asked her why she didn't hang it somewhere, she said, rather wistfully, "It's still unfinished."

The purpose of this visit was the Mediterranean sun, but also to put an ocean between himself and a woman in town with whom he had fallen fully in love, had planned to divorce my mother and then marry her, but at the last minute decided he couldn't, grabbed his brood, and left for Europe. A survey of his short stories from this era reveal a man in mourning, lovesick with his loss, though through a child's eyes, he seemed happy enough. My mother? From this visit, I retain a poignant memory: for some reason I was alone with her one day, on an expedition down into Antibes, next to the stony beach and the chilly sea, and I must have requested a ride on a merry-go-round there. As I went around and around on my frozen horse, I would look over at her at every passing, but she was looking out over the slate gray sea, not at me, lost in thought, and each time I looked at her I wanted to jump off and distract her, rescue her, bring her back to me, to the present, and away from whatever dark thoughts she was having. Eventually, the ride was over, and I ran to her, and the car, eager to get back up the hillside to the house where we were living. More than my siblings, I was told years later, I was aware of their marital troubles, and back in Ipswich I had once walked into the kitchen just after my mother had smashed a dinner plate, and when I asked what was wrong was told, "Daddy wants to leave us and marry Mrs. Harrington!"

By the time we moved to England for a year, in 1968, it was not to escape a woman but a book, *Couples*, which, my classmates happily informed me, was a 'dirty' book. He had been paid handsomely for the movie rights (never made) and so, aside from being famous, he was at least rich enough to rent an expensive house on Regents Park, send all of his children to private school, and buy a new Citroen station wagon, that had to be shipped back across the ocean to America.

By this time, my siblings were demonstrating talents in the arts, painting and drawing, and my brother had begun to make small amusing animal figures of a material called 'sculpy'. My mother praised whatever her children produced, put it on display in our house and conveyed the strong sentiment in everything she did that art is something worthy of pursuit. (Even I used to draw before my artistic interests turned to the somewhat more literal medium of photography.) She lavishly praised our work (perhaps beyond its merits, in some cases), put it on display around the house, and encouraged us to continue, made art appear to be a worthy life-long pursuit. At a very recent graduation party for one of her seven grandsons, Sawyer Updike, freshly minted from the University of Vermont, she expressed the hope, in her congratulatory toast, that, wherever else his career might take him, he continue to pursue his artistic pursuits, because his work was 'quite wonderful'.

As a result of her encouragements, in part, we are all now artists of one sort or another: my brother Michael is a designer and sculptor, my elder sister a painter and teacher, my younger sister, Miranda, a late blooming full-time painter. I am a full-time English teacher who writes on the side, and pursues photography as an avocation, for which I am sometimes even paid. My father, too, of course, was a visual artist, a writer whose real, childhood ambition was to be a cartoonist. His own mother was an aspiring, practicing writer who, in middle age, began to publish stories in *The New Yorker* and elsewhere, eventually gathered in two collections,

Enchantment and *The Predator*: the first was published when she was in her sixties, the latter months after her death, in 1989.

In 1974 my parents separated, family drama and trauma well chronicled in my father's short stories of the time, and they eventually divorced two or three years later. Whatever vicissitudes their marriage had undergone, in their 22 years together, during that time he had gone from being a very good college student, to one of the most important American writers of his generation, and she had provided the domestic stability, and the labor—cooked, cleaned, ran the household, raised the children, read his stories when asked and gave advice, and into the bargain was also beautiful, charming, kind, and his intellectual equal. I don't believe she complained overly much when his 'fiction' suggested there were extra-marital relationships. An artist must feel free, he had somewhere written, to be true to him or herself, regardless of the collateral injuries. And for these twenty plus years, she had sublimated her own artistic aspirations, her quest for beauty, to his.

It was in the turbulence of their separation and then divorce that I—spurred on by an encouraging girlfriend, and the shifting landscape of the family—began to write, rather unexpectedly, and even less expectedly, I published a few short stories in my early twenties. As always, my parents were encouraging, and after reading one of these stories, "Apples", my mother said, "Well, that's a perfect story." I'm not sure a story can be perfect, and I'm sure that this one isn't, but I was grateful for the praise. The only real problem was I had never really aspired to write, or be a writer, and as a child I had been much more interested in photography, and my mother had put my pictures around the house for display. My father had always given me photography books for Christmas, not novels, and probably felt, as I did, this was a more promising artistic path. In any case, we take our successes where we find them, or they find us, writing led me to teaching, helped me get a full-time job in a community college teaching English, and this—vocation wise—is where I have happily landed.

When my mother remarried, it was to a tall, earnest Englishman who reminded me of her own father, a handsome, pipe-smoking Unitarian minister from Indiana. He adored her, lavished her with love and praise and admiration, as well as her painting. He also left the house each day at 7 a.m., got dropped off at the train station, and did not return until 6 or

7 p.m., leaving her, for the first time in her adult life, with time and psychological space to paint. She set up a studio in an underused room on the first floor, knocked down a wall, and this would become her studio, a room of her own, for the next thirty-five years, and counting. In her fifties she began to show her work, in galleries in town, and had several solo exhibitions, and began to sell her work. When she turned seventy we approached the curator of a gallery space at the Schlesinger Library at her alma mater, Radcliffe, for a one-woman 'retrospective', with a large, opening night reception attended by family and friends. She was, I believe, in her quiet, New England, understated way, thrilled.

That was seventeen years ago, and she has continued to paint, and show her work, and sell it, only slowed by her husband's illness and managing his care, and then by a couple of falls of her own, causing a cracked pelvis, broken hip. She is thin, but growing stronger this summer, and remains beautiful, and is also, I have been slow to realize, extremely resilient and tough. She was of the generation of women whose job it was—a college degree or not—to create a stable and pleasant environment for the husband, whose job it was to have a career and make money and, if possible, attend the children's sporting events. She did so for two men— the first a famous American writer, John Updike, the second a transplanted Englishman, Robert Weatherall, a well-educated, affable, intellectually curious college administrator, the director of the office of career planning. Since Bob died two years ago, she has lived alone in the house, and for the first time in her life is not taking care of someone else. She is also the last of her generation in her family, and at the ends of their lives she nursed and cared for each of her family members: both of her parents, then her aunt, Antoinette Daniels, then her only sibling, a sister, Antoinette Pennington Fisk, then her husband Bob.

This past May, of 2017, was her reunion year, her sixty-fifth from the Radcliffe class of 1952. Logistics—transportation, tickets she paid but kept not arriving—all weighed heavily on her, but one rainy humid morning in May we attended a morning event on "fake news", and then, during a large, tented lunch, an awards ceremony for PBS Anchor women Judy Woodruff and Gwen Ifill, who had passed away the previous winter at the age of 61. It was all rather moving, to sit in this large tented space with the smell of crushed grass, surrounded by mostly women in their eighties and seventies and younger, all the way down to my youthful generation which, I needed to remind myself, had just embarked on their sixties. And when Judy Woodruff spoke of Gwen Ifill, and another close friend and colleague made a moving tribute, my eyes kept filling with tears, but I hoped my mother (dry eyed, as far as I could tell) did not notice. She is—outwardly at least—very stoical, and I cannot remember a time when I have seen her actually cry.

Her own mother outwardly wept every time we packed up our station wagon, after a week at their summer house in Vermont, still dabbing away the tears when we rounded the corner of enormous pine trees, and they disappeared from sight.

Among the jobs she has assigned herself in the house is to go through her family possessions—letters and photographs and documents—to decide what to donate to the Schlesinger Library at Radcliffe, and when I visit she often has something to show me, or tell me about. Another box of such things recently arrived from my cousin, in California—her own mother's things, which my mother then works through when she feels able. It is emotionally laden work, I have found, sifting through these artifacts of the past, reading letters and gazing at photographs of people who have not been alive for decades: someone we will never meet, long since dead, but here she is, a beautiful baby on a wicker chair under a grape arbor on a lovely veranda; and then, not so long after, the same person as a beautiful twenty-five year old, holding on her lap another beautiful baby, who was my mother's mother, who I knew as a child. In short, you can only do this sort of work for so long, before it drains you, and you need to put all of these things back into the box from which they have come and go out for a walk.

One morning my mother and I were looking through some letters when she showed me one she had recently found, one that her mother, Elizabeth Entwistle Daniels, had sent to her own grandmother, on December 31st, 1908. My mother's eyesight is not great, and not getting better, and so I read to her the letter aloud.

Her mother was eight or nine, in Sausalito, California, visiting her parents, who are there because her father is captain of a coast guard ship which is stationed there, and they are spending the winter with a woman named Mrs. Gabbet. There was no way of knowing, of course, that within three years she would lose both of her parents—her father, from the after effects of accident as sea, and her mother, after childbirth, to a baby sister who also was lost. She was then raised with her sister, Antoinette, by her mother's mother and her Aunt Polly, in the family house in Saxonville, Massachusetts. As I read, I am aware of a curious jumbling of time—reading a letter, aloud, to my mother, at eighty-seven, written by her mother, at age nine, to her grandmother, in the year 1908, when she would have been in her fifties, I would guess, one hundred and eight years ago.

> "Thursday Dec. 31, 1908
> Sausalito California
> Dear Grandma:
> I hope you had a happy x mas and will have a happy New Year. I am sorry I did not write before. I am writing at Mrs. Gabbet's desk for there is no good place in our room to write. We had a Christmas tree in Mrs. Gabbet's; I got a Parcheesibored and a dolls set and a pink hair ribbon in a little box and a little looking glass and a brownie camera and a prayer book. I am going to sing in the choir. I can't think of anything else to say so I will close with much love from your dear little girl Elizabeth.
> PS I will write to others some other time"

When I look up, my mother is smiling, and for an instant it is as if things have been inverted, or made for a moment to stand still, as if she is the mother of this child and not the other way around; my mother is still quietly smiling, and when she speaks it is in the present tense, as though her mother, and everyone else in this constellation of women who have loved and raised us—mothers and daughters and grandmothers and aunts—are all still here, somehow, in a nearby room, or not so far away.

"She's such a good girl!" she says.

21

Dreams of a Mother and Daughter

Lyndall Gordon

I am to be my mother's sister. Not a writer. Such a life isn't thought of in our colonial town. Ships from Cape Town take fourteen days to reach anywhere that matters. Only the likes of Alan Paton can venture to be a writer; *Cry the Beloved Country* has the resonance to catch an 'overseas' ear—that magical 'overseas', arbiter of values we can't judge for ourselves. Builders on the roads improvise in Xhosa or Zulu, chanting in unison to the beat of the pickaxe; they lift, bend back, let fall—audible, but hardly in print.

'I'm only a housewife at the bottom of Africa', my mother says, mindful of womanly modesty. Like other women of her generation, she will not put herself forward. All the same it's a statement of sorts to her daughter who knows that she 'scribbles'. More secret, confided alone to my upturned face, is that she, a suburban housewife with no credentials, is Chosen like the prophets in the Bible. To take on life as a series of 'Tests' implies that she merits the attention of her Maker.

To the faithful who surrounded her early years on the veld, the Bible is 'the Book'. Not only that, she says, the Bible is 'a whole library of books'. For here are family stories, history, biography—'Abraham is the first great

Adapted from *Divided Lives: Dreams of a Mother and Daughter* (Virago Press, 2014).

© The Author(s) 2018
D. Salwak (ed.), *Writers and Their Mothers*,
https://doi.org/10.1007/978-3-319-68348-5_21

biography'—and above all the Prophets with whom she feels an affinity. Like Joseph in Egypt, she has 'prescient' dreams.

As a child, I'm to be my mother's 'sister' because she wants one so. My part is to be there if she's ill. Morning is the darkest time of her day. My mother looks back to the veld dawns of childhood with longing because these days she has to be drugged as soon as she wakes. The 'powders' dull her, she explains, a temptation not to take them, and no one knows if she does or not.

Suddenly she calls in her danger-voice, 'Help, oh-h, help me. Quickly!' It's a Test she might fail, and if she does she might go mad, or something worse might happen. I fly to her side and find her on her knees. I grab the glass jug on her bedside table and toss water in her face. It doesn't matter if it splashes the bed or spills over the floor. If she doesn't revive I must dig in her handbag for a large, blue Mason Pearson hairbrush, and push its bristles into her wrists. I never do this hard enough. Is it because I don't have the strength or can't bear to hurt her? She wrenches the brush from my hand and drives the bristles back and forth across her wrists—until she comes round. Sooner or later she does come round. Then she pulls herself up from the floor, and lies on her bed moaning. Lenie, the cook, hears the commotion, and comes pitter-patter on small feet. I'm relieved to see Lenie, and ashamed too for Lenie to see 'madam' so. Lenie sucks her tongue in dismay, and brings a cup of sweet, milky tea. Lenie never says a word, but has her share in our helplessness. None of us say a word. It happens, and we go on till the next time.

My mother is slow to get up in the mornings, slow to dress. She splashes her face on and on to the measure of slap, slap, drip, slap, slap, drip, to counteract the miasma of the powders; then draws seamed stockings over her feet. All her underwear, including the silky petticoat, is purest white. Her 'smalls' are washed separately every day; nothing unclean touches her skin.

In the forties and fifties, husbands of housewives have a right to complain. My father Harry is easy-going and enjoys (as my mother puts it) 'fullness of life', but he does grumble if breakfast does not appear as he ties his shoelaces, putting one foot and then the other on his dining-room chair. The grumble isn't made directly to Lenie but to his wife who has nothing to do but take charge of the servants and yet, at this moment, is reading Wordsworth and reaching out to a girl who 'dwelt among untrodden ways'.

Harry's grumble is routine, for he's looking forward to the office, ready for his next legal case, as in youth he'd stood ready, swinging his arms in his one-piece racing costume: the first whistle took him to the brink of the pool, toes curled around the edge; at the second blow of the whistle, his arms swung back, knees bent, as he tensed his shoulders for the dive; and then—GO. Other whistles blew him about the pool in games of water-polo.

When Berelly (Dr Berelowitz), with a mouth like a twisted rope, comes to examine my aching ears, he's perfunctory. Without warning he jabs an inflamed drum. He's clumsy because he's enthusing about literature with my mother. He'd prefer to examine her books. My mother has chosen him because he reads and she trusts him all the more for his indifference to sport. Shaking his head, he peers at my father's collection of swimming trophies.

As Rhoda Press, my mother was born to a different world like the parched landscapes of the Bible. She likes to remember, 'I opened my eyes on a shepherd's world with flocks of bushes stretching to the curve of the veld.' The horizons of Namaqualand are often so cloudless you can see line upon blue line of mountains and, looking up at night, 'a river of stars'. In 1917 there were only far-flung farms at the end of the railway line, running more or less parallel to the harsh west coast. A number of my mother's poems and stories emerge from this landscape, so that when she dies, I will choose these lines for her grave:

> Like a tree born in dawn's dark crystal stillness
> Roots clasping native stone
> My spine, my staff
> For I am home.

I am to be a channel for my mother's writings. It's impossible to remember at what age this emerges into consciousness. All that can be said with certainty is that a sisterhood as child-carer changes during my schooldays in the fifties into a sisterhood of poems and stories. There seems no divide between the 'Colossal substance of Immortality' in the visionary poets she loved—Emily Brontë, Emily Dickinson—and her own 'scribbles'. These she reads aloud with modest disclaimers, and yet I'm party to an intention that overrides her lifetime. She will not attempt to publish her writings, she says, and this may be in part fear of failure, but the reason she gives is that the twentieth century has shut off to the spiritual journey in her poems. She does know this is not wholly true, for she traces a similar journey in Eliot; all the same, she believes that I (or descendants in the future) might bring her to light in time to come.

Let me be clear: my role as her channel has less to do with love than reliance. I am heavily freckled; not a light spray but splotched all over despite the floppy-brimmed hat on my head. When the sun is at its zenith each December, impeccable Aunt Berjulie, who was brought up by her own impeccable aunts in Northern Rhodesia, comes to the Cape. In well-matched outfits from John Orr's in Johannesburg, Aunt Berjulie never fails to alert my mother to my ruined face. My mother, whose dark skin is untroubled by sun, never thinks much about looks. This makes it comfortable to be with her. I'm a conscientious child, not winning, not brainy but exercising an earnest intelligence—not the most attractive of qualities, yet it includes attention to phrases like 'the river of stars' and 'the curve of the veld' that fountain from my mother.

To take in poetic words is also to know how mundane I am. In truth I don't want the poetry of my mother's pained existence apart from the world. Her freakishness—shaping me as her familiar—prompts a counter-dream of normality.

A channel then. My mother never explains how this channel is to be constructed between her shut-off invalid existence and some far-off future when her voice will emerge.

As a child I'm filled with my mother's barely veiled boredom when men jabber about business, the same boredom that deadens the air around my father when he and swimming cronies put heads together over stop-watches. I promise myself that I will never settle for a blocked off man like husbands of my mother's generation (their reading confined to law reports, sport and war) and then, glancing in a mirror, see that I may have even less choice than she had.

On Sundays, when our father takes us to the beach, he's shaking hands with listeners to his 'Sports Round-Up' on the wireless. While his back is turned, other children, from a safe distance, yell 'freckle face'. Is that me? It has to be, for who else—certainly no one in sight—is so splotched with brown marks. These children assure me of a disfigurement others pretend not to notice.

I watch my mother put on make-up, as she stands short-sightedly peering at her serious blue eyes and high nose in the mirror of the three-corner cupboard in the bathroom. There's rouge in a small round pot and a tube of red lipstick. Too red. It's like putting on a mask before she can be seen.

We live in a colonial world with servants, where middle-class women have little to do. Women 'drop in' of a morning to pass the time. Before the bell starts ringing, my mother parts her hair on the side, and puts a finger along the unruly bits to make them wavy not wiry. She pats down and scrunches her dark curls, and if not in a hurry, rolls up a lock in a bendy brown curler to make it behave. Her thinness looks fragile, but passes as feminine delicacy in the turquoise muslins or shades of tea-rose she likes to wear.

No one outside the house knows how ill she is. It's a resolute performance as a wife and mother, but concealed in this casing lie dreams and visions. This much she intimates, but I have no access to secrets in her past. So, often, I lean on the insensibility of Granny Annie and my father who provide a cast-iron armour of normality. The daily marvel of their oblivion is the ease with which they don't see what they don't have to see. I'm less adept at concealment than my mother. The deception of normality—barely convincing as I know it to be—makes me ill at ease with people who come to the house.

My mother broods darkly in a way that can provoke an attack. Although it's not possible to press her with questions, the extremes of her self-portrait leave a gap between her early years on the veld, with 'children's voices chipped out of silence', and what she terms, in her cryptic way, 'suffering' and 'illness'. Each word comes freighted with explosive: the danger of what actually took place. It's her way to hint—a nightmare journey to Europe; misguided doctors; a man who died—so that I glance ineffectually through a fog of unfocused feeling shaded by alarm. If only I could calm her; give her pleasure. In a small way it contents her that I fall in love with *A Child's Garden of Verses*: I know by heart 'how do you like to go up in a swing', and 'on goes the river', bearing the child's paper boats to 'other little children' who'll 'bring my boats ashore', and the invalid child who lives in his imaginary 'Land of Counterpane'. My mother is drawn to writers like Robert Louis Stevenson and Katherine Mansfield who contend with illness.

All she will say about the onset of her own illness was that it 'befell' her at the age of seventeen, and that it was bound up with a 'bereavement'. Who was it she had lost? There is an air of things that happened before I was born, an air that her real life is over—as though her lips are kissing her hand to a person I can't see.

The Jewish Orphanage is filled to capacity during the war. Not all the children are orphans; some have parents who can't keep them; some were evacuees during the Blitz. They are housed in a three-storey building backing on Table Mountain.

In my sister role, I accompany my mother who goes twice a week to run the library.

'Librar-ee...librar-ee...', she sings up and down the long corridors, putting her head into dormitories with rows of whitewashed iron bedsteads and uniform, white bedspreads. Her heels tap-tap along the polished floor.

Children come running, books under their arms. They cluster around as she asks them what books they like. Biggles, say the boys. *Pollyanna* or *Anne of Green Gables*, say the girls who like to read about orphan girls whose opinions disconcert their elders. My mother fires up with eagerness to introduce them to the spark *Jane Eyre* keeps alive throughout her chilling and starving at Lowood charity school, and to another favourite, *David Copperfield*, as an orphaned victim of Mr Murdstone.

'Mr Murdstone', she says, drawing out the fearful first syllable, alarm in the cast of her face.

The children's eyes fix in reflected alarm as the bully torments the child; then, from deep within, questions well up. Questions about adult cruelty. Impossible questions because, towards the end of the war in Europe, the Allies come upon the Nazis' extermination camps, and there are no answers for Jewish children. It's enough that Rhoda takes up each question with attentive seriousness. A child who comes to this library has its beak open, ready. Each child gets a kiss when they line up to check books out.

It's not sentimental; more a ritual. 'Have you had your kiss?' Rhoda asks as though it's a right. Some return with a second book, to receive another kiss.

My mother, in purposeful mode, trailing children, tap-taps through a dank classroom with a key in her hand. As she unlocks the library, the children crowd closer, and help to push open the reluctant door. All at once we're enfolded by what I've thought of ever since as the library smell—print and paper—with its promise of worlds to enter. I associate the enticing smell with books for my mother's generation: all the sequels to *Anne of Green Gables*, running to Anne's children in *Rilla of Ingleside*, where spoilt, lisping Rilla has to grow up when she adopts a baby with croup.

I run my finger over old-fashioned bindings, which have images tooled on them in gold or silver: chums wearing gym-tunics in school stories by Angela Brazil. Away at boarding school, English girls appear not to miss their mothers because they are level-headed and have their minds on midnight feasts and helping those in trouble. These self-sufficient chums in books I can't yet read absorb me through illustration.

Emily, in *Emily of New Moon*, is open to 'the flash'. My mother recalls her excitement to find a girl in a book who'd had the same intimation that came to her as 'gold-smoke' across the veld when she'd been a child sweeping the sand off the stoep.

I listen as one who's not up to 'the flash'. People remark how I look like my father, a sun-baked, outdoor look of readiness that's common at the

Cape. I'm not rare, moonlike and fragile with large, glowing eyes like Emily who means to be a poet, and is climbing 'the Alpine path'—taking her gift to its heights—in a sequel, *Emily Climbs* (1925). This has been a model for my mother who, like Emily, 'scribbles' in secret and is suitably delicate with crisp, dark curls.

Was it solitude that developed her sensitivity to truth? This question comes only later when I read Virginia Woolf's essay *On Being Ill*: 'what ancient and obdurate oaks are uprooted in us by the act of sickness.' She makes bold to seize one gain of long illness, its subversiveness. She inveighs against what her society accepts: 'getting and spending', racism—she belongs to Alan Paton's party advocating the vote for the majority excluded by their colour—and brutish husbands.

On rare afternoons when my mother is up to it, she takes Pip and me to one of three shelly beaches between Muizenberg and St James. It's a treat to descend into a white tunnel under the train line. The tunnel echoes and magnifies the sound of the ocean; at its far end is a vision of the blue rim of the sea melting into a clear blue sky, and then, as you emerge, there are rocks interspersed with pools big and small, covered with fronds of green seaweed. It's a water-baby paradise.

When Rhoda reads aloud from *The Water-Babies*, published in grimy Victorian London, I stare at the colour plate of the sooty little sweep, Tom, descending through the chimney into Ellie's gauzy bedroom: the astonishing sight of middle-class comfort. We follow Tom's transformation into a water-baby, along with other fantasy babies in their snug home-pools.

My mother suggests that we prepare a water-baby pool for the likes of Tom to discover. I imagine his delight to find a cradle (a rocking shell) and inside it a lump of smoothed green glass for a pillow, a silvery 'venus ear' for a looking glass and curtains made of frilly seaweed.

One afternoon my mother collects a party of children playing on the beach and sets up a competition to see who can create the loveliest water-baby pool. I can't now recall who won because winning didn't matter, only an intense absorption, when you become what you make. You hear it in a child's hum—my mother calls it 'a cosmic hum'. It's a kind of bliss that has visited me again two or three times as a writer—once, tuned to the surges of Eliot's sea-quartet, *The Dry Salvages*.

The shelly beaches are afternoon beaches: no swimming here; the rocks lie close together and sometimes, at high tide, there's almost no sand. The wonder of these beaches lies in their secrecy, smallness and tidal obliteration: no names; no signs; simply steps down to the damp, rather smelly tunnel and a rising anticipation if the tide is low; the chance to hunt the rarest treasures: an anemone, waving its salmon tendrils in a rock pool and sucking your finger; a shell with the roar of the sea when you put it to your ear; the 'venus ear' with its dotted curve and, on the inside, a pearly sheen of silver-grey-pink; and the round green shell of the sea urchin, so fragile that it's a triumph to find one intact.

'Close your eyes', Rhoda says, 'and count how many sounds you can hear.' Concentrating on sound alone, I hear more than one might with eyes open: the gulls of course; the whirr of a fishing-rod as a solitary fisherman on a rock reels in his catch; footsteps along the cement floor of the tunnel; the whine of a dog tugging on its leash; the tickety-tack of a passing train, and cries coming my way that make me open my eyes to look up at black children in the third class tail of the train (where blacks must travel) who are waving from a window as they sweep by.

As I grew up, the fog around my mother's condition did block questions in a way that must have become habitual. My brother trots off to nursery school and our father drives away to his law office in town, so he too is not a witness, or not by day; nor is he told on his return. Nor is my grandmother present in my memory of these times. I'm alone with my mother as she falls on her knees next to her bed or on a rug in the dining-room.

Curious to me, looking back, is that my father and grandmother must have known that these emergencies would occur from time to time. Why did they say nothing? Might they have hoped she'd exert more control in the presence of a child? More likely, I think, was their reluctance to imagine what might happen when they weren't there—what George Eliot meant when she says that most of us go about well-wadded with oblivion. George Eliot actually says 'stupidity' but that's too dismissive, and her link of herself with 'us' doesn't ring true. It tells us more about the frustrations of George Eliot herself as an intellectual in a provincial society. Harry and Annie were certainly not stupid. Their extrovert high spirits simply overrode the intrusion of troubling thoughts. Their wadding may even have been of benefit. It ensured a cover for anything out of the ordinary.

It will happen quite casually when I'm fourteen that my eye will fall on words my mother has set down. Mid-afternoon, the house is quiet. The servants, having cleared up after lunch, have gone to their rooms off the yard at the back. Wearing school uniform, a white panama hat and a green cotton dress that looks rumpled by the end of the school day, I'm returning home, through the gate, across the stoep festooned with heavy boughs of vine, and quietly pushing open the front door. In a corner of the hall is a round, pedestal table, and on it are three exquisitely illustrated books between carved wooden bookends: *The Happy Prince and Other Tales* by Oscar Wilde, *The Bells* by Edgar Allan Poe and the plays of Shakespeare. I often stop at that table to look at Millais' 1852 painting of Ophelia singing as she drowns ('Her clothes spread wide, /And mermaid-like, awhile they bore her up.'), and this time, I notice that my mother, in her absent-minded way, has left a half-finished poem there, before she closed her door for her afternoon rest. It's usual for her to be sleeping, or trying to and easily disturbed, when I tiptoe back from school.

As I glance at the poem, a word leaps out. The word is 'epilepsy'. Instantly, it strikes me: 'That's what it is.'

Until that moment the problems besetting my mother seemed various—tension, fatigue, anxiety, falling, jerking awake, sleeplessness, 'dry-sickness' (the last a made-up word that she associated with Eliot's *Waste Land*, and familiar long before I read that poem)—so that it has never occurred to me that one symptom could take precedence. My next thought is surprise that there might be a word for it, after all. Something that definite; something by then made known to my mother, who at that date was thirty-eight. I never mention this discovery. It is somehow understood that the word is not to be uttered.

In the poems of Rhoda Press silence and utterance are central to the soul's trials. When she pulls herself together to leave our house, she carries a small, wire-bound notebook in her handbag, and sometimes she stops in the street to set down a character she's noticed or a line of a poem that comes as she sniffs the sour-sweet tang of the fynbos with face uplifted. The challenge is to voice what has been voiceless.

> The veld is voiceless
> Africa is dumb;
> flat and far as space can reach
> mountains that bless
> await in the sun
> a poet's speech.

Sealed in a car, cut off from the veld by her suburban marriage, she spies a gazelle with its long eye-tendrils. Native of the veld, its eye meets hers as it

> sucks from sourbush and scent of clod
> a poet's song.

These poems and the life that brought them onto the page bore on the kind of biography I was to write. I could not omit Eliot's silencing of

Emily Hale, a teacher of speech and drama, as a 'Lady of silences'; nor could I fade out James's silencing of the woman he called 'Fenimore', great-niece of James Fenimore Cooper and a companion in exile, by sinking her dresses in the Venetian lagoon—a strange, guilt-ridden story he relayed after Fenimore's suicide, picturing how the dresses with the huge 1890s sleeves came back to the surface swelling like 'black balloons'. What these women actually were and what they became in poems and fictions was a vital part of these lives.

The attacks do not of themselves define my mother's life so much as the way she saw them: a Chosen being like Jacob in the Bible wrestling all night with an angel. In one poem it's an encounter so fraught, it nearly wrecks the wrestler, who holds on by reciting the 23rd Psalm:

> ...Turn
> on the edge of death and walk on the tightrope psalm
> steadfast to the end: 'surely goodness
> and mercy shall dwell'
> till the clayhouse body knows
> the Inrush of the Spirit
> and the fountaining of love.

As a child I can't fathom what she's saying beyond an unspeakable horror I'm reluctant to know. The tenacity is clearer, and I'm somewhat relieved when she moves on to love. And of course I'm glad that she's making me into a person who, she says, 'will one day understand'.

So it happens that while my mother scribbles in her notebook, I become a watcher of her chrysalis. Years later, as a biographer, this will put me in sympathy with others who watched at the side of writers and seers: Emily Hale, who watched Eliot, and waited for him; and Fenimore, who watched Henry James; and Charlotte Brontë, watching her sister Emily, who was herself a watcher of the night, awaiting the 'wandering airs' at her window—reminding me how Rhoda each night opens her window to the roar from the ocean's throat.

Lives I will watch as a writer turn on the private life of that room, its moral character, its sufferings and resilience, above all the 'fountaining' of a writer's voice.

22

Her Programme

Tim Parks

The Cover—Page 1
SS PHILIP & JAMES PARISH CHURCH, WHITTON

Saint Philip was the fifth apostle of Jesus. It was he who asked Jesus how on earth he was going to feed the five thousand and in this he was not unlike my mother who spent much of her life worrying how to feed people, though without the benefit of miracles. My mother died of a long and miserable cancer but I have no doubt that had the opportunity arisen she would have preferred to be crucified upside down like St Philip whose tormentors offered to cut him off his cross after hearing him preach very persuasively in this inverted position, but he refused. My mother could also be very stubborn.

St James might be James the Just, brother of Jesus (who Catholics insist was actually his cousin, otherwise how could Mary have held on to her virginity?) or James the Great, son of Zebedee, brother of John the Apostle and an apostle himself, or James the Less, son of Alphaeus, another apostle, though sometimes identified in fact as James son of Clopas. However, the SS Philip & James Parish Church Whitton website has nothing to say about which man is meant, nor is it clear why Philip

© The Author(s) 2018
D. Salwak (ed.), *Writers and Their Mothers*,
https://doi.org/10.1007/978-3-319-68348-5_22

and James's names often end up together as joint patrons of Christian churches all over the world, except for the fact that they share the same feast day: May 3rd in the Catholic tradition and May 1st in the Anglican tradition, something that hardly seems important now since our programme refers to a ceremony in late November. This particular SS Philip &James, I should say, is an Anglican church, but high Anglican, meaning candles and holy water, and so almost Catholic in a way, and certainly not low Anglican as was my clergyman father whose middle name was James and who considered candles and incense and turning to face the altar while reciting the Apostle's Creed superstitions on a level with witchcraft, but also, strangely, the prerogative of the presumptuous upper classes, who, as he saw it, had always held back the evangelical mission of the English church, perhaps because they just didn't care whether the poor were saved or not and considered themselves saved by birth. The fact that my mother, after my father's death, spent the last thirty years of her life attending a high rather than low church (to whit SS Philip & James, Whitton) was not a betrayal of her late husband's principles, which she fervently shared, but rather to do with this church's proximity to the house of her widowhood, which was definitely low, lowly in fact, though always stacked with religious commentaries, bibles and wall texts, one of which, placed beside a photograph of my father, says:

> Death hides –
> But it cannot divide,
> Thou art but on
> Christ's
> Other side.
> Thou with Christ
> And Christ with me
>
> And so together
> Still are we.

Philip & James aside, the church itself is a quaint stone structure inaugurated in the 1860s but aspiring to look as if it were built four hundred years before, with a quaint little spire and quaint little pews, and so on. No feature, it seems, is not gratefully copied from ancient models, in much the same way that SS Philip & James were happily plucked from a long tradition of possible church names. It is by no means an unpleasant place.

Whitton is a nondescript suburb developed in the 1930s around a village situated halfway between Twickenham and Hounslow. It is hard to think of anything else to say about it, except that it was here, at the end of a poky cul-de-sac that my mother, made homeless when my father's death obliged her to vacate their vicarage in Finchley, found a house cheap enough to buy with the aid of a two-thirds contribution from the Church Commissioners Pension Fund. And it was in that cul-de-sac that a hearse and two funeral cars had considerable trouble reversing and turning when they came to pick up the mourners for her funeral. As my brother and sister and I, reunited for only the second time in forty years, all climbed into the first car, each of us held in his or her hands a copy of the programme that began

SS PHILIP & JAMES PARISH CHURCH, WHITTON.
A Service of Celebration and Thanksgiving for the Life of
(Here, there is a 2" × 2½" photo of my mother in her late seventies wearing a turquoise cardigan and black beret, smiling cheerfully)
JOAN ELIZABETH PARKS
1922–2013
Monday 25th November 2013 2.00 pm

The word funeral does not appear on the programme, though everybody has been speaking of the event as a funeral; everybody has been saying things like, 'Tomorrow is Mum's funeral,' or 'John, you really must make it to Mum's funeral, however arduous the trip.' My mother would have been 91 on November 30th, that is next Saturday, but warned me in early October that she doubted this birthday would be celebrated. In fact she had written the programme we now hold in our hands some months before and if it doesn't have the word funeral anywhere on it, this is because she chose not to put it there. It was important to insist that death had lost its sting.

Behind the name Joan Elizabeth, etc., in faded background on sepia paper, is a round photograph showing two yellow roses. My sister, who together with her husband has been largely responsible for organizing the funeral, since 'the boys' (myself and my brother) live abroad, John in America, I in Italy, has chosen yellow roses for the main wreath and hence also for the cover of the programme. 'They're so much less depressing than white lilies,' she explains and she tells me she is eager to recover these yellow roses, if possible, after the service, since it seems a shame to leave them to rot at the crematorium, with what they cost as well. 'Yes, lilies do make one think one must be at a funeral,' my brother quips, fresh from his transatlantic flight. Rather to our surprise John has responded to the call and come to be with us at the ceremony and now we are all three in the funeral car as the driver patiently turns his long vehicle around in the narrow Close. At the bottom of the programme's cover page, just inside the round frame of the roses photo, italicized and in capital letters, are the words:

GOING HOME TO GLORY

This, as I recall, was the title of a biography of Dwight D. Eisenhower, written by his grandson David, though what exactly glory might be—a place? an aura? a celebration?—or how my mother might be said to be going home there, I am not sure. Glory is one of those words whose emphatic enunciation seems to have more reality than anything it might refer to. What could home mean for my mother if not 5 Willowdene Close, Whitton, and before that 658 High Road, Finchley, and before that again, 163 Kingscote Drive, Blackpool? Or more in general perhaps home for my mother was south-west London, Chiswick, where she grew up and spent the war, or even more in general England, a country in which, aside from one or two missionary excursions, she spent all her life and which she firmly believed to be the best, most civilized and most beautiful in the world, despite the deafening noise of jet engines over Willowdene Close, situated as it is right beneath the flight path for Heathrow, not to mention a neighbour who thought of endless ways of making it difficult for her to use her garage that he wanted to buy from her and knock together with his own.

But we are in the posh funeral cars now, cars that my mother, with typical generosity and foresight, not wishing her family to be financially burdened by her death, paid for herself a couple of years back, along with a standard funeral package that included her coffin, now visible in the hearse in front. And in the coffin is my mother, going home to glory, via SS Philip & James, Whitton.

As it turns out this is the first time any of us three children has seen the coffin, despite the fact that it has been on show, with the body inside of course, embalmed for viewing, for some days now. My mother had not included embalming in the funeral package she paid for because, along with her distaste for candles and incense, she also disliked the idea of the body made an object of reverence and possibly even veneration. For my mother, head and shoulders, torso and limbs, were merely the husk from which she would be released into glory, whatever and wherever that might be. It is important to have words to anchor our aspirations. However, having chosen cremation rather than burial, again out of a wish to undo any iconic significance the body might have (that I know of my mother never visited the graves of her own parents), the funeral could not take place until at least two weeks after her decease, this so that any number of doctors and authorities could certify that there was nothing suspicious in the circumstances of her departing this world, since of course once cremated the forensic folk can hardly dig one up again to check. Hence, if, when the time came, anyone wanted to view the body before the funeral, "something people do like to do these days," the undertaker had persuaded my sister, "and your mother was a popular person," the body would have to be embalmed.

"At ninety pounds it wasn't expensive," Helen reassured me, unnecessarily, on the phone and she explained that since, on Mother's own instruction, she and her husband had used mother's cash card to take most of the remaining money—not much—from her current account during the three days when she was clearly dying, this unexpected expense was in fact covered by my mother who hadn't asked for the service and didn't want it. Uncle Alec, Helen added, my mother's brother, had been to see the body and reckoned they had done a good job and she looked peaceful and had colour in her face. Which was good. However, Helen herself did not wish to see it, or her. She wanted to remember mother as she was alive.

"Are you joking?" my brother retorted when I asked him, via email, if he was planning to see the body. To my brother seeing Mother in her coffin was unthinkable. But ever since I had arrived at Whitton Station three days before the ceremony, and spied the undertaker's directly across the High Street and realised that my mother, whom I had last seen on her deathbed, indeed dead, was in there, behind that rather dingy façade, in a box, chemically altered to avoid the smell and generally made to look, so far as is possible, her old self, no doubt wearing, if one can speak of wearing, one of the smart dresses she used for church, perhaps even to preach in at church, with a flower in the button hole no doubt, perhaps a bonnet on her grey hair, smart stockings and shiny shoes, I had thought of little else. On three or four occasions I had walked back and forth in front of the undertaker's where there was a phone number for making appointments to view the dear departed, but without ever quite being able to make up my mind to go in. I wanted to see her, my mother, her body, out of a vague sense of duty and respect, a desire for ritual perhaps, and again out of curiosity—how had they made her look?—and again because I was never going to have another chance to see her, or even her husk, ever again; then perhaps at some deeper level I wanted to see her because I loved her and felt very much that there was still, if not precisely unfinished business between us, nevertheless a whole area of communication that had simply been off limits, a territory we had never been able to meet on, and that territory was precisely the territory of death, the territory of coffins and corpses and what it means to be a corpse in a coffin, what it means, if you like, to not be, or not to be. It wasn't that my mother and I were never able to mention death when talking to each other, quite the contrary, merely that when it was mentioned we were both immediately aware that it was here that our visions of life differed radically, that I felt death would be the end while she insisted it was only the beginning. But of these two positions—the dead quite dead as I saw it, the dead more alive than ever as she believed—the first is accepted with resignation and requires no great effort to sustain, while the second must be constantly fed with fervency and hope; and as her cancer advanced and her pains became unbearable these qualities were no doubt in short supply; one looks for a little help from one's friends, from one's clergyman, from willing fellow believers who will speak to you of the golden streets of paradise and the pleasure of being reunited with your long dead husband, now on Christ's other side, or again from a daughter like my sister Helen who is always ready to tell you that Jesus is watching over us and all is well; alas, I could not be one of those reassuring people, and hence there had been a sort of estrangement between myself and my mother over this matter of her dying during her long illness. Not that I would ever have advanced my thoughts on death unasked, or even perhaps if asked, but merely that she knew my thoughts and could see well enough that I felt the way I do, could see it, perhaps, most clearly in my sadness and even kindness, for I can be kind, as her death approached, my more frequent visits, my greater and greater solicitude, and this sadness and kindness of mine became a problem for her perhaps, speaking as it did of my conviction that she would soon be, as I saw it, no more; and no doubt it was because of this that the word 'goodbye' was never actually spoken between myself and my mother in the hours spent together those last days of her life as her mind came and went and finally went, for good. One says, for good.

So now, outside the undertakers opposite Whitton Railway Station, I felt compelled to go in and see this seraphic face they had arranged for her, the face of one in glory perhaps, lying in the polished wooden box that she had paid for. What was driving me perhaps was the hope that, as I stood over the coffin and looked down on her cheerful, made-up face, all that previous and, I had always felt, stupid tension between us might magically dissolve. But having arrived at the undertakers I did not go in. I kept walking, on one occasion to draw money from Barclays cash machine at the next street corner, on another to enjoy a coffee at Costa which has just opened on Whitton High Street, alas too late for my mother who loved good coffee and always lamented that the cafés in Whitton were hopeless. Actually it was the cakes she liked, more than the coffee, but that's as maybe. It wasn't fear, I thought, that stopped me from going in to the undertakers opposite the station to view the body, or again from phoning the number and making an appointment to view it. Isn't 'view' a strange word to use here? As if she were a painting. Or something for sale. I had seen corpses before. I wasn't afraid that the sight would impress itself in some unhappy or terribly permanent way on my mind. Nothing could have been more disturbing than the sight of my mother as she was that last exhausting night of her life, yet I had quickly put it aside, it was not haunting me. No, if I didn't go in to the undertakers, although I felt strangely compelled to go in, it was because another part of me had decided that this 'viewing of the body' was just not on, Mother hadn't wanted it; it was ghoulish and false; I would be doing something in the hope of bringing about a resolution that couldn't possibly occur; Mother was dead and the time for resolutions was over. How could the tension between us dissolve, if she wasn't there? Surely the tension should have dissolved anyway, with her passing, and if it hadn't, it had nothing to do with my mother and everything to do with me. She had not wanted to be embalmed, had not wanted to be 'viewed' and never wore make-up. Case closed.

I walked back and forth in front of the undertaker's quite a number of times in the three days before the funeral, always feeling absolutely compelled to see the body and always knowing that there were excellent reasons why, on arrival at the undertakers, I would not in fact go in to see it. One concern, for example, was that by seeing her, viewing her, what I was really trying to do was to confirm that I had always been right about death, it really was the end—here she is reduced to a painted dummy—and that she had been wrong; I wanted to win the argument with my mother, at last. Which amounted to kicking the old girl when she was down. It was not honourable. And so now, as I sit in the funeral car and it draws up to the hearse in front and we all see for the first time, through magnificently polished glass, as if in a motorized display case, my mother's fine coffin, with the splendid wreath of yellow roses on top that must not be left to rot at the crematorium, I simultaneously feel, exactly as I knew I would, which is to say regretful, because it is now too late to see her dear face that one last time; and relieved because the dilemma is finally over, I need think about it no more and can concentrate on grieving. Mother is dead, in her coffin, on her way home to glory.

One thing I didn't expect was that the undertaker himself would walk in front of the hearse in his dress suit all the way from 5 Willowdene Close to SS Philip & James Parish Church, Whitton, a distance approaching half a mile. Immediately I begin to wish that I too was walking ahead of the hearse, or beside the coffin. Apparently the under-taker asked my sister if any of us children wished to help carry the coffin from the hearse into the church and she, or rather her husband, Humphrey, who has very generously been handling the arrangements on her behalf, at some detriment and cost to the little company he runs no doubt, had said no, we didn't, though actually it would have been a great relief for me to do something, anything, to contribute to this funeral in whatever way, because the worst part of a funeral is feeling that there is no way to participate really, actively, if not by crying your heart out, which for some reason is frowned on in men in their late fif-ties. My sister sitting to my right in the middle of the seat has told me she is determined not to cry, in part because she does not want to make an exhibition of herself, an expression we often heard from our mother's lips, and in part because it would cause her make-up to run so that she would then look a 'right state' at the reception which has been arranged afterwards in the church hall out of respect for all the people who knew my mother through her church work and will have come, some of them, from afar, and thus face a long journey home and deserve some refresh-ment. My brother also seems determined not to show too much emo-tion and is again making quips about the funereal quality of lilies and the Dickensian demeanour of the undertaker in his dress coat. John is one of those people who believes the best method of defence is attack. The more provocatively he jokes, the more we can be sure he is in dan-ger of howling.

We pass the Admiral Nelson on the right, where I never managed to persuade my mother to join me for a drink, then turn north at the roundabout onto Whitton Road just as a 747 rumbles over, apparently as slow and steady in cold winter air as the hearse is on the recently re-tarred road surface. To pass the time, I start to look at the programme they have put in my hand, and as I turn the first page my sister, who by the way has rather attractive pink highlights in her hair, tells me that Gordon, her son-in-law and quite a computer whiz, was up half the night with Photoshop, turning Mum's simple programme notes into something that looks like a professional publication complete with art-work of one kind or other on all eight of its crisp A5 pages. "Hasn't he done a fantastic job!" she exclaims. On the first inside page I find a wel-

coming address signed by my mother, as if she were actually there leading the ceremony.

Page 2
Welcome dear friends,
Thank you for coming and joining in; what I desire above all things is that
this should be a service of celebration—not of my life and achievements—
but of the wonderful Lord who has been my strength and stay, all my life.

Reading this I'm immediately reminded of my mother's voice and
reminded what's more of how she always created a mood of such kindness
that the simple fact of disagreeing with her, or worse still of pointing out
an awful cliché like 'strength and stay', always made you feel distinctly
unkind. It goes on…

> I have always loved the words of Jacob, who after a long and chequered life,
> could say as he blessed his grandchildren, "The God who has been my
> shepherd all my life to this day, the Angel who has delivered me from all
> harm, bless the boys". The Lord has certainly been my shepherd, saved me,
> blessed me, guided and delivered me. I heartily recommend my dear
> Saviour to you.
>
>   Joan Parks.

On reading this, the words that bring unexpected tears to my eyes are,
bless the boys. Why the boys and not the children? Were they in fact only
boys Jacob blessed? I can't remember. But whatever the exact nature of
the Bible story, and despite the fact that we are her sons, not grandsons,
I feel at once this blessing is intended for my brother and myself, the family's two unbelievers, 'the boys'. My mother is using her funeral programme for one last sermon. The boys are to sit obediently in church, as
of old, and listen.

As it happens we are to sit by the wall, in the short front pew on the
right. My brother is actually leaning against the masonry. I'm next to him
with Helen to my left and husband Humphrey beside her at the end of
the row by the central aisle, because he will have to leave his seat to read

the lesson. In the pew behind us is Uncle Alec's family, but again with my sister's son, Daniel, at the end of the row because he too has to give a reading. My sister's family, then, all of whom share my mother's evangelical views, will be active in the service. This is no doubt what Mother wanted. Her boys, though blessed, must play no part, in case they say anything out of line. Church is not a place for us to speak. I had told my brother-in-law that if it was that kind of funeral, I would be very happy to say a word or two in memory of Mum, but he had said mother specifically stipulated that she did not want eulogies. When I replied that what I said would not be exactly a eulogy, he did not respond.

Waiting for the coffin, my brother turns round and jokes some more with my cousin immediately behind him. I stare about me at the familiar trappings of an Anglican church and the less familiar paraphernalia of the high Anglican variety. Lighted candles. A crucifix. My father hated crucifixes. He hated a dead Christ. I haven't been in a church in England or thought about this stuff for years. Decades. Suddenly an old aura is upon me. An old force field has me on the defensive. This is what adolescence was like. Doing one's duty in church, feeling vaguely guilty, waiting to be free. Now the organ strikes up sombre. It was always part of the package. At last one senses the shuffle of coffin bearers, a hush of heightened attention. I turn and there she is, in her box, the woman who wrote 'Welcome dear friends', and in fact as the coffin is set down a woman appears at a mike stand on the chancel steps and reads the greeting out, mother's welcoming address, in a sweetly sanctimonious voice. "The God who has been my shepherd all my life to this day, the Angel who has delivered me from all harm, bless the boys," she reads, unaware of any hidden message. Then, straight out of the pages of Barbara Pym, a young clergyman, tall, blonde and blandly handsome, announces the hymn, and we are on our feet singing, Thine be the glory...

I have decided to copy down everything my mother wrote for her funeral programme. The next forty minutes was such a storm of emotions for me, I want to go back over it slowly and carefully. So here is the hymn. On my feet, I am sharing my programme with my brother, who has contrived to lose his. He concentrates on singing in a rather fruity, posed voice, participation mingling with irony—I'm in this, but definitely not in this. It's almost a continuation of his jokes. I try to do the same but I can't stop my body shaking. Church music has a powerful effect on me at the best of times, propelling me straight back to a childhood of Matins and Evensong, choir practice Tuesdays, and the slowly dawning suspicion that much of the music and all of the words were awful. Anyway, here is mum's first hymn.

Page 3
Thine be the glory, risen, conquering Son;
endless is the victory, thou o'er death hast won;
angels in bright raiment rolled the stone away,
kept the folded grave clothes where thy body lay.
Thine be the glory, risen conquering Son,
Endless is the vict'ry, thou o'er death hast won.

Lo! Jesus meets us, risen from the tomb;
Lovingly he greets us, scatters fear and gloom;
let the Church with gladness, hymns of triumph sing;
for her Lord now liveth, death hath lost its sting.
Thine be the glory, risen conquering Son,
Endless is the vict'ry, thou o'er death hast won.

No more we doubt thee, glorious Prince of life;
life is naught without thee; aid us in our strife;
make us more than conquerors, through thy deathless love:
bring us safe through Jordan to thy home above.
Thine be the glory, risen conquering Son,
Endless is the vict'ry, thou o'er death hast won.
                            Edmond Budry 1884

To my left, beneath her pink hair, my sister is singing softly. Beyond her, her husband's voice is powerful and full of faith. To control myself, I count the archaisms and clichés: thine be ... bright raiment ... o'er death. This hymn, if I remember rightly from my choirboy days, is translated from the French. I start to look at it with a professional eye. The translator seems to have used the original as a prompt to assemble a collage of pre-existing English formulas, in much the same way as the church I'm standing in is an aggregation of architectural mannerisms from centuries before. It's curious how this aping of the ancient is supposed to be reassuring. My brother soldiers on, rhyming tomb and gloom, life and strife, though I can see he's getting into troubled water now. He's afraid he might cry. Death hath lost its sting, he wavers. Naught without thee. Safe through Jordan. Home above. It's depressing to think that such hackneyed platitudes have to be repeated at such an important moment, though we are singing them of course because my mother in her coffin wanted to believe all this and wanted us to believe it too. Towards the end of the last verse I manage to get my voice into gear again and even give the refrain a little oomph. Thine be the glory. Endless the vict'ry.

Page 4
SCRIPTURE READING
John 11: 12-27: "Do you believe this … ?"

These words make me sit up. What a dangerous challenge? Do you believe this? What a risk, from Mum! My brother-in-law leaves the pew and goes beyond the coffin to the chancel steps and the mike stand. He apologizes to my mother, he begins, for reading from the Contemporary English Version of the Bible rather than her beloved Authorized version. Everybody knows my mother preferred King James. But he wants, he says, for everything to be comprehensible. Indeed! And he begins to read the story of Lazarus.

> A man by the name of Lazarus was sick in the village of Bethany. He had two sisters, Mary and Martha. This was the same Mary who later poured perfume on the Lord's head and wiped his feet with her hair. The sisters sent a message to the Lord and told him that his good friend Lazarus was sick.
> When Jesus heard this, he said, "His sickness won't end in death. It will bring glory to God and his Son."
> Jesus loved Martha and her sister and brother. But he stayed where he was for two more days. Then he said to his disciples, "Now we will go back to Judea."

"Teacher," they said, "the people there want to stone you to death! Why do you want to go back?"

Jesus answered, "Aren't there twelve hours in each day? If you walk during the day, you will have light from the sun, and you won't stumble. But if you walk during the night, you will stumble, because you don't have any light." Then he told them, "Our friend Lazarus is asleep, and I am going there to wake him up."

They replied, "Lord, if he is asleep, he will get better." Jesus really meant that Lazarus was dead, but they thought he was talking only about sleep.

Then Jesus told them plainly, "Lazarus is dead! I am glad that I wasn't there, because now you will have a chance to put your faith in me. Let's go to him."

Thomas, whose nickname was "Twin," said to the other disciples, "Come on. Let's go, so we can die with him."

When Jesus got to Bethany, he found that Lazarus had already been in the tomb four days. Bethany was only about two miles from Jerusalem, and many people had come from the city to comfort Martha and Mary because their brother had died.

When Martha heard that Jesus had arrived, she went out to meet him, but Mary stayed in the house. Martha said to Jesus, "Lord, if you had been here, my brother would not have died. Yet even now I know that God will do anything you ask."

Jesus told her, "Your brother will live again!"

Martha answered, "I know that he will be raised to life on the last day, when all the dead are raised."

Jesus then said, "I am the one who raises the dead to life! Everyone who has faith in me will live, even if they die. And everyone who lives because of faith in me will never really die. Do you believe this?"

"Yes, Lord!" she replied. "I believe that you are Christ, the Son of God. You are the one we hoped would come into the world."

What a curious passage it is. Full of non sequiturs. Why does Jesus come out with the riff about light and stumbling when his disciples want to know why he is risking the trip to Jerusalem? Why do they say of Lazarus, if he is asleep he will get better? Sleep is hardly an illness. Unless they mean he will sleep his way out of illness. Why does Jesus let someone die just so he can raise him from the dead? If he needed to show off his powers, there could hardly be any lack of opportunity. Most of all, why has my mother wanted, at her funeral, a passage about being raised from death back to this earthly life when what she claimed she always wanted was a place in paradise.

'Do you believe this?' my brother-in-law raises his head. He's a good reader and makes it challenging. Again I feel the question is meant for us boys. Do you believe, Tim. "Yes, Lord!" The affirmation is my mother's. No doubt when she wrote the programme she imagined the words ringing out as she went to meet her Maker. My mother lived a very humdrum, domestic life, but always charged with a sense of metaphysical drama. True she was stewing plums, but she was also wrestling with the devil. All the same, she didn't ask her son-in-law to read the rest of the story: the visit to the tomb, Jesus's weeping, Martha reminding him that the corpse will smell bad ('Lord, by this time he stinketh'—I remember those words sinking into my infant head fifty and more years ago), Jesus ordering Lazarus to come forth, and finally the dead man appearing in his grave clothes, including the cloth that covered his face, and so, presumably, his eyes. Mum did not ask Humphrey to read this part, I suppose, because, aside from being unbelievable, it all feels a little messy and improvised. Not like the powerful rhetoric about death and resurrection. Once raised up, poor Lazarus will still have to die again. And why did Jesus weep, if he knew there was no problem?

Quite suddenly, the Italian expression *botte di ferro* comes to mind. *Sono in una botte di ferro*, the Italians say. I'm in an iron cask. And, no, it doesn't mean a coffin; it means, I've secured myself against all attack. My enemies can't get me here. They can't penetrate these iron walls. Writing this programme, planning every detail of her funeral, Mother has put herself in the proverbial *botte di ferro*. Our grief, our sadness, our disbelief, can't get her now. The iron barrel bobs about on a bright stream of faith. I've been to many funerals where I felt the religious ceremony impeded an expression of mourning, but none where the deceased herself is running the show. When I go, I suddenly decide, and what I mean is when I die, my own kids can organize whatever funeral they want, wherever they want, to express whatever grief they may or may not feel, or no ceremony and no funeral at all. What will it matter to me? Let them be free. But now a woman in black cassock and dog collar stands and walks to the microphone.

HOMILY
The Revd Elizabeth Greenwood

She is in her sixties with drab grey hair cut in a fringe across her forehead and round spectacles. Beneath them she has two large pools of black under her eyes. I have honestly never seen anything like this before. They're not bags, but as it were deep bruises, beneath the eyes and as if resting on thin, drained cheeks. If you saw it in the cinema, you would think it a make-up job. They're very black and very round. No, they're oval. Quite probably my mother, embalmed in her *botte di ferro*, has a better complexion than this preacher. But the Revd Greenwood begins brightly and sweetly enough and immediately it's clear she knew my mother well and loved her. She talks about Joan's faith, Joan's charisma, Joan's preaching, Joan's wisdom, the help she always gave people, the numbers of 'young folk' she 'brought to Christ'. All this I recognize well enough, though without enthusiasm. It's right that it be mentioned, but it has nothing to do with the things a child might appreciate of a mother. When we were small it was painfully clear that the pleasure my parents took in their preaching was precisely what left them distracted in our regard, frustrated and perplexed when Helen fled from school every day, downright angry when John abandoned A levels for art college, anxious and accusing when I was more interested in Beckett than the Bible. But watching this woman preach, efficiently and pleasantly, producing the eulogy my mother hadn't wanted—and for a moment I imagine her gently wrestling the microphone from mum's hands—I can't help wondering why my mother didn't become a clergywoman herself. She always spoke of her 'ministry', after all. She was only 58 when my father died. The same age I am now. Why didn't she? Then I remember a conversation in which she said that although women could be excellent preachers, many folk still preferred a man for the position of authority. I had the impression she was including herself in those many folk.

These thoughts are pleasantly innocuous and get me through the rest of the homily. But there is a toxic sea beneath them. I do not feel I am in a *botte di ferro*. Perhaps after the funeral it will be possible to grieve. Will it? What is the difference between a homily and a sermon? Is one a commentary on the scripture reading, the other freestanding, as it were? But the Reverend Greenwood said nothing about Lazarus. Perhaps the less said the better. Lord, he stinketh. What worries me is that we will get to the end of the funeral, the cremation, without really grieving. Without catharsis. I'll be stuck with oceans of bottled up grief, like chronic catarrh. Now the blonde clergyman is telling us for at least the third time that the ceremony is not to be one of sadness but celebration. Can't we be sad that Mum is gone, damn it? Even if she has gone to glory? Isn't it still a loss to us? Didn't Jesus weep for Lazarus, even if he was about to raise him from the dead? The clergyman invites us to stand to sing "Just as I am without one plea," written in 1851 by Charlotte Elliot, but with a last verse, he announces, and his lips spread into a warm, indulgent smile—a last verse written by my mother. Again, I hadn't expected this. Not only has she written the programme, but now she's changing the texts she's chosen. For a moment I wonder if she mightn't even have added a verse to the Bible.

"Just as I am, without one plea." As a choir boy I always thought two verses were quite enough for any hymn, or at a push three. After which a terrible plodding sets in. "Just as I am" has five verses, plus mum's. She's put it at the end for effect, but maybe it should have gone in earlier. Actually there's a choir here too, at SS Philip & James. But no choirboys. A dozen voices, mostly women; no one under fifty. They sing well enough, holding their hymn books (not the programme), in that lovely posture on open hands, lips and teeth enouncing the words more carefully than these words deserve. Here they are, the words to the hymn, I mean. It would be unkind and unrealistic of me to ask you to read them all. Just remember I am trying to sing all this at my mother's funeral—my mother has really died—and that I do so sharing the programme with my brother, from America, whom I love but rarely see, and who again is managing to sing, straight-faced, determinedly posed, while I keep giving way to waves of emotion. It is so extraordinary that mum is dead.

> Just as I am—without one plea,
> But that Thy blood was shed for me,
> And that Thou bidst me come to Thee,
> – O Lamb of God, I come!

Just as I am—and waiting not
To rid my soul of one dark blot,
To Thee, whose blood can cleanse each spot,
– O Lamb of God, I come!

Just as I am—though toss'd about
With many a conflict, many a doubt,
Fightings and fears within, without,
– O Lamb of God, I come!

Just as I am—Thou wilt receive,
Wilt welcome, pardon, cleanse, relieve;
Because Thy promise I believe,
– O Lamb of God, I come!

Just as I am—of that free love
The breadth, length, depth, and height to prove,
Here for a season, then above,
– O Lamb of God, I come!

Just as I am, old tired and frail,
To see Thy face beyond the veil,
I climb on still though steep the hill
Oh Lamb of God I come, I come.
                    Charlotte Elliot 1851

Final verse Joan Parks 2013

Lamb of God, I reflect, for my daughters at least, who are in the second pew from the front on the other side of the coffin, will mean above all the heavy metal band, from the USA. I've always wondered why the expression crops up so much in Christian rhetoric. Lamb of God. Am I the only one who finds it creepy? No doubt in the distant past people would immediately connect lambs with weakness and sacrifice and a good meal. A lamb was the epitome of powerlessness, defencelessness. They would have bought lambs live and had them killed for this or that celebration. So in that inversion of hierarchies typical of Christianity, you have people worshipping the humblest, weakest creature, the sacrificial lamb, who actually turns out to be God.

Does that make sense? And how ridiculous the verse rhyming spot and blot and waiting not! How did Christianity get so attached to second-rate nineteenth-century doggerel? Not that heavy metal bands are much better. As we sit down, the blonde clergyman who is barely ten feet away from me, facing me, hence inevitably aware of my tears, my growing unease with this ceremony, remarks that members of the congregation will never have thought of Joan as old tired and frail. 'However great her pains,' he says, 'however exhausting her sickness, once Joan climbed the chancel steps here to preach—only two months ago! Exactly where I stand now—her body seemed to grow taller, didn't it? and to shed twenty years.' He stops and beams. 'She was an inspiration to us all.'

Again I recognize this of my mother, but I also remember a woman who had to struggle to get out of her armchair to answer the front door when I visited, a woman who seemed ashamed to confess that she was 'losing her battle' with the cancer, that she was struggling with depression, grateful for injections of cortisone, desperate for painkillers. 'It's agony, Tim,' she told me. She had tears in her eyes. This woman will find no mention in the programme. 'I climb on still though steep the hill'. There is something dangerously infectious about hymn-speak. Cancerous. It multiplies ad infinitum.

'Now we have a poem,' the clergyman says, as if this was our treat after the main course. His face is set in rejoicing mode. From the pew behind me, my nephew steps to the front. The programme says:

Poem
I know Jesus, that I'm called,
The Message was quite clear
And yet I cannot see, the How, the Why,
I feel so small and weak, so ill-equipped
For such a task.
And yet I am prepared to say my "Yes"
And undertake the risks and enter the unknown

> Trustfully treading your path,
> The only one that leads to life—to You

There is no attribution here, so that I wonder for a moment if it might not be my mother's, my mother who is still in the coffin about ten feet to my left. Very still. This business of someone you knew for so long screwed down in a box with a heavy lid, really is a mystery. Her but not her. Here but not here. However slow and tired she had become towards the end, however much she suffered, even when she was vomiting blood, there was still the exchange of glances and it was her, mother and son aware of each other's presence. Or mother and daughter no doubt. Mother and friends. Mother and nurse. There was something there, recognition, and now, mysteriously, life is gone and we have the lump of flesh in its box soon to be burned to bits while her handsome grandson reads, with just a trace of embarrassment, this poem I'm thinking might be hers. The foregrounding of her weakness—small, ill-equipped—the miracle of her being chosen—self-esteem—the emphasis of her accepting the challenge, the weird sentimentality of this projected meeting with a personal creator, very much a male authority rather than a woman. These are all familiar ideas, though she had become even more careful than I was to avoid mentioning them when we were alone together these last years.

REFLECTION, The Revd David Cloake, the programme now says. We're at the bottom of page 5. We're getting there. Since I'm sitting now and he standing in voluminous robes a few feet away and above me, he seems very tall and young and blonde, very complacent and ruddy and solid and cheerful. 'Joan asked not to have a eulogy but she is jolly well going to get one, actually two,' he laughs. 'Enough modesty. We can't let her leave us without celebrating her life.'

The Revd Cloake proceeds to poke a little gentle fun at my mother's low church foibles. 'No, we wouldn't have dreamed of poisoning her funeral with incense. She was very worried about that. Trust me, Joan, I said.' He's laughing. It's actually rather fun. He recalls how Joan used to help him with his sermons, offering suggestions and feedback. 'The Lord has laid out so many rich foods, David,' she told me, 'All you have to do is choose which you are going to serve up each day.'

No doubt, I reflect, this was how Mum felt when family or friends came to visit. What foods would Helen or John or Timothy like her to serve up in her microwave, since the Willowdene kitchen was too small for an ordinary oven? And what would I serve up I suddenly ask myself if they were to let me say something? I try to think. I would say Mum was always generous, she always remembered everyone's birthdays, she never complained if you didn't phone and visit for a while. In fact she never phoned you at all, which was rather extraordinary in a mother, but always waited for your calls, then was always delighted to get them. But she never complained in general. Never complained. Above all, in her last years, now that we were undeniably adult, she learned to stop talking religion to us, myself and my brother, at least most of the time, learned just to be happy eating rhubarb crumble together, with cream of course, or enjoying a little sherry, or playing a game of Scrabble or Rummikub, or watching a detective yarn on TV—she always used the word 'yarn'—learned, in short, to be a reassuring and facilitating presence, even if she did always try to make you eat too much. And when she had at last stopped preaching to us it really was good to be with Mum and to help her out and ask her if there were any odd jobs around the house she needed doing, or any heavy shopping, and when she was well it was good to take the bus together to Marble Hill and enjoy a cake at the café in the park, hopefully outside in the sunshine and talk a little politics, or discuss the family, and the sad state of the Church of England synod. This is about all I would have said about Mum at the funeral service, if I had been invited to. I wouldn't have troubled the crowd with the way she always expressed negative opinions of my girlfriends. Not one girlfriend did she ever like. Or the fact that she thought yoga the work of the devil and AIDS a divine punishment for perversity. Skip that. I would say that Mum had learned and I had learned to be happy together, as mother and son, putting aside she her evangelism and me my resistance to her evangelism, and I would say the fact that we managed to do that together, in unspoken agreement, was really something rather wonderful. And no doubt with others too she came to the same wise compromises. And on Mum's headstone, if ever there was to be a headstone, I would put: Her Christmas presents always arrived early.

This eulogy of mine more or less matched the reverend's in time. So I didn't hear what he had to say. Thinking of mum like that, I had of course made myself tearful again, but cheered myself up too. Because it seemed at last there had been a point in being here. Meantime another, older clergyman has begun reading the collect.

O MERCIFUL God, the Father of our Lord Jesus Christ, who is the resurrection and the life, in whom whosoever believeth shall live, though he die; and whosoever liveth, and believeth in him, shall not die eternally; who also hath taught us (by his holy apostle Saint Paul) not to be sorry, as men without hope, for them that sleep in him: we meekly beseech thee…

What a relief this is after the nineteenth-century hymns! Even if the content is the same, at least the *Book of Common Prayer* does not leave the reader feeling a fool. And how ironic that the wilful archaisms of the nineteenth century never have the steady conviction of the sixteenth. Hymn-speak as the last refuge of denial perhaps. Rock of doggerel, cleft for me. Let me hide myself in thee.

As the man's voice follows the familiar rhythms, I inevitably begin to hear my father, who of course had intoned these very words on any number of occasions when I sang in the choir at funerals to earn myself a half a crown. In Blackpool that was. So for just a few moments we were all back together, Mother in her coffin, father in my head, my brother and sister in their entirely alien minds and worlds, but very close, one each side of me.

And now we are at the last hymn, printed over a woefully unflattering photo of my mother in inky black and white, her nose an old potato, her teeth evidently false.

HYMN

Tell out, my soul, the greatness of the Lord!
Unnumbered blessings give my spirit voice;
tender to me the promise of His word;
in God my Savior shall my heart rejoice.

Tell out, my soul, the greatness of His Name!
Make known His might, the deeds His arm has done;

His mercy sure, from age to age to same;
His holy Name—the Lord, the Mighty One.

Tell out, my soul, the greatness of His might!
Powers and dominions lay their glory by.
Proud hearts and stubborn wills are put to flight,
the hungry fed, the humble lifted high.

Tell out, my soul, the glories of His word!
Firm is His promise, and His mercy sure.
Tell out, my soul, the greatness of the Lord
to children's children and for evermore!
                    Timothy Dudley-Smith 1962

I confess I don't know this hymn. Perhaps because, being written in 1962, it was too new for my church childhood. The diction does not seem to have greatly changed from the mid nineteenth century, but it is definitely harder to sing. I can't seem to follow the music at all. I'm all over the place. Still we are almost there, now, so it hardly matters, almost through. Only one more page of the programme. And this thought brings both relief and urgency. Unable to go on singing, I suddenly take my brother's hand, something I have wanted to do all service, and squeeze it, and still singing, he squeezes back, very warmly. Then I take my sister's hand on my left and squeeze that, and she too squeezes back with immediate and intense warmth. And now it occurs to me I should take both hands, so that we can all three be united. But immediately I shelve the idea. The hell with symbolism. And my sister leans toward me and whispers, 'Don't be sad, Tim. It will all be all right.' As if her little brother were worrying about something that could be put right! And I tell her, 'It's ok, Helen. It's all right now.' And actually it was. Right and ready for the final words.

FORASMUCH as it hath pleased Almighty God of his great mercy to take unto himself the soul of our dear sister here departed: we therefore commit her body to be consumed by fire—earth to earth, ashes to ashes, dust to dust—in sure and certain hope of resurrection to eternal life, through our Lord Jesus Christ, who shall change our vile body that it may be like to his glorious body, according to the mighty working, whereby he is able to subdue all things to himself.

To subdue all things to himself. What a strange notion. The holy water they are sprinkling on the coffin is not something Mother would have approved of. But she can't stop them. She's gone. Already the bearers have her on their shoulders. Her vile body subdued, her programme over, Joan has no more cards to play.

Index[1]

[1] Note: Page numbers followed by 'n' refer to foot notes.

© The Author(s) 2018
D. Salwak (ed.), *Writers and Their Mothers*,
https://doi.org/10.1007/978-3-319-68348-5

Index

Printed by Printforce, the Netherlands